Praise for Gayle

and her delectable Daphne

"A sweet treat for cozy mystery fans."

—Fresh Fiction

"For people who love a tasty cake and a cozy murder mystery, *Murder Takes the Cake* is a delicious read."

—Suite101

"The breezy story line is fun to follow. . . . Daphne is a solid lead character as she follows the murder recipe one step at a time."

—The Mystery Gazette

"The folksy names, dialogues, settings, and characters all promise a good cozy (culinary) mystery. This was an easy, entertaining read. It reminded me a bit of a comfortable, enjoyable game of Clue."

—A Bookworm's World

"Trent has written an absolutely captivating cozy, complete with all the traditional elements of the genre. . . . I hadn't even read past page seven, and I had laughed out loud numerous times. The dialogue in this book is filled with snappy wit."

—Pudgy Penguin Perusals

This title is also available as an eBook

Killer Sweet Tooth

A Daphne Martin Cake Mystery

GAYLE TRENT

GALLERY BOOKS

NEW YORK   LONDON   TORONTO   SYDNEY   NEW DELHI

Gallery Books
A Division of Simon & Schuster, Inc.
1230 Avenue of the Americas
New York, NY 10020

First Gallery Books trade paperback edition October 2011

GALLERY BOOKS and colophon are registered trademarks of Simon & Schuster, Inc.

For information about special discounts for bulk purchases, please contact Simon & Schuster Special Sales at 1-866-506-1949 or business@simonandschuster.com.

The Simon & Schuster Speakers Bureau can bring authors to your live event. For more information or to book an event contact the Simon & Schuster Speakers Bureau at 1-866-248-3049 or visit our website at www.simonspeakers.com.

Manufactured in the United States of America

10 9 8 7 6 5 4 3 2 1

Library of Congress Cataloging-in-Publication Data

Trent, Gayle.
   Killer sweet tooth / Gayle Trent.—1st Gallery Books trade paperback ed.
      p. cm.— (A Daphne Martin cake mystery ; 3)
   1. Martin, Daphne (Fictitious character)—Fiction. 2. Bakers—Fiction. 3. Murder—Investigation—Fiction. 4. Virginia—Fiction. I. Title.
   PS3620.R4454K55 2011
   813'.6—dc22   2011013024

ISBN 978-1-4516-0002-5
ISBN 978-1-4516-0004-9 (ebook)

This book is dedicated to Deborah A. Bassham, DDS, MS.
Without a late-night weekend visit to her office, the idea for
Killer Sweet Tooth *would not have been born.*

CHAPTER

One

IT ALL began with a little bite of innocent sweetness. It was mid-January, and Brea Ridge—deep in the heart of Southwest Virginia—had been experiencing the type of "Desperado" days the Eagles would describe as "the sky won't snow and the sun won't shine."

Ben—my boyfriend . . . significant other . . . man I date?—was working late to make sure an article was included in the Saturday edition of the *Brea Ridge Chronicle*. He's not only the newspaper's editor in chief, he also writes articles and is a perfectionist who has trouble delegating. This isn't the first Friday night he's had to call and cancel our plans at the last minute. We'd only been planning to go see a movie in nearby Bristol, but I was still disappointed. However, there were worse things than disappointment. My ex-husband Todd's idea of a fun weekend evening had been to berate me and to prove how superior he was to me in both size and strength. Oh, yeah . . . good times.

Violet, my sister, was visiting her mother-in-law Grammy Armstrong this evening with her hubby Jason and their twins, my precious tween nephew and niece Lucas and Leslie. Anyway, Grammy was celebrating her seventieth birthday. I'd made the cake for the occasion. It was a ten-inch round cake with a basket-weave border and an assortment of flowers—roses, carnations and daisies—in the center. I'd finished it off with a *Happy Birthday* pick in the center of the flowers. Violet and her family, as well as the rest of the Armstrong clan, were having a small gathering to wish Grammy Armstrong well.

I must selfishly admit, I felt as if everyone had left me out in the cold that night. Pardon the pun. But I was lonely. Lucky for me—or at least I thought so at the time—Myra was lonely too. Myra is my favorite neighbor. She's a sassy, sixtysomething (you'll never get her to admit to any specific age) widow who knows everything about everybody in Brea Ridge (or can find out), who has a heart of gold, and who is as entertaining as they come. I saw her arriving home (she lives right next door), gave her a call, and she agreed to come over around eight for some freshly made cashew brittle and a game of Scrabble. Myra tends to make up words when playing Scrabble, but that merely adds to the challenge of the game.

At the sound of the doorbell, Sparrow, my one-eyed formerly stray gray-and-white Persian cat, raced down the hall toward my office. She has a little bed in there under the desk, and it's her favorite hiding place. She has begrudgingly made friends with me, but she isn't comfortable around other people yet. Don't worry about the one eye. The veterinarian said she was probably born that way. Plus, it's how she got her name. My nephew and niece, Lucas and Leslie, named her Sparrow in honor of Captain Jack Sparrow, Johnny Depp's character in *Pirates of the Caribbean*. They said having one eye made Sparrow look like a pirate.

I opened the door and Myra came in wearing jeans, an oversized blue sweater, and a pair of tan Ugg boots. She deposited the boots by the door and rubbed her hands together.

"I'm so glad you called," she said. "I've been bored out of my mind today. That's why I went out to the mall for a while."

"Did you buy anything good?"

"Not a thing. I just window-shopped until the stores started closing. That made me even more depressed."

"I know what you mean," I said. "Cake orders have been slow since New Year's . . . even with the Daphne's Delectable Cakes lawn sign I put up last week. Do you think I should add 'It's okay to stop by anytime and order a cake' to the sign?"

"Nah. Things'll pick back up. Valentine's Day will be here before you know it," Myra said as we walked into the kitchen. "Who knows? You might even get to make a wedding cake."

"That would be wonderful," I said.

I'd only been back in Brea Ridge for four months—after more than a twenty-year absence—and opened a cake-decorating business, which I run out of my home. I hadn't had the opportunity to make any wedding cakes yet, although I had been given the privilege of making a large, tiered cake for a guinea pig's birthday celebration. It was the closest thing to a wedding cake I'd prepared so far.

I had the Scrabble board set up on the island with the two stools set on opposite sides. The cashew brittle and chocolate-covered raisins were plated and on a tray to the right side of the board along with a large bowl of popcorn. The Scrabble tiles were to the left.

"What would you like to drink?" I asked.

"Something hot. That wind chilled me to the bone on my walk over," she said. "How about a decaf café au lait?"

I smiled. "Sounds good to me."

Myra sat down and began choosing her tiles. "Great. Nearly all vowels. How am I supposed to make a word out of this mess?"

"Just put those back and draw some new letters." I have a single-cup coffeemaker, so I began making Myra's café au lait.

"No, now, you know I don't cheat," she said. "I'll make do with the letters I have. Maybe some of this cashew brittle will help me think."

The next sound I heard was a howl of pain.

"Myra? What is it?"

"Owwww, my tooth . . . my filling . . . fell out!" She shoved her fingers in her mouth, trying to retrieve the metal filling.

I turned the coffeemaker off. "Who's your dentist? I'll call him and ask if he can meet you in his office." Don't think I was being sexist when I said "him." There were only two dentists in Brea Ridge, and they were both men.

"Bainworf."

I got "Bainsworth" out of the mumbled word and rushed into the living room to retrieve my phone book from the end table. I called the dentist's office first and then dialed the emergency number that was on his answering machine. Dr. Bainsworth answered the call immediately.

"Hi, Dr. Bainsworth. I'm Daphne Martin. My friend Myra Jenkins is a patient of yours. She is here at my house and she just bit into a piece of cashew brittle and lost a huge filling. She's in terrible pain."

"Ah, yes, I know Myra well." His voice was deep and rich and contained just a hint of amusement. "Tell her I'll meet her at my office in three quarters of an hour. In the meantime, do you have any clove oil?"

"I believe so."

"Then apply a little of the oil to the tooth with a cotton swab," he said. "It'll help dull the pain until you can get her here." He chuckled. "Good luck."

"Thank you." Apparently, he *did* know Myra well.

I returned to the kitchen. "Dr. Bainsworth will see you in his office in forty-five minutes."

"It's gonna be almost an hour?" she asked. "I'll be dead by then, or at least passed out from the pain."

I opened the cabinet where I keep my spices and got the clove oil. "He told me to apply a little of this to your tooth. He said it will help dull the pain."

"Eashy for him to shay." She continued moaning as I went to the bathroom for a cotton swab.

"Come on," I said when I had returned. "Dr. Bainsworth says this will help. Take your hand down, open your mouth, and show me which tooth."

She opened her mouth. "It's this toot." She pointed to her second bicuspid on the left. "The one drobbing wit pain."

I dabbed clove oil on the tooth. "There. Feel better?"

"No."

"Well, just give it a minute," I said. "Go ahead and slip your boots back on, and we'll head on over to the dentist's office."

She got down from the stool, went into the living room, and put on her boots. It took a laborious effort, but she managed somehow. Myra should have been an actress. She was a regular drama queen.

I took my coat from the closet, grabbed my purse and car keys, and off we went.

Myra gasped and covered her mouth when the cold air hit her tooth.

"I'm sorry," I told her, "but the dentist is meeting us, and you'll be feeling better in no time."

She nodded as I opened the passenger-side door of my red Mini Cooper and helped her get in. I hurried around to the driver's side, started the engine, turned on the lights, and backed out of the driveway. The traffic was surprisingly heavy for a Friday winter's night in Brea Ridge.

When we got there, I was relieved to see lights blazing in the back of the office. Dr. Bainsworth was already there and, presumably, had everything ready to fix Myra's tooth.

Myra pulled her scarf up over the lower portion of her face before stepping out into the cold air. I walked ahead so I could hold the heavy door open.

We stepped inside and looked around the empty office. Empty offices always look creepy at night, don't you think? There was only one light on in the entryway, and in the waiting area, the long, skinny windows allowed muted light from streetlamps to filter in, casting shadows throughout the room.

"Dr. Bainsworth? It's Daphne Martin and Myra Jenkins. Would you like us to come on back?"

He didn't answer, and I supposed maybe he couldn't hear us.

"Let's go on back," I said to Myra.

She nodded slightly, and we walked toward the examining rooms.

"Dr. Bainsworth?" I called again. "Are you back here?"

I looked inside the first room. My eyes widened, and my hand flew to my throat. I turned to Myra in shocked silence.

"Wha?" She followed my gaze to where Dr. Bainsworth was lying facedown on the floor. A trickle of blood emanated from his head. "No!"

"It's okay," I said, putting my arms around her. "I'll call 911. I'm sure he'll be all right."

"My toot! Who'll fiss my toot!" she cried.

I heard a thud in the lobby as if someone had tripped over a piece of furniture. I froze, and Myra did too.

"Whoever did this to Dr. Bainsworth is still here," I whispered.

She nodded.

"We have to find something to defend ourselves with." I stepped into the examining room and grabbed a huge plastic toothbrush.

Myra armed herself with a model of a molar so big she could barely hold it. She raised it up to eye level so she'd be ready to strike someone with it if need be.

It was at that moment that we heard the sirens. Which was odd because I hadn't called 911 yet.

I looked from my giant toothbrush to Myra's giant molar to the dentist bleeding on the floor. "This is not good."

I had no more than gotten those four words out of my mouth when two policemen, neither of whom I knew—which is also odd, given my past experiences here in Brea Ridge—came around the corner with their guns drawn. Had we wanted to, Myra and I could not have escaped. We'd brought a toothbrush and a molar to a gunfight.

I will say, however, that we had the element of surprise on our side. The officers were too stunned to speak. So I took the initiative.

"Hi," I said, trying to smile but probably grimacing. "I know this looks crazy, but—"

"Be quiet and drop your weapons," the taller, older officer commanded.

I put down my toothbrush and raised my hands.

Myra was a little slower. "Weapons?" She frowned at her plastic molar. "Hiss is no weapon; it's a plastic tooth."

"Drop it," the officer said. "Now. And put your hands where I can see them."

She shrugged and dropped the tooth. It bounced across the floor and hit the officer's left shin before coming to rest at his feet.

"Hands," he said.

Myra rolled her eyes and held up her hands. I silently prayed she wouldn't get us both shot.

"My tooth," she began. Then she looked at me. "Tell 'em."

"Um . . . yes, Officers. Myra—this is Myra Jenkins, and I'm Daphne Martin—she hurt . . . well—" I cleared my throat. "Lost a large filling, actually, out of one of her teeth. So, I called—"

"Save it," he said harshly. "I need you both to step away from the body."

"Can you re-ive him?" Myra asked.

The officer looked from Myra to his partner to me. "What?" he asked.

"Re-ive! Wake him up . . . fiss my tooth!"

"Step away from the body now," he demanded.

The other officer—shorter, trimmer, and clean-shaven—stepped forward and lowered his gun. "This way, ladies. We'll go into the hallway until Officer Halligan can see to the victim."

"Ought to be out catching who did this," Myra muttered as we followed the younger man to the end of the hall near the waiting room.

I could see the road beyond the picture window, and a light blue or silver car was speeding down the road. Could that speeder be Dr. Bainsworth's attacker?

"Did you see that?" I asked. "That car racing down the road . . . it could be whoever did this. Shouldn't you call somebody?"

"We get our fair share of speeders on the weekends," the officer said. "Mostly, they're kids in a hurry to get to Bristol or Johnson City or somewhere. Did you get a good description of the car? Make? Model?"

"No," I told him. "Do you think Dr. Bainsworth will be all right?" I hoped to show the nice officer that we were really more concerned about the dentist than about ourselves and Myra's hurt tooth.

"Hard to say, ma'am," he said. "Did you see anyone else when you arrived?"

"No," I said. "Of course, we weren't looking for anybody. We were just hurrying here to see the dentist about Myra's tooth. We did call him ahead of time. We spoke to him less than an hour ago. There should be a record of our call."

Darn! Should I have said that? Will he think the call was a ruse to lure Dr. Bainsworth here so we could bash him over the head and take . . . take what? Toothpaste samples? I was panicking. It was obvious Myra *had* lost a filling and that she was in pain.

I noticed he was holding his gun at his side, but he hadn't holstered it yet. The other officer came into the hallway. His gun had been put away—at least, for now—and he was removing latex gloves while talking into a microphone on his right shoulder.

"Yeah," he said. "Get Crime Scene out here right away." He turned to the three of us. "Let's all step into the waiting area. We need to secure this location and wait for the crime scene techs."

"Will Dr. Bainsworth be okay?" I asked.

"No. He's dead."

At that, Myra just flat-out started to cry.

"It's gonna be okay," the younger officer—Officer Kendall—told Myra, trying to reassure her, as he eased us into the back of the patrol car. "I called the station and we have a doctor on call who happens to be there right now. We had a patient fall against his toilet and chip a tooth, so we called in the dentist." He smiled at Myra. "So, you're in luck. Since we need to take you to the station for questioning so Crime Scene can go over Dr. Bainsworth's office, you get some free dental work on behalf of the Brea Ridge Police Department."

"Yay," Myra said sarcastically.

I glared at her.

"Wha?" she asked. "He's had his hans in a prisoner's mouf and maybe a toilet."

"You're talking like Scooby-Doo," I said.

"You ought to know . . . Raphne."

I sighed and rested my head against the back of the seat. I shuddered to think what might be on it—blood, spit, snot, vomit—and decided I'd scrub my scalp raw in a scalding shower as soon as I got home. I thought about whether or not this was the worst night of my life. Sadly, this night didn't even make my top-ten list.

I suppose number one on the list would have to be the night my ex-husband shot at me. Fortunately, he missed . . . which is why he's now serving time for attempted murder in a Tennessee prison and why I moved back to my hometown in Virginia to start life anew at the tender age of forty.

If you're wondering why he shot at me, it was because the mileage on my car wasn't where it should have been at the end of the day. On my way home from work, I'd gone four-tenths of a mile out of my way to a bookstore—which turned out to be eight-tenths of a mile after I got back on the route home, naturally—so I knew I was busted before I'd even gotten home. But I was so tired of having my every move controlled . . . tired of having to ask permission to stop at the grocery store or to schedule a hair appointment . . . tired of being told what to do and when to do it . . . tired of signing and turning over my paycheck to someone who wouldn't even allow me to have a checking account or a credit card . . . tired of not being able to voice an opinion . . . I was just plain tired. So, I did it. I knew there'd be a price to pay, but I was at the point of being willing to pay it. And the title of the book I'd bought? *Regaining Your Self-Respect: A Ten-Step Plan.*

So, you see? This night was cake compared to that one.

Cake. I almost laughed at the irony of my thoughts. That's my claim to fame here in Brea Ridge—Daphne's Delectable Cakes. Well, that and seeing dead people. Not like the kid in that movie with Bruce Willis but rather literal dead people. Since I'd set up shop here, my first customer had been murdered, and a bagger from the town's grocery store had been poisoned. Neither of those incidents had anything to do with me; they were just wrong-place-wrong-time situations. Like tonight.

Myra elbowed me in the side. "You awake?"

"Yes."

She nodded toward the windshield to show me that we'd arrived.

The officers parked the squad car and opened the doors to remove Myra and me. Officer Kendall, the nice one, said Dr. Huffington would fix Myra's tooth while they were interrogating me.

Officer Halligan punched in a code, and we entered the jail. We were in the back part, so we walked down a concrete floor past holding cells on the way in. It wasn't pleasant. In fact, it was downright creepy. The entire area smelled like urine and sweat. A few disheveled, drunken people (mainly men) yelled things (mainly obscenities) at us as we passed by their cells. I so did not want to wind up sleeping over at this establishment.

An oversized man barreled down the hall and exuberantly

greeted Myra. "Hey, Ms. Jenkins! Remember me? Mark Huffington?"

Myra's eyes widened. "Btter?"

"Yeah!" He laughed. He looked at me. "Back in the day, Myra's son Carl Jr. and the other kids called me Butter—you know, short for 'butterfingers'—because I couldn't hold on to a football or a basketball to save my life." He chuckled again, reminding me of a cross between John Candy and Christian Slater. "Better hope I'm not as clumsy with a drill, eh, Ms. Jenkins?"

I recalled Myra saying that Carl Jr. had attended Abingdon High School. They hadn't moved to Brea Ridge until he was in college.

Poor Myra looked terrified as "Butter" led her away. I didn't feel much more at ease as I stepped into the interrogation room and heard the heavy metal door slam shut behind me.

CHAPTER
Two

MYRA AND I spent the next several hours at the police station. We were fingerprinted, so our prints could be compared with others found in the office. They questioned me, then waited for Dr. Huffington to fill Myra's tooth and for her anesthesia to wear off so they could talk with her alone and understand what she was saying. After interrogating us separately, they questioned us together. This after leaving us alone in the interrogation room for an hour or so to see if we would say anything incriminating. We'd both seen enough crime shows to know better than to say anything at all to each other.

Naturally, our stories matched up. We were telling the truth. And we had both—separately and jointly—told the exact same story, down to where we'd picked up the dental props because we'd heard something in the office. They had then taken our formal, sworn statements. Finally, they'd agreed we could be released. Officer Kendall had kindly offered us a ride to the dentist's office to pick up my car.

"It's been a long night," Officer Kendall said as he ushered Myra and me into his patrol car. "I'm used to it. I work twelve-hour shifts from six P.M. to six A.M. every evening. But I reckon you ladies are tuckered out."

"We're tuckered, all right," Myra said.

"I could probably take you home rather than to the dentist's office," he said. He turned to look at me. "Is there somebody who can drive you over to pick up your car later today?"

"No," I said. "I mean, yeah, somebody could, but I want to get my car now."

"You're sure you're up to driving home?" he asked.

"I'm fine," I insisted.

"How about you, Ms. Jenkins? Would you like me to take you home?" he asked.

"Gosh, no," Myra said. "After being out all night, can you imagine what god-awful things folks would say if I came rolling up in a police car? I'd rather take my chances with Daphne."

"Gee, thanks," I said. "You so give me the warm fuzzies."

Officer Kendall drove us back to . . . well, to the scene of the crime, where yellow police tape had been affixed across the front door.

I ran my hands over the knees of my jeans. "How did Dr. Bainsworth's assailant get in?"

"The crime scene techs said there was no sign of forced entry," Officer Kendall said. "They figure either Dr. Bainsworth allowed the person or persons in, that the murderer had a key, or that someone had neglected to lock all the office doors when they left yesterday."

"Then you think it might've been an inside job," I said.

"It's too early to form a definitive conclusion at this time," he said.

"I wanna go home," Myra said.

"All right. Let's go." I thanked Officer Kendall for the ride as he let us out of the patrol car.

We got into my car, and I started the engine. It felt good to be behind the wheel—back in control—of something. I noticed that Officer Kendall followed us for a while to make sure I was okay to drive.

After I had seen Myra safely home, I drove the few remaining yards to my house and pulled into the driveway. The sun hadn't come up yet, but the sky showed that it was considering doing so. I was so weary it was all I could do to put one foot in front of the other as I walked to my front door. I still wanted that shower, but I didn't know if I could stay awake long enough to manage it. I fumbled as I tried to put my key into the lock.

"Well, hey there, pretty mama," a warm, mellow voice said from behind me.

I turned around quickly to see who had sneaked up on me. It was Elvis. Elvis Presley. And it appeared as though he'd just stepped out of a pink and white 1955 Cadillac Fleetwood with whitewall tires. This was the young, thin Elvis, and he was wearing black leather pants, a matching jacket, and a white and black striped shirt.

I was so tired I simply started laughing, and I couldn't stop.

Tears flowed down my face, and I couldn't catch my breath. The fact that I was so exhausted I was seeing Elvis and a pink Cadillac should have had me worried, but, oddly enough, I found it hilarious. I guessed it beat pink elephants.

Elvis frowned. "What's so funny, darlin'? Was it something I said?"

"It's everything you said. Either the paperboy has really stepped up his game, or I'm hallucinating. That, or I'm dead. Are you Elvis?"

"Well, yeah . . . I mean, no. I'm an Elvis impersonator and a member of the Elvis Impersonators' Evangelical Interdenominational Outreach. . . . We're a national charity organization otherwise known as the EIEIO."

That sent me into another fit of laughter, and Elvis chuckled right along with me this time.

"The founder's last name was MacDonald," Elvis said.

I had called my boyfriend Ben when we were leaving the police station and told him briefly what had happened to Myra and me. Moments later, Ben pulled up to find me and Elvis huddled together laughing hysterically with me holding my door key.

He got out of his white Jeep. "What's going on?"

I held up my hand. "Do you see this guy?"

"Yeah," Ben said.

"Does he look like Elvis?" I asked.

"Yeah," Ben said, planting his hands on his hips.

"Thank goodness," I said. "I haven't lost my mind."

"Is it so strange to find an Elvis look-alike at your door?" Elvis asked.

"It's not even light out yet," Ben said.

Elvis tilted his head. "You've got a point there, buddy. But I was just driving by and I saw this young lady pulling into her driveway, and I stopped." He shrugged. "I was planning on talking with her sometime today anyhow. I got her name from Aaron, one of our local boys. When I saw the sign in her yard, I knew I was in the right place." He shrugged. "Seemed like this was as good a time as any since she was here and I was here."

"What did you want to see me about?" I asked him. "Are you looking for a cake?"

"Well, I just told you about the EIEIO. We're in town this week at the Brea Ridge Hotel for a convention, and we'd like you to make us a cake for next Friday night's gala."

I turned and unlocked the door, then invited Ben and Elvis in and stifled a yawn as the men followed me inside.

"What's the EIEIO?" Ben asked.

"The EIEIO is a group of missionaries who dress up and perform as Elvis," I explained.

I sat my purse on the counter and took a magnetized notepad off the refrigerator door. "How many people will your cake need to serve?" I asked as I slid the bowl of last night's popcorn on the island over to make room to write.

"Well, there are twenty-five of us in town for the convention. Those who have wives or girlfriends will bring them to the gala." He looked up at the ceiling as he calculated. "Some of our event coordinators will be there. Let's make it seventy-five just to be on the safe side."

"All right. Is there a particular design you'd like?" I asked.

He grinned. "Yes, ma'am. A pink Cadillac."

I smiled. "I should've known it would be that or blue suede shoes."

"Yep." He stuck out his hand. "Just dawned on me I haven't properly introduced myself. I'm Scottie Phillips."

I shook his hand. "Daphne Martin."

Ben extended his hand. "And I'm Ben Jacobs."

I looked at Ben as he and Scottie shook hands. "What are you doing here this time of the morning?" I asked Ben.

He glanced at Scottie and then back at me. "We'll talk about it after you finish your business here."

"Okay." I turned my attention back to Scottie. "What flavor cake would you like?"

"Can you make a peanut butter and banana cake?" he asked. "You know, Elvis loved his peanut butter and bananas."

"I've never made one before . . . but if there's a recipe out there for peanut butter and banana cake, I can certainly make it," I said.

"You are an angel," he said with a smile.

"She certainly is," Ben said.

Scottie gave me his cell number and told me to call him if I had any questions. He invited Ben and me to a performance at the Brea Ridge Hotel on Sunday night, and then he left.

Ben wanted lots of answers as soon as Elvis—I mean, Scottie—left. But I simply couldn't talk about last night's ordeal yet.

"Thanks for coming over, Ben, but, please, can we wait until I've taken a shower to get into it?" I asked. "I was scared half to death, then I was in the back of the squad car. And then I had to mingle in the jail with other people who'd been hauled in." I shuddered. "I really need to bathe."

"Of course. Sorry."

"Do you mind opening a can of food for Sparrow and putting it into her bowl?" I asked. "She won't eat it unless you go into the living room, though."

"Is she ever going to get used to me?" he asked as he opened the small can of food and dumped it onto her plate by the kitchen door.

"Eventually."

I heard him toss the can into the recycle bin before going into the living room to wait for me. I took my nearly scalding shower, washed my hair, rinsed, repeated . . . repeated . . . and repeated just one more time for good measure. Then I scrubbed my body with a loofah and even went over and under my fingernails with a nail brush.

I towel-dried my hair and dressed in black yoga pants, a teal sweatshirt, and shea-butter-infused lavender socks. I didn't figure I'd win the Damsel of the Day award, but then, I wasn't vying for it. I was more tired than I thought by now and was hoping to answer Ben's questions so I could turn the ringer off on my phone and go to bed.

I walked past Sparrow furtively eating her breakfast in the kitchen. She looked up at me as if to admonish me for being out all night. Cats can look so haughty and condemning. Then, as if her expression hadn't spoken volumes, she nonchalantly went back to eating.

I went into the living room and found Ben sitting on the couch watching an early morning news show. I sat down beside him, and he put his arm around me.

"Good morning," he said.

"Hi," I said. "Now, are you going to tell me what brings you by so early this morning?"

"I just wanted to check on you and make sure you're okay. You want to talk about it now?"

"There's not much to say." I stifled a yawn and nestled my head on his shoulder. "Myra lost a filling . . . we called the dentist . . . and he said he'd meet us there. . . . So we . . . went to his office . . . and found him. It was terrible. I thought he was only unconscious."

"And you said earlier on the phone that he died from a blow to the head. Did the police find the murder weapon?"

"Not that I know of. They weren't exactly forthcoming with Myra and me." My eyelids were so heavy. I went ahead and let them shut. "Tell me they'll find whoever did this."

"They will," he promised.

WHEN I AWOKE, I was lying on the sofa covered with a fleece throw. There was a note from Ben on the coffee table.

> *Hi, sweetheart. You're obviously exhausted. I'll be back*
> *later with dinner.*
>
> *—Ben*

I looked at the clock. It was nearly two in the afternoon. I rubbed my eyes and went into the kitchen to make myself a cup of coffee. While the coffee was brewing, I cleaned up the Scrabble game and the almost-untouched refreshments. What should have been a night of relaxing fun had turned into a nightmare. Poor Dr. Bainsworth. I wondered who'd want to hurt him. He'd seemed really nice over the phone, super-indulgent toward Myra. . . . I couldn't dwell on that now, though. After a long dry spell, I had work to do. And since baking is the best form of therapy I've found yet, I was glad I'd found Elvis and his crazy cake order on my porch that morning.

I took my coffee and the notes I'd made about Scottie Phillips's Cadillac cake into my office and turned on the computer. Carving the cake wouldn't be easy, especially with the fins and all the other angles. Still, a template would help. I just hoped I could find a peanut butter and banana cake recipe.

To my surprise and delight, there were a number of peanut butter and banana cake recipes online. I scanned several until I found the one I felt would both taste the best and be the best consistency for carving. I made myself a grocery list and printed the recipe.

Before shutting off the computer, I checked my e-mail to see if anyone had requested a cake quote. No one had. That made me realize that "the King" and I hadn't discussed my fee. I decided to give him a call before heading out to the Save-A-Buck. Unfortunately, I got his voice mail. I left a message quoting a price and went on to the grocery store. Right now, any business was business. Plus, while I was at the Save-A-Buck, I could talk with the manager, Steve Franklin, about making some cakes and cookies for the store. The Save-A-Buck is a smaller store and doesn't have an in-store bakery, so Mr. Franklin allows me to bring in baked goods with my logo and contact information on the boxes and sell them on consignment.

I went into the bathroom, splashed some water on my face, and then put on a little makeup. I still looked pale and tired eyed, but at least I was wearing mascara and lipstick. People couldn't accuse me of not trying. I pulled on my boots, coat, and gloves, grabbed my purse off the counter, and headed out.

*   *   *

As I walked across the Save-A-Buck parking lot, I was greeted by China York, who looked like a female Willie Nelson. The tiny little woman was wearing her typical ensemble—jeans and a white tee under a red and black flannel shirt—but today she was also wearing a quilted jean jacket and men's work gloves. She sort of looked like a cross between a pixie and a lumberjack. She had a plastic bag hanging from each arm.

"Hi," she said. "You doin' all right?"

"I'm fine," I said. "How about you?"

"I'm good. It must've been rough on you and Myra finding Dr. Bainsworth like that last night," China said.

"How'd you know?"

"Heard it over the scanner." She shifted her weight from one booted foot to the other.

"They gave our names?" I asked.

"No, but as soon as they gave the descriptions, I knew it was you and Myra."

I smiled wanly. "Yeah, it was a rough night."

"How's Myra doing?" she asked. "Did she get that tooth fixed?"

"Yeah, the dentist—a Dr. Huffington—was there at the jail to help an inmate, and he refilled the tooth for her."

"Butter Huffington?" China laughed. "I'd have loved to have seen the expression on Myra's face when she saw that Butter would be her dentist."

"You know, he seemed really capable," I said. "I think he did a good job."

"Oh, I don't doubt he's a good dentist, but when you know

someone in one capacity, it's hard to imagine them in another." She cocked her head. "Take your niece and nephew . . . do you know any of their friends?"

"I know a few of them."

"Now imagine going to the gynecologist twenty years from now and having one of those kids come into the exam room," she said.

My eyes flew open in horror. "Ewww!"

China grinned. "Exactly."

"So, let's change the subject quickly," I said. "Do you know anyone who might've wanted to hurt Dr. Bainsworth?"

"I wanted to hurt him last year when he did a root canal on one of my teeth. But I got over it." She shrugged. "I'll keep my ear to the ground and let you know if I come up with anything. By the way, I've got some potato soup in the slow cooker. I'm going to take some to Myra later on. Want me to bring you some?"

"I appreciate the offer, but Ben said he'd bring dinner later."

She nodded. "That's good. Let him take care of you. It'll make him feel strong, and it'll make you feel cherished."

"Let me know if you hear anything about Dr. Bainsworth," I said.

China waved as we went our separate ways.

Before doing my shopping, I asked my favorite checkout girl, Juanita, if I could speak with the manager, Mr. Franklin. She paged him, and he came to the front.

"Hi, Steve," I said. "I thought I'd see if you need any cakes, cookies, or candies while I'm here. You haven't ordered brownies in a while."

He nodded. "How about some football-themed stuff? The Super Bowl is coming up in a couple weeks. Maybe people getting in the spirit of the game will give up their New Year's diets and give in to temptation."

"Okay. Would you like a few cakes and some dessert party platters with cookies, candies, and mini brownies?"

"Sounds good, Daphne. Can I count on five cakes and five party platters to start with?"

"Sure," I said.

"Great. Bring the invoice when you bring in the cakes." With that, he returned from whence he came as if he were a man of great importance with scant time to spend on the little people. I wondered if the fact that he was dating the well-to-do Maureen Fremont had contributed to his increased sense of self-worth. Maureen was the sister-in-law of Belinda Fremont, the rich client for whom I'd made a guinea pig birthday cake. The guinea pigs are "champion cavies" and have their own suite in the Fremont home.

After Mr. Franklin left, Juanita said, "I'd like to talk with you before you leave. I want you to cater my sister's *quinceañera*."

"A *quinceañera* . . . that's her fifteenth-birthday celebration, right?"

"Yes," she said. "It's a very special occasion."

"That's wonderful, Juanita. When is it?"

"It is next Saturday. I know this is very last-minute. My mother and I had planned to make the cake ourselves, but I know you could do such a great job," she said.

"Why don't you come by my house after work and we'll look at some books for ideas?" I asked.

"I can't today, but maybe I can come tomorrow?"

"Tomorrow sounds super." I grinned. "Well, I'm off to buy lots of bananas."

She gave me a quizzical look. "You've adopted a monkey?"

I laughed. "No, but I'm making a peanut butter and banana Cadillac cake for the Elvis Impersonators' Evangelical Interdenominational Outreach."

"Oh, I know the EIEIO," she said. "My boyfriend is a new member. He learned of them through our church."

"So your boyfriend looks like Elvis?" I asked.

"Not so much. He is better, I think. But when he puts on the wig and sunglasses and flashy clothes, yes, he does resemble Elvis Presley . . . at least, as much as some of the other EIEIO people I've seen," said Juanita. "And he has a beautiful singing voice. That's how he won my heart—singing to me."

"Sounds romantic."

"He is romantic." She lowered her eyes. "Sometimes I feel I do not deserve him."

"Yes, you do. You deserve the best, Juanita."

WHEN I GOT home, I put away my groceries and made enough batter for three large peanut butter and banana sheet cakes. I was only able to put one cake into the oven at a time, so I covered the rest of the batter and put the mixing bowl in the refrigerator.

While waiting for that first cake to bake, I called Myra.

"How are you today?" I asked when she answered.

"I'm feeling much better, thanks."

"I'm sorry my cashew brittle caused you so much pain and aggravation," I told her.

"Me too," Myra said. "Want to know the worst part? I didn't get to eat any of it. I messed up my tooth with the first bite. Save me some?"

"Of course . . . if you aren't afraid to eat it," I said. "I think if I were in your position, I'd never want to see another piece of cashew brittle for as long as I lived."

"Not me. I don't hold grudges against food," she said. "I'll just chew my brittle on the other side of my mouth. I think those fillings are in pretty tight."

"So I never got around to asking last night, did Dr. Huffington do a good job?" I asked.

"He did all right," Myra said. "I just had to get my mind around the fact that he's not a little, clumsy football player anymore. Now he's a big, clumsy dentist." She giggled. "He liked you, by the way."

"He did?" I asked. I hadn't been aware he'd really even noticed me.

"Yep. Asked if you were married. I told him you were divorced but that I believe you're seeing someone."

"Thank you. I mean, he seemed nice enough, but I *am* seeing Ben and . . ." I let the sentence trail off.

"Right. So were you too tired to bake today?" Myra asked.

"As a matter of fact, I have a cake in the oven right now." I explained to her about the EIEIO and the cake I was making for their Friday-night end-of-convention festivities.

"Sounds interesting. I used to love Elvis," she said. "Not literally *love,* you know, but I sure thought he was the berries."

"Lots of people did. Lots of people still do, I guess," I said.

"Scottie—my client—invited Ben and me to go to the show at the hotel tomorrow night."

"Are you going?" she asked eagerly.

"Maybe," I said. "I'll ask Ben this evening. He's bringing over dinner."

"If you decide to go, ask if he'd mind my tagging along."

"If we decide to go," I said, "I'm sure he'd love to have you tag along." Actually, I wasn't *sure* of anything. But I felt obligated to take Myra to the Elvis concert the next night either way.

CHAPTER

Three

BEN CAME over to my house at about seven o'clock that evening and brought dinner from Dakota's. It's the only steakhouse in Brea Ridge, and the food is terrific. Ben had a prime rib, and he brought me my favorite, the filet mignon. He'd gotten us house salads, fries, and rolls to go with the steaks. I'd have to spend an extra thirty minutes on the treadmill tomorrow morning, but it was worth it.

I went to the refrigerator and got a Diet Coke for me and a regular one for Ben. "Did you go into the office today? Was everyone talking about the murder?" I asked as I sat down at the table. I noticed he'd changed from the jeans and sweatshirt he'd been wearing that morning into dress pants, a blue and white striped button-down shirt, and a sport coat.

"I went in for a little while," Ben said. "Neil is doing fine as assistant editor, but he's still new at it." He sighed. "Of course, there was quite a bit of buzz about Dr. Bainsworth, but it's all speculation at this point. The police aren't giving us much to go on."

"About Neil . . . don't you think you might be giving him the impression you're not confident in his abilities?" I cut into my steak. "You *are* confident in them, aren't you?"

"Yes and no." Ben took a drink of his soda. "He's a good editor, but he's young and inexperienced."

"And so were you at one point. Besides, that's why you have a cell phone," I said. "So he can call you if he has any questions. You're going to have to give him some wings if he's ever going to fly, you know."

"I get what you're saying, Daph, but it's my name on the masthead. When all is said and done, my name as editor in chief is what people see. I'm ultimately who they blame or who they praise for the paper's content."

"Yeah . . . okay." I knew I was fighting a losing battle, so I began to eat in silence. Ben and I had been over this before. If he'd delegate more of his responsibilities at the newspaper— the responsibilities that had already been assigned to other people anyway—then he and I would be able to spend more time together. Don't get me wrong. I was glad Ben took such pride in his work and that his job was important to him, but I'd like to think spending time with me was a priority to him too.

"What?" he asked after a few minutes. "Are you mad at me now?"

"No, I'm not mad." Maybe I was just trying to resign myself to the fact that Ben Jacobs was a married man . . . married to the *Chronicle*.

That might even explain why he'd remained single all these years. What a dope I'd been to think even for a second that maybe Ben had never gotten over me when we'd broken up all those years ago.

"You are," he said. "You're mad. Daphne, you know my job entails working some long hours. I can't help that."

"Let's please not discuss this right now. Let's just eat dinner in peace," I said.

Ben huffed. "Fine."

As we were finishing up, the doorbell rang. I got up to answer it and was surprised to see Scottie Phillips on my doorstep for the second time that day.

"Hey," he said as he came in the door. He shook off his leather coat and handed it to me.

Okaaay. "Hi." I hung the jacket up on the rack beside the door.

"Got your message," he said. "Sorry I had my phone off. Whatever you want to charge for the cake is fine. EIEIO is going all-out for this party. We just ask people to remember we're a missionary organization."

"Sure. I'll . . . uh . . . give you the fifteen percent missionary organization discount," I said. "Does that sound about right?"

"Sounds good to me." He nodded at Ben. "How you doing this evening?"

"Fine," Ben said tightly. "I'm doing just fine."

"Man, those fries look good." Scottie looked back at me. "You gonna finish those?"

"No. Be my guest," I said.

He sat down at the table opposite Ben and dug into my remaining fries. "I love big ol' thick steak fries. They're the best."

"Yeah. They're good." Ben glanced at me in exasperation, but I couldn't very well be rude to a client, the only client I'd had in two weeks besides the Save-A-Buck. It was a work thing. Certainly he could understand *that*.

"So," Scottie said to Ben, "are you and long, tall Sally here coming to the performance tomorrow night? The EIEIO will rock your socks off."

"Sorry," Ben said, sounding anything but sorry. "I have to cover a council meeting tomorrow evening."

"My neighbor Myra and I are going to try to make it, though," I said.

Scottie smiled. "Super."

Ben merely stared at the man.

After he'd finished my fries and my Diet Coke, Scottie wiped his mouth and hands on my napkin and got up from the table. "It's been real, folks, but I have to get back to the hotel. We've got one last rehearsal before tomorrow's show." He kissed my cheek and grabbed his jacket. "See you there, Daphne."

With that, he was out the door . . . and yet he left behind a silence that was palpable.

"Had you ever seen that guy before this morning?" Ben asked.

"No," I said.

He blew out a breath as he was shaking his head. "What a jerk! He asks for your leftovers and then kisses you like we've all been old friends for years. Seriously, who does he think he is?"

"I guess he thinks he's Elvis." I shrugged.

"I don't like him. There's something smarmy about him," Ben said. "Did you *have* to tell him you'd come to that concert tomorrow night?"

"As a matter of fact, I did. You didn't leave me a way out— you said *you* have to be somewhere, not that *we* have to be somewhere," I said. "Besides, when I mentioned to Myra today that I had a new client who had invited us to the EIEIO concert, she asked if she could go with us."

"Then you're actually going?" he asked.

"Of course I am. I have to. One, he's my client; and two, I'm the reason Myra lost her filling yesterday and had to go to the dentist; which means that, three, I might be the reason Dr. Bainsworth is dead."

Ben ran his hand over his face. "How did you get from going to an Elvis concert to killing a dentist in three easy steps?"

"It wasn't hard," I said. "Isn't there any way you can get out of this council meeting? Can't someone else cover it?"

"I'll see, but I doubt it," Ben said. "Everyone else has their own assignments."

I could've pointed out the times since I'd been back in Brea Ridge when he'd had to—or volunteered to—take on the assignments of others, but I didn't. Instead I took his hand and led him into the living room. "What's being said about Dr. Bainsworth today at the newspaper? You said the police weren't giving you much to go on, but do they have any suspects?"

"Besides you and Myra?" he asked. "No."

"Oh, come on. There has to be somebody."

"I know, but they don't have any leads yet," said Ben. "The

police are going over the office, interviewing Dr. Bainsworth's staff members, and talking with everyone who had appointments scheduled during the past couple weeks."

"Well, that's good." I sighed. "But what if they don't find anybody? Will they arrest Myra and me?"

"From what I gather, I don't think so. They don't have any real evidence against you at this point."

"But they're looking," I said.

"Sure, they're looking. They're asking around to see if you or Myra had a prior connection to the man or a motive to harm him. It's standard procedure."

"Myra was his patient. Is every patient he had on the suspect list?" I asked.

"At this point, they could be. But the cops aren't going to find any evidence linking you or Myra to Dr. Bainsworth's murder." He squeezed my hand.

"Since I've only been back in Brea Ridge a few months, I never even met the guy. What was he like?" I asked.

"I didn't know him that well either. I go to Farmer—the other dentist. But Bainsworth seemed like an okay guy. I interviewed him for the paper a few times." Ben stretched his legs out in front of him. "I did an article on him when he moved his practice into a new building—where it is now—because it was in the historical section and he was remodeling. I also spoke with him about the mission trip he took a couple months ago."

"A mission trip? He wasn't an EIEIO, was he?"

Ben smiled. "I don't think so. He was doing dental work for the poor, which was really magnanimous of him given his circumstances at the time."

"What circumstances?" I asked.

"Well, his wife had left him a few months prior and was in the process of taking nearly everything the two of them had," Ben said.

"That doesn't seem very fair." I leaned back into the sofa.

"He was cheating on her," Ben said. "Angela, his wife, caught him with one of his hygienists."

"That bites." I laughed at my own joke, but Ben didn't.

"Anyway, the mission trip had already been scheduled, which is why I suppose he still went. Once the divorce was more fully under way, I don't think he could have afforded it," Ben said. "That's a shame too, because from the way he talked he'd really enjoyed helping those people."

BEN LEFT FAIRLY early since he had to get up and go to work the next morning. I was a little tired but restless. I went into my office to search online for a large model of a 1955 Cadillac I could use to make a template for the EIEIO cake.

As I searched, I wondered about Dr. Bainsworth. Maybe his wife killed him. She could still harbor feelings of hurt and jealousy. Surely the police would check her alibi.

Or since he was cheating on his wife, perhaps the other injured party—the hygienist's husband or boyfriend—had gone to the office to confront Dr. Bainsworth. But why would he wait so long? From the way Ben had talked, Dr. Bainsworth's wife had discovered the affair and started divorce proceedings more than four months ago. Wouldn't anyone entangled in that volatile situation have lashed out before now?

What if one of Dr. Bainsworth's patients told him something while under anesthesia? What if the dentist confronted the patient about it later, and the patient got angry? That could make sense. But then, even if the police questioned every single one of the dentist's patients, the guilty person wasn't going to speak up and say something stupid like "Yeah, I slipped into his office to bash him on the head because I confessed to him that I was embezzling from my company while I was all hyped up on nitrous oxide."

I wondered if Myra was up for some undercover investigation. Fortunately, before I could dwell on Dr. Bainsworth's murder suspects any more, I found the car I needed for my template. I printed it out and went to bed, resolving to start carving the cake first thing tomorrow morning. This way, I could give it a trial run. And if the cake went wrong, I could make another in plenty of time for the party.

THE NEXT MORNING, I hurried outside to get the newspaper to see what was being written about the Bainsworth investigation. There was the handsome dentist's face plastered on the front page with the headline POLICE SEARCH FOR DENTIST'S KILLER. The article related how "two local women, one of whom was a patient of Dr. Bainsworth," had found the body Saturday night at the dental office. Thankfully, they hadn't named Myra or me in the article. I didn't need bad publicity to further drive down the market for baked goods in Brea Ridge.

The *Chronicle* went on to list Dr. Bainsworth's attributes before saying that police were pursuing several leads in connection with his murder. They weren't specific about those leads, but at least the paper didn't say "especially the patient and her friend."

After reading the paper, I made myself a task list. Mr. Franklin wanted five football-themed cakes for the Save-A-Buck and five party trays to psych people up for the Super Bowl. I decided I would make one yellow, two chocolate, and two white cakes—all sheet cakes. I'd go with chocolate chip, oatmeal raisin, and snickerdoodle cookies for the party trays, along with the brownies and some white- and milk-chocolate-covered pretzels.

The phone rang. I hadn't put on my headset yet, so I picked up the receiver.

"Did you see it?" Myra asked excitedly. "We made the front page of the paper!"

"Was that us? I thought it was Dr. Bainsworth."

Myra huffed. "Oh, you know what I mean. Did Ben mention anything about the suspects?"

"No," I said. "Actually, he told me that the police were being kind of cagey on the subject."

"On *Law and Order* that always means they don't have any suspects at all," she said.

"Not even the two lovely costars who made the front page of the paper?" I asked sarcastically.

"That would only work if one of us had been having a fling with Dr. Bainsworth. I wasn't. Were you?"

"Yep."

She blew out a breath. "Oh, you were not. And don't say you were, not even joking! You'd be arrested for sure."

I laughed. "I'd better get back to work. I'll talk with you later."

"Call me if you find out anything," Myra said.

"Likewise."

Before I got started on all that baking, I needed to start carving on the peanut butter and banana cake. I retrieved my template, slipped on my apron, and put on my telephone headset. Then I stacked the three sheet cakes with buttercream between the layers to hold them together, and I started carving.

To be honest, I was nervous about the carving. I haven't done all that many three-dimensional cakes. But as I carved, I became more confident. The cake was actually starting to look like a car.

I was using a round biscuit cutter to make the wheel wells when the phone rang. "Daphne's Delectable Cakes, how may I help you?"

"It's me, Daph."

It was my sister, Violet, and she sounded exasperated.

"What's wrong?" I asked.

"I just read about you and Myra Jenkins in the paper. You found the dentist dead night before last? I can't believe you didn't call me first thing!"

"How could you tell from what was written in the paper that Myra and I were the ones who found the dentist?" I asked.

"Educated guess. Whenever anything weird happens in this town lately, you and Myra are at the heart of it. Now, why didn't you call me?"

"Well, I didn't call you from the jail because you were at Grammy Armstrong's party," I said. "How did that go, by the way? Did she like her cake?"

"It went fine, and she loved the cake. Everyone did," she said. "Don't change the subject though. Why didn't you call me?"

"I didn't get home until almost seven yesterday morning,

and then I went to sleep. When I got up, I had to go to the Save-A-Buck and then get started on a cake I'm doing for a new client."

"The *Chronicle* said Dr. Bainsworth had been bludgeoned to death with a blunt object. Was it horrible?" she asked.

"Of course," I said. "But it wasn't as gory as all that. In fact, I thought he'd only been knocked out when I saw him. He didn't appear to be hurt all that badly."

"Oooh, that's so scary that it happened just before you got there. I mean if you'd been just a couple minutes earlier . . ."

"Tell me about it," I said. "Myra and I thought we heard the killer in the waiting area."

Violet gasped. "What did you do?"

"We grabbed the only things we could find to use to defend ourselves, a tooth and a toothbrush."

"Daphne!"

"What would you have done?"

"I honestly have no idea," she said. "I'm just glad you're all right. Let's change the subject. So, who's the new client?"

"The EIEIO," I said.

"That bunch of Elvis impersonators that have descended on the town? Are you making a cake shaped like Graceland?"

"No; fortunately, the Elvis I spoke with apparently didn't think of that. He's getting a pink Cadillac," I said.

Violet laughed. "Be sure and take pictures. This I've gotta see."

"I will. Hey, they've invited me to their concert at the hotel tonight," I said, going back to working on the wheel wells. "Would you like to go?"

"No, thanks. Once Jason and I were eating dinner in a restaurant in Gatlinburg—it was before the children were born—and an Elvis impersonator started performing. He tried to give me his sweaty scarf. It was sopping wet—and it smelled!" She made a gagging noise. "I've never been able to look at Elvis impersonators the same way since."

"Gee, thanks for getting me all excited about the event," I said. "I can only hope I'll be offered a scarf."

"Sorry," she said with laughter bubbling into her voice. "Didn't mean to ruin it for you. Some of those impersonators are really good . . . just not the one we saw."

"I'm taking Myra. I feel I owe it to her since it was my cashew brittle that caused her to lose her filling and have to go to the dentist in the first place."

"Daphne, you have to stop blaming yourself for every little thing," Violet said. "If the filling was in that bad of shape, she'd have lost it anyhow."

Even though Violet was my younger sister, she often took a maternal tone with me. I guess being a mom had done that to her over the years.

"True," I said, "but maybe it wouldn't have been Friday night and maybe we wouldn't have found Dr. Bainsworth bleeding on the floor of exam room one."

"You've got a point. But still . . ." She trailed off, apparently unable to think of anything to counter my point.

"Ben said Dr. Bainsworth was going through a messy divorce," I said. "Do you think his ex-wife might've murdered him? I mean, maybe it wasn't even on purpose. They could've been arguing over the resolution of their property or whatever, and she could've lost her temper and hit him with . . . something."

"I doubt it. I sold Angela her new house on the outskirts of town, and she seemed like a really nice person," Violet said. "Plus, despite the way their marriage ended, it appeared to me that Angela and Jim had a pretty amicable parting. The way she talked, he was giving her just about anything she wanted."

"Of course she was going to tell you everything was rosy, Vi. You were her real estate agent."

"I think if Angela had been going to kill Jim," Violet continued, "she'd have done it when she found out about the affair— the first affair, I mean. I could see her acting in the heat of passion then but not killing the guy four or five months after the fact."

"Wait. You said the first affair," I said. "There was more than one?"

"Oh, yeah. After the hygienist he was seeing left her husband thinking she was destined to be the next Mrs. Bainsworth, Jim started dating someone else—a patient, I believe." She thought a second. "Yes, it *was* a patient. It was Maureen Fremont."

"Maureen Fremont?" I asked. "I thought she was dating Steve Franklin."

"She is now. This was before that. Her divorce had just become final, and she was vulnerable and apparently more than a little stupid," Violet said. "I mean, she had to have heard all the gossip about Jim and the hygienist. Anyway, their little fling didn't last long either."

I didn't want to talk about Dr. Bainsworth anymore. "How are my sweethearts?" I asked, speaking of Lucas and Leslie.

"Hoping every single morning for a snow day. At least, it has them glued to the morning news until after schedule changes are announced, and I can pretend they have a keen interest in current affairs."

I laughed. "Do you think they might like peanut butter and banana cake balls if I dip them in white chocolate?"

"Peanut butter and banana cake balls?" She groaned. "Maybe. They like to try weird things."

"It's the flavor of cake Elvis requested. Actually, I tasted a bit that I carved off, and it's pretty good."

"Really? Want the kids to come over one evening this week and help you make the cake balls?" Violet asked.

"I'd love it. Their aprons are by the door waiting for them," I said. "Does Wednesday work for you?"

"Wednesday is great."

We said our good-byes and hung up. Well, she hung up. I pressed *end* on the headset.

Violet's twelve-year-old twins, Lucas and Leslie, love to make and decorate cakes, cookies, candy, cinnamon rolls . . . you name it. I think they like the eating part better than the baking and decorating these days, but that's okay too. I love to have them over.

I don't have children of my own. Given my troubled marriage to Todd, it was a blessing we'd never had children. But at forty, I felt like my chances at motherhood were dwindling. I sometimes wonder what I've been missing out on.

My thoughts turned back to Dr. Bainsworth. I tried to picture what he must have looked like when he wasn't lying on his white tiled examination room floor with a small puddle of blood stemming from a head wound. He'd been tall—I imagine he was over six feet—he had an athletic build, and he had thick, dark brown hair. He looked youngish. I'd have taken him to be in his early thirties. Violet knew of one affair he'd had with a patient. Had there been others?

Three hours and an aching back later, I had finished carving the Cadillac and had covered it in peanut-butter-flavored buttercream frosting. It looked good. I could really envision it coming together. I loosely covered the cake in plastic wrap and put it into the refrigerator. I'd tint some fondant pink and cover the car tomorrow.

I made enough batter to make a chocolate half-sheet cake. Cut in half, it would provide the two fourth-sheet cakes—or roughly nine-by-thirteen-size sheet cakes—for Save-A-Buck. While the cake was baking, I cleaned up the kitchen and got ready for my meeting with Juanita.

I keep cake samples in the freezer, and I'd set some out this morning to thaw. I had also found some cake-decorating books with *quinceañera* cakes in them. With some families, a *quinceañera* is almost as important as a wedding.

By the time Juanita came at five, the cake was on the island cooling. I'd even taken a shower and gotten ready for the Elvis concert. I didn't want to call too much attention to myself—Violet's sweaty-scarf anecdote was still too fresh in my mind—so I was wearing all black. With my dark hair and eyes, I hoped my ebony sweater and wool pants would help me blend into the background. Black boots and a heavy silver braided necklace and matching earrings rounded out my outfit.

"Oh, you look elegant," Juanita said when she arrived. "Do you have plans this evening?"

"Actually, Myra and I are going to the hotel tonight to see the Elvis concert," I said. "Are you going?"

"Yes, I am. I don't want to show up alone, though. Would it be okay if I ride with the two of you?" she asked.

"That'll be great," I said. "I spoke with Myra earlier, and she thinks China York will be going with us too. So it'll be a foursome."

Juanita put her hand to her mouth and tried to suppress a giggle. "Ms. York? Ms. York is an Elvis Presley fan?"

I smiled. "That's what I thought, too. But then, Elvis fans come in all varieties, I suppose. Remember that little Hawaiian girl Lilo in that Disney movie?"

"I do." She shook her head. "Still . . . Ms. York? She doesn't strike me as the type of person who would go in for Elvis impersonators. Some of them are . . ." She struggled to find the right expression.

"Over the top?" I asked.

"Yes," she said. "Very much over the top."

I shrugged. "I imagine we're in for an interesting performance. For now, though, let's get to work on your sister's *quinceañera*."

We pored over the three cake books in which I'd found *quinceañera* cakes. Juanita informed me that her sister, Isabel, would be wearing white and that her *damas*—the young ladies in her court—would be wearing rose. Juanita finally decided on a cake consisting of seven tiers. The main cake would be three tiers tall and set on a pedestal above a fountain. Two two-tiered cakes would be placed on either side—with dolls representing the *damas* standing on staircases on the sides of the main cake leading from the main cake to the smaller cakes.

After tasting the cake samples, Juanita chose a white cake with strawberry filling and vanilla buttercream frosting.

She clasped her hands to her chest and smiled at me, eyes glistening with tears. "This is so exciting! Isabel's party is going to be wonderful."

"Tell me about your *quinceañera*," I said. "What was it like?"

"I did not have one."

Fortunately, the awkwardness of that moment was interrupted by the doorbell ringing. Unfortunately, it was Myra . . . and she had completely and totally lost her mind.

CHAPTER Four

JUANITA AND I looked at Myra and then at each other with a mixture of alarm and amazement. Myra was wearing tight black cigarette pants and a bright red low-cut sweater that can only be described as va-va-va-voom. She had on a curly strawberry-blond shoulder-length wig. In addition, I think she'd had someone at a mall cosmetic counter do her makeup because it had obviously been applied with the intent to sell her one of everything in the cosmetic case. She'd been given "smoky cat's eyes," bright red lips, and contoured cheeks. But what really concerned me were the scarlet, strappy stilettos.

"Do I look like a sex kitten?" she asked, clawing the air in what I imagine she saw as a catlike gesture.

When Juanita and I merely continued to gape at her, she asked, "Don't you see? I'm Ann-Margret!" She smiled and tottered around in a circle.

"You're going to hurt yourself in those shoes," I said.

"Nonsense." She lifted her chin. "I believe the Bible, and it says, 'He will make me walk on my high heels.' New King James version."

"Myra, they didn't have high heels in biblical times," I said.

"It's the last verse in Habakkuk." She nodded smugly. "If you don't believe me, look it up."

I cannot simply let a challenge like that slide. I went into the bedroom, got my New King James–version Bible, and returned to the kitchen. I fumbled around until I finally had to look Habakkuk up in the table of contents. Then I flipped to the last verse and read aloud:

The Lord God is my strength;
He will make my feet like deer's feet,
And He will make me walk on my high hills.

"It says *hills*," I said, placing the Bible on the table so both Myra and Juanita could read the verse for themselves. "High hills . . . like little mountains."

Myra huffed. "Look down at my dear feet. If these shoes ain't little mountains, I don't know what are."

Juanita pursed her lips. "She's got you there."

"Are you ready to go?" Myra asked.

"I am. Juanita, are you?"

"Yes, I am ready," she said.

"Good," Myra said. "If China will come on, we can get

there in time to get a good seat." She considered Juanita and me for a moment. "You two probably have time to glam up a little bit if you'd like to. This is a live performance, you know. And you can bet those Elvises will be dressed to the nines."

Juanita had on jeans and an ivory fisherman's sweater. She looked lovely in a natural way.

"I'll be fine," I said. "I believe you're glammed up enough for all of us."

"Yes, so do I," Juanita said. "You look lovely. . . . Very . . . Priscilla, did you say?"

"*Ann-Margret,*" Myra said. "She and Elvis were in love before he married Priscilla. Ann-Margret is the one who got away." She looked wistful. "But tonight, maybe he'll get a second chance."

I shook my head ever so slightly at Juanita. There was no point in reiterating to Myra that she was not Ann-Margret and that the real Elvis Presley was dead. Myra was in her own little fantasy world at this point.

And when China showed up, she appeared to be in a fantasy world of her own. She'd left her silvery hair unbraided, and it was hanging in loose waves nearly to her waist. She'd also traded in her blue jeans and man's flannel shirt for a lavender wrap dress. She wore flat-soled boots and carried a black wool trench coat over her arm.

"China," I said when I found my voice, "you look incredible."

"Thanks," she said. "They were able to work me in down at Tanya's—she's not usually open on Sunday, you know, but she made an exception today with everybody wanting to go to the concert. And I thought I might as well fix up a tad . . . you know, put on a dress, smear on some lipstick."

Tanya's is the informal name for Tanya's Tremendous Tress-Taming Salon.

"You do look nice," Myra said, looking at me from the corners of her eyes.

"And isn't Myra something?" I asked.

"She sure is," China said with a shake of her head. "Y'all want to get started?"

"We'd better, if we're going to get a decent seat," Myra said. "And, no offense, Daphne, but I don't believe we'll all fit comfortably in that little drawn-up car of yours. That's why I brought my Buick."

I chuckled. "We should've rented a Cadillac for this special occasion."

"Yeah, well," Myra said, "I can't think of *everything* myself."

Juanita and I got into the backseat of Myra's huge white Buick and, through a series of shared looks, communicated our acknowledgment that she and I were the only sane people in this car and could possibly wind up being the only sane people at this concert.

"Say, Juanita," Myra said, glancing into her rearview mirror at us, "weren't you a patient of Dr. Bainsworth?"

Juanita lowered her head. "I was for a while, yes, but then I transferred to Dr. Farmer."

"Why's that?" Myra asked.

"I just wanted to," Juanita said. "Why do you ask?"

"Well, you've probably heard that Daphne and I are the ones who found the dentist's body," Myra said, turning her attention to the road. "I'm asking people all over town about him because we need to figure out who killed him before the cops try to frame us. I mean, we *were* the ones who found him."

"Yeah, and even though the *Chronicle* didn't mention our names, everybody seemed to know it was us," I said.

"And, of course, this is not the first dead body Daphne's ever found," Myra reminded us. "Nor is it the first time she's been investigated for murder."

"Thanks for pointing that out." I wondered if she'd catch my sarcasm this time. She usually didn't. "I talked with Ben about suspects last night too. He told me the police are going through Dr. Bainsworth's files and are talking with his staff and patients. If anybody had a reason to kill him, they'll find it. I hope."

"They're going through his files?" Juanita asked. "But why? I mean, what would someone's dental records have to do with the dentist's death?"

"I don't know," I said. "After Ben gave me some of the gory details about Dr. Bainsworth's divorce, I thought the killer might be his ex-wife. Violet doesn't think so, though. She likes Angela and doesn't think the woman would fly into a rage at this stage of their divorce."

"I agree with Violet," China said. "I believe Angela was smart enough to put the whole mess behind her and start all over . . . kind of like you, Daphne. Anyway, the salon was buzzing with dentist talk today."

"What did everybody there have to say?" Myra asked.

"The general consensus is that Dr. Bainsworth fooled around with the wrong patient and that the girlfriend—or more likely, her husband—got fed up with the dentist's frisky behavior and confronted him," China said. She took a deep breath. "I have to tell you, though, some officers came into the salon while I was there. They were asking questions about Dr. Bainsworth . . . and they were asking us questions about the two of you."

"What kind of questions?" I asked.

"Pretty general stuff," China said. "They wanted to know if any of us knew you—and of course, we did—if either of you had a beef with Dr. Bainsworth or had been romantically linked with him, what type of people you are . . . that sort of thing."

"I hope you put in a good word for us," Myra said.

"I did." China huffed. "I told them you were both nice as pie and that I didn't think either of you had it in for Dr. Bainsworth."

"Thank you. I hope they'll leave Daphne and me alone and follow other leads. I heard there's a woman who works the night shift at the Sunoco claiming a man came in there with blood on the sleeve of his jacket just as the police went roaring by on their way to Dr. Bainsworth's office," Myra said. "Ivy, who works at the post office, was telling me about it. The Sunoco woman asked the man if he'd hurt himself, and she said he'd acted surprised. She pointed out the stain on his sleeve, and then he said, 'Oh, no, I was with a buddy whose nose started to bleed.' That sounds awfully suspicious, if you want my opinion."

"I agree. What did the man buy at the Sunoco?" I asked.

"Just a bottle of pop," Myra said.

"What sort of car was he driving?" China asked.

"Ivy said the Sunoco woman didn't see a car," Myra said. "She said the man was acting like he was looking for somebody. She didn't know if he'd parked out back or was waiting for a ride or what."

"Or if he was looking to see if the police were after him," I said. "The Sunoco is only a few yards away from Dr. Bainsworth's office. If the police could take a look at their security video—"

"I don't know whether or not that would be of much help," Myra said, interrupting. "The man was dressed as Elvis."

DESPITE THE FACT that a crowd had already gathered by the time we reached the hotel, we had a table near the left side of the stage thanks to Juanita's boyfriend. He'd reserved it for her and had even left her a single red rose.

I had no idea what to expect from this concert. I was under the impression that most Elvis impersonators worked alone, came out and did a set of Elvis songs, maybe handed out sweaty scarves, and then everyone went home. I was apparently somewhat correct in my assumption because when the announcer came out to introduce the EIEIO members, he called the concert "unprecedented."

The lights dimmed and in a hushed, reverential voice, the announcer introduced the Elvis Impersonators' Evangelical Interdenominational Outreach. A blue spotlight shone on an Elvis who was standing in the center of the stage.

"One for the money," he sang.

A red spotlight shone on an Elvis to his right. "Two for the show."

The Elvis to the left was spotlighted in white. He picked up the next line.

The lights came up, revealing an entire stage full of Elvises. Some were young, some were old; some were skinny, some were fat; some wore black leather, and some wore white jumpsuits with rhinestones and fringe. I tried to pick Scottie Phillips out of the crowd, but I couldn't. I saw Myra's point. If an Elvis had committed a crime in Brea Ridge within the past three days, barring a confession, you'd be hard-pressed to figure out which Elvis it was.

The Elvises finished singing "Blue Suede Shoes," and then one of them stepped forward to explain the EIEIO's mission. I thought maybe this man was Scottie, but the voice wasn't quite right.

"The Elvis Impersonators' Evangelical Interdenominational Outreach, also known as the EIEIO, tours all over the world, ladies and gentlemen," he said. "We travel to areas of need. In those desolate places, we use our talent to entertain and to spread love, hope, and happiness to a weary world." He closed his eyes and dropped his head.

The audience applauded.

The Elvis impersonator raised his head and continued. "Tonight, friends, we're asking for your help. As you enjoy the performance, ladies and gentlemen, look into your hearts. Realize how very blessed you are. And then, if you're able to do so, please make a monetary donation to the EIEIO. Please . . . help us help the world."

Again, the audience applauded. I glanced around at my tablemates. China and Juanita looked solemn and thoughtful. They truly believed the EIEIO organization was doing valuable work. I didn't see how going places and giving Elvis performances enhanced the world, but maybe there was more to it than that. I personally wanted to see a brochure, especially before I contributed any of my hard-earned money to the cause.

Looking at Myra, I could see she simply wanted this Elvis to hush so the concert could continue. She soon got her wish.

About halfway through the concert, an older Elvis wearing a white jumpsuit and sporting an orange and white lei came onto the stage and began singing "Viva Las Vegas." He walked down the stairs and into the dining hall. As soon as he noticed Myra/Ann-Margret, he conga-ed over to our table. He held out his hand, and she took it. No big surprise.

"Ladies and gentlemen, Ann-Margret!" he shouted as a spotlight shone on the two of them.

Myra did a little bow and then began to conga with Elvis. Thank goodness, he had his hands on her waist. She did the most wobbly conga I'd ever seen on those "high hills" of hers, and I was happy Elvis was there to keep her from falling and breaking a hip or something. After he'd finished his performance, Elvis led Myra back to our table, took off his lei, and put it around her neck. She beamed—at him, at us, at the audience, and then back at us. That last smile lingering in my direction contained a hint of I-told-you-so triumph. I raised my soda glass in salute.

Later, Juanita's boyfriend—whose real name, she whispered, was Aaron—came onto the stage. He was a cutie—one of the slimmer, leather-clad Elvises. I wondered what he looked like without the wig. He was fair skinned, and I thought maybe he was a blond.

"I see a lot of beautiful people in this audience tonight," Aaron said, "but the most beautiful girl in the world to me is sitting right there, friends." He pointed at Juanita, and a spotlight shone on her.

She covered her blushing face with her hands as the audience cheered and applauded.

He continued as the spotlight turned back to him. "Tonight, I'll be performing a song that Elvis sang in his last TV appearance just six weeks prior to his death." He went on to sing "Unchained Melody."

"Juanita," I whispered as the applause finally died down after his performance, "he did a fantastic job. What a voice."

She was still blushing. "I know. Thank you."

Another Elvis took the stage. "Not many people know this, but 'Heartbreak Hotel' was inspired by a suicide note. The note said simply, 'I walk a lonely street.' The song became Elvis's first number one hit on *Billboard*'s pop chart and earned him his first gold record for sales over one million."

He went on to sing the song, jumping off the stage and going from table to table crooning to all the ladies, including China, whose hand he kissed. Her cheeks flushed prettily, but she didn't seem terribly surprised or impressed to be included in the Elvis impersonator's attentions.

Amidst all the fun, I kept thinking about the woman who worked at the Sunoco and had sold a bloody-sleeved Elvis a bottle of pop. If I was an Elvis impersonator who wanted to commit a crime in Brea Ridge, this was the ideal time to do it. Even if I *wasn't* an Elvis impersonator, what better time could there be to dress up as Elvis and commit a crime?

Who robbed the bank? Elvis! Which Elvis?

But then, what motive would an Elvis have to kill a dentist? No, I had to agree with China. Cherchez la femme.

The concert was almost over, and I'd yet to see Scottie Phillips. I hoped he was part of the concert. I'd hate to think my biggest client—okay, my only client—in two weeks would miss my show of support.

A few Elvises later, I would live to regret that sentiment.

Once again, the lights dimmed dramatically. A single trumpet played "Taps" softly in the background as a yet-unseen person spoke softly from the stage.

"This next song's origins date back to the American Civil War. The tune 'Aura Lee' was published in 1861. Elvis released the single 'Love Me Tender' to this tune in September of 1956."

"Taps" faded, the lights came up, and there stood Scottie Phillips as Elvis, dressed head to toe in black leather.

"This is the ultimate love song . . . a song where the singer pours his heart out . . . asking for a chance at love." Scottie looked over at me, and I gave him a little wave.

Scottie walked slowly down the steps of the stage to the main floor. "I have a confession to make." He gazed around the room. "I'm asking for that chance at love tonight myself, ladies and gentlemen."

Like everyone else in the hushed room, I began looking around to see who Scottie wanted to have a chance at love with.

He walked toward our table. "Daphne, my little confectionery queen, come here." He held out his hand. "Please."

Wide-eyed and slack-jawed, I merely sat there.

Scottie smiled at the audience. "I think my lady is a little overcome, folks. Please give her your encouragement. Won't you?"

As the audience erupted in applause and wolf whistles, Scottie put his arm around me and led me to the stage.

"Come on, help me out here," he whispered to me. "It's part of my act."

While Scottie had been wooing me out of my seat, someone had put a straight-backed wooden chair in the center of the stage. Scottie ushered me onto the chair. He sank to his knees in front of me and began singing 'Love Me Tender' as if he meant every word.

Halfway through the song, he took my hands and pulled me to my feet. There was an instrumental interlude. Scottie pushed the chair aside with his boot and waltzed me around the stage. After the instrumental section, we stopped dancing back at center stage. Scottie held me in one arm and held the microphone in the other. He sang the rest of the song and then sang the last verse again.

By the time he'd finished that last verse, we were standing face-to-face. And he was close. You couldn't have slid a playing card between us without it bending. He put the arm holding the microphone around me too.

"What did you think?" he asked in a husky voice.

"Um . . . that was . . . a great performance," I whispered.

That's when he kissed me. Not a simple peck on the cheek this time, but a Scarlett-Rhett-curl-your-toes kind of kiss. On-stage. In front of all those people. And all those people started cheering and whistling and clapping.

I couldn't help but laugh. Scottie was a showman, and I'd been given a starring role in his latest performance. He laughed too.

Keeping one arm around me, he turned to the audience. "Thank you. Thank you very much."

I looked out at the audience too. I was surprised to see that many of the women were actually crying. They'd bought Scottie's entire song and dance. They really believed this was a man pouring his heart out to a woman he loved.

"Take a bow, Daphne," he said.

I did a quick bow. This was kind of fun, but now I was ready to go back to my little table in the corner and hide.

Scottie winked at me and started to lead me off the stage.

But I pulled up short. Ben was standing at the back of the room. Scottie followed my gaze. Then, instead of continuing to lead me off the stage, he swept me up into his arms and carried me backstage. Once again, the audience went crazy.

"Get 'er done, Elvis!" one male audience member yelled. I was 99 percent sure that male audience member was not Ben.

Scottie sat me down backstage. "That was pretty awesome, huh?"

"I need to go explain this to Ben," I said.

"Why?" Scottie asked. "You don't think he loves you enough to come and get you?"

"I'm not sure he loves me at all . . . especially after this," I said.

He grinned. "Well, then, lucky me."

"I have to get out there," I said.

"I'll send a note to your table to let your friends know where you are. Go out back and meet them at the car," Scottie said.

"But—"

"If you don't, those women will mob you when you go back out there. They'll want to know how we met, how long we've been seeing each other, when the wedding will be. . . ."

"I'm not the first woman you've 'loved tender,' am I?" I asked.

He chuckled. "No, but you're my favorite . . . and you could be the last if you play your cards right."

"Right. I haven't even been dealt a hand in this game. Which way do I go to get out of here?" I asked.

He led me to the backstage door. "Thanks, Daph."

"You owe me," I said.

"After that kiss? Don't I know it," he said with a grin. "Good night."

I hurried over to Myra's car. She, China, and Juanita hadn't come out yet. I walked around the parking lot hoping to spot Ben. I needed to tell him that things weren't what they'd looked like.

I didn't get a chance, though. I saw his Jeep speeding away.

CHAPTER
Five

W HEN MYRA, China, and Juanita finally came out, I explained to them what had happened.

"I need to call Ben," I said. "I've never seen him that angry.
At least, not at me. Not even when we were kids."

Ben and I grew up in the same neighborhood. He, Joe Fen-
ally, Violet, and I played together nearly every day. Then Ben
and I dated all through high school.

"Are you sure Ben is the one you want?" Myra asked. "That
Elvis just poured his heart out to you."

"Myra, it was a joke," I said.

She shook her head. "Didn't look like a joke to me."

"Not to me, either," China said. "Although I do believe Ben is the one who holds your heart."

"Me too," Juanita said. "Don't let this Elvis come between you and Ben."

"Guys," I said, "Elvis—Scottie—*isn't* interested in me. His so-called declaration of love was simply part of the performance. If I hadn't been there, he'd have chosen someone else."

"I wish it had been me," Myra said.

"So do I," I replied.

As we piled into the car, I said, "I've got to call Ben as soon as I get home."

"Let me just drop you off at his place," Myra said. "You need to do this kind of making up in person instead of over the phone."

"She's right," Juanita said. "He needs to see the sincerity in your eyes."

"But what if he didn't go home? What if he went back to the office or somewhere else?" I asked.

"Well, I won't leave you at his house if there's no one home," Myra said. "Gee whiz, it's January. Do you think I'd leave you stranded?"

"No," I said. "I'm just nervous. That's all."

"You should be nervous," China said.

"Thanks," I said. "That helped."

She laughed softly. "Sorry. I'm only thinking I'd be nervous too if I had to explain to one man why another was kissing me in front of a room full of people as if he were shipping off to war tomorrow. And that declaration of love might have been a joke, but the kiss wasn't."

"Amen," Myra said with a sigh. "That was a great concert, don't y'all think? That Elvis I danced with—his real name is

Cecil—he asked for my phone number. I think we might be going to lunch tomorrow."

"Be careful," said Juanita. "These men travel a lot. He might break your heart. He could have a woman in every town."

"You're a good one to talk," Myra said. "What about Aaron? He's an Elvis. Aren't you worried he'll break your heart?"

"Yes," Juanita said. "But at least he lives here in Brea Ridge. Plus, he has a job here at home so he does not go out of town as much as the others."

"Not every man who travels will roam," Myra said. "My Carl had to travel for his job fairly often, but he never strayed outside the boundaries of our marriage."

"Carl was a good man," China said.

"Not all men are," said Juanita.

We arrived at Ben's house, and Myra eased into the driveway. There were lights on in the house, and his Jeep was parked out front.

"Would you like us to wait?" China asked.

"Of course we're not waiting," Myra said. "If we leave her here, he'll have to take her home. He won't be able to bull up and not talk to her if he has to drive her home."

"What was that talk about not leaving me stranded?" I asked. "What if Ben refuses to drive me home?"

"He won't," Myra said. "He's a gentleman."

Hoping she was right, I got out of the car and walked hesitantly to the door. I rang the doorbell and could hear Sally, Ben's golden retriever, barking. I looked over my shoulder to see Myra backing the Buick out of the driveway. She, China, and Juanita waved, and then they left me standing there on Ben's doorstep. I'd been dropped. Now I knew—at least in some small way—how my poor cat Sparrow must have felt.

I spotted a patrol car moving slowly down the road behind Myra's car. It had been following us.

Ben didn't come to the door right away, so I rang the bell again. The porch light came on, making me squint against the sudden brightness. Ben opened the door. He stood there shirtless and barefoot, wearing only a pair of jeans. His curly, dark brown hair was wet. His well-defined chest and abs were glistening. He looked good. My throat went dry.

Sally, tail wagging a hundred miles an hour, tried to nudge around Ben to tell me "hello" but he wouldn't let her.

"What're you doing here?" he asked me.

"I came to explain about the concert," I said. "About Scottie. It wasn't what it looked like."

"It looked like he was making out with you onstage."

"Right. That's how he *wanted* it to look," I said.

"Then he did an excellent job," Ben said. "He got precisely the effect he was going for."

"It wasn't like that," I said. "It was an act. He chose me because we'd already met. If it hadn't been me, it would've been someone else."

"But it was you," Ben said.

"Do I have to stand out here in the cold while we discuss this?" I asked. "You left the concert angry at me, and I'm here to tell you there's nothing to be angry about."

"Put yourself in my shoes. If you showed up somewhere unexpectedly and found some woman kissing me, how would you feel?" Ben asked.

"I'd feel horrible," I said. "But I'd give you a chance to explain."

"Explain what, Daphne? How do you explain standing on a stage in front of all those people kissing a man who has just declared his love for you?"

"I wasn't kissing him. *He* was kissing *me*."

"You weren't pushing him away," Ben said.

"Because it was an act. He whispered as much to me as he pulled me to the stage. He's a performer, Ben. It didn't mean a thing. It was a joke."

"It wasn't a joke to me. I need to get to sleep; I've got a lot of work to do tomorrow. Good night, Daphne."

I sighed. "Good night." I turned and started walking down the driveway. I had my cell phone in my purse. I'd call Myra or Jason, Violet's husband, to come and get me if I had to.

"Wait!" Ben called. "Where's your car?"

"At home!" I yelled over my shoulder. "Myra dropped me off here."

"Come back here. I'll take you home."

"No, thanks," I said. "I'll be fine."

With a growl of frustration, he stormed out the door and down the driveway, flung me over his shoulder, and took me back up to the house. I had to almost literally bite my tongue to keep from asking if every man in Brea Ridge considered me his own personal rag doll tonight.

"Sit down until I go in here and get on a shirt and some shoes," he said. "Then I'll drive you home."

"I can call Myra," I said.

His response was to slam a door.

Darned if I was going to wait, and darned if I was going to call anyone I knew and have them witness my humiliation. I left Ben's house and began walking. The patrolman was either making another pass, or someone else was tailing Myra. I flagged him down. It was Officer Kendall.

"Hi," I said. "Could you please give me a ride home?"

"Get in."

"Why have you been following Myra and me?" I asked as I buckled the seat belt. "By the way, being up here in front with you is way better than getting stuffed in the back."

"I imagine so," Officer Kendall said. He put the car in gear and headed in the direction of my house.

"Would you mind telling me?" I asked.

He shrugged. "Who says I've been following anyone?"

"Well, I'm not saying it's you in particular, but I have seen more law enforcement vehicles on the road since Friday night."

"Just keeping the town safe, ma'am," he said with a grin.

"You don't really think Myra and I had anything to do with Dr. Bainsworth's death, do you?"

"You tell me," Officer Kendall said.

"Okay, then no, we unequivocally did not." I watched his face, but his expression didn't change. "How can I make you believe me?"

"Let me do my job. If you're innocent, you have nothing to hide, right?"

I sighed.

He pulled into my driveway, and I got out of the car. "Thank you for the ride. Have a safe evening."

"You too," he said.

He waited until I unlocked the door, got inside, and turned on the lights before he left. I guess that was thoughtful. While I despised the notion of being watched, I had to admit it was convenient that Officer Kendall had been tailing me tonight. I wondered if his partner, Officer Halligan, had Myra duty.

I went to the bedroom and kicked off my shoes before returning to the kitchen. The phone was ringing. I knew without even looking at the caller ID that it was Ben. I turned the ringer off. I'd tried to explain; he'd blown me off, and I didn't want to deal with it anymore tonight.

I needed comfort. I needed decaf café au lait and chocolate chip cookies. Fortunately, I had chocolate chip cookies in the freezer. All I had to do was thaw them in the microwave for a few seconds. While the café au lait was brewing, I took the cookies out of the freezer.

As I began to warm the cookies, the doorbell rang. I went to the door and turned on the porch light. It was Scottie. I opened the door, keeping the locked storm door between us. It was late, this guy was practically a stranger, and I was tired.

"Hi," he said. "I'm here to apologize."

"Apology accepted," I said. "Have a good night."

"Um . . . can't I come in?" he asked.

"Not tonight, but I appreciate your coming by to tell me you're sorry."

"All right." He hesitated. "Do you want me to call . . . what's his name? Ben?"

I shook my head. "No need."

"Really? He looked pretty steamed when he left the banquet hall."

"He's fine," I said.

"Well . . . see you tomorrow then?" Scottie took a step back but looked at me to make sure I hadn't changed my mind about his coming in.

"See you." I closed the door.

After he left, I took my cookies and café au lait and curled up on the sofa. I decided I hadn't ever really examined my feelings for Ben. Of course, now it looked like I might never have to. But I wondered if I'd begun dating Ben because he had seemed like such a safe man after my stormy relationship with Todd. After all, this past Friday night wasn't the first I'd spent either alone or with Myra because Ben was working late or attending some newspaper-related function or was otherwise too busy to see me. Maybe he wasn't that into me. Maybe this incident with Scottie simply gave Ben an excuse to end our so-called relationship.

It could be that I was destined to be alone. I had to admit, though, being by myself was much better than being with Todd had ever been. When I was living in that marriage, I'd never felt as alone in my entire life.

My thoughts drifted back to Dr. Bainsworth and what had been said about him in the car. When Myra had asked Juanita why she'd changed dentists, she'd seemed terribly uncomfortable. Could Juanita have been one of Dr. Bainsworth's numerous conquests? Is that why she'd switched dentists? And was that why she was so adamantly convinced that all men cheat? I couldn't imagine gentle little Juanita bashing a man's head in, but I guess stranger things have happened.

I definitely had to get together with Myra tomorrow. Hopefully, after her lunch with Elvis/Cecil, she and I could meet and try to figure out who might have had it in for Dr. Bainsworth. We needed to get this investigation under way. No offense to Officers Kendall and Halligan, but I wasn't very confident in their abilities.

CHAPTER
Six

WHEN I got up Monday morning, I looked like death on a cracker. More specifically, I looked as if I'd tossed and turned all night feeling sorry for myself. This was mainly because I'd tossed and turned all night feeling sorry for myself. It was a good thing that I'd adamantly studied Bobbi Brown's makeup book shortly before my thirty-eighth birthday and knew all about using yellow-based corrector and only lining your upper lids to help camouflage dark under-eye circles. I know most women freak over turning forty rather than thirty-eight, but I was pretty much over the age thing by the time I turned forty. It's probably because I was dealing with arrest warrants and trials by jury as my fortieth birthday approached.

I followed the memorized makeup instructions and then peered into the mirror. "Well, now what, Bobbi?" I asked, as if the famous makeup artist would magically appear and fix the rest of my face.

She didn't. Left to my own devices, I did the best I could—added some lipstick and mascara—and then shuffled into the kitchen. While the coffee was brewing, I stepped outside to get the morning paper. The front-page headline was POLICE STILL STUMPED OVER DENTIST'S MURDER. The article went on to say that they were aggressively pursuing all leads. There was no mention of the fact that police were following Myra and me around all over town and acting as interim taxis when necessary.

The bottom-right corner of the front page showed a photo from last night's concert with the header ELVIS INVASION LEAVES BREA RIDGE "ALL SHOOK UP." I inwardly groaned. I'd had my fill of the concert—thank-you-very-much—so I didn't read the article, but I did check the byline. The article had been written by Suzanna Leonard, a newbie who was interning at the paper while studying journalism at one of the nearby colleges. Most of the work she was given was fluff pieces.

I thumbed through the rest of the paper before tossing it in the recycle bin. It was time to get to work.

I didn't feel like working on the Cadillac cake today. I was too tired and irritable to do something that required that much thought and precision. I decided to make the brownies and cookies to put onto the party trays I was preparing for the Save-A-Buck. Once the house smelled like chocolate, maybe I'd start feeling better.

I got out my favorite blue mixing bowl and my chewy chocolate fudge brownie recipe. I put on my headset before spraying the bottom of three brownie pans with baking spray. I intended to triple the recipe in order to have enough brownies for all five party trays.

The phone rang, and I stopped spraying midair. Should I sound chipper, contrite, pleasant, professional . . . ? I went with professional, since the caller might not be Ben after all. It turned out to be a wise choice. It was Myra.

"Good morning, honey," she said. "How did things go with Ben last night?"

"Things went pretty much right out the window," I said. "We had a big argument and haven't spoken since. I even hitched a ride home with Officer Kendall, who seemed to be following us around."

"Yeah, I spotted Halligan tailing me when I dropped China and Juanita off at your house to pick up their cars," she said. "Didn't Ben even call to find out how you got home?"

"He called a couple times, but I didn't answer, and he didn't leave a message. Maybe he saw the squad car taking me away. He wasn't concerned enough to drive over here and see for himself that I got home okay."

"That's all right," Myra said confidently. "That means he's good and jealous. If he didn't care about you, he wouldn't be jealous."

"I guess you've got a point there," I said.

"I know I do. Oh, honey."

My lips curled into a smile. When Myra said *oh, honey,* you could count on getting a good story. I sat down on a stool at the island.

Myra continued. "One time me and Carl went to a Valentine's Day dance at the Moose lodge. Well, I looked as pretty as a picture . . . had on a sparkly red dress with an A-line skirt and a white crinoline underneath so that when we danced I could spin around and show my crinoline instead of my butt—I'd done practiced it in front of the mirror and everything."

"Good thinking," I said.

"I know. I'd thought of everything," she said. "Anyway, Carl didn't have any reason whatsoever to have a straying eye that night, but he did. That old Mary Breedlove was there with a hot-pink minidress on that was cut down nearly to her belly button. While I was worried about people seeing my butt, she'd apparently been worried that people *wouldn't* see hers . . . along with everything else the good Lord gave her. And one of the things He'd given her was apparently a push-up bra, because otherwise her boobs would've been down there at her belly button with the neckline of that dress."

I giggled. I had no clue who Mary Breedlove was, but Myra was obviously still mad at her and at Carl for whatever indiscretion he'd made, even though he'd been dead for five years.

"Well, you will absolutely not believe what Carl Jenkins did," Myra said. "He asked that trollop to dance! Oh, yes! It wasn't bad enough for him to ogle her, he actually asked her to dance. And, of course, she did. Old home-wrecking hussy."

"So, what did you do?" I asked.

"I got up and sashayed over to Will Pennington. He'd always had a thing for me, and his wife was dead. He'd showed up at the Moose lodge to look for love in all the wrong places, I reckon, so why Mary didn't set her cap for him instead of my Carl is beyond me. 'Will,' I said, 'I'd like for you to take me home, please.' Well, his eyes lit up like . . . like . . . like two big porch lights, and we left."

Like two big porch lights? Oh well, no one could accuse Myra of using too many clichés. "You didn't tell Carl you were leaving?" I asked.

"No, indeed, I did not tell Carl," she said.

"What did he say when he got home?" I asked.

"I don't know, because I wasn't there."

"You weren't there?" I asked. "You were actually out with Will?"

"Yes, I was. Once we got in the car, I said, 'Will, I'd really rather not go home just yet. Why don't we go see a movie?' And that's what we did. In fact, we saw a double feature," Myra said.

"Are you kidding? What time did you get home?"

"About one in the morning," she said.

"Was Carl still up or had he gone to bed?" I asked. *Or had he left home?* was what I was really wondering.

"Oh, yeah, he was up," Myra said. "He was sitting there in his recliner as mad as an old one-horned bull. I asked him if he and Mary Breedlove had enjoyed themselves at the dance. He said he'd felt like a fool when he came back to our table and I was gone. I said, 'You looked like one out on the dance floor with that trashy Mary. It's a wonder your eyes didn't pop plumb out of your head and into that push-up bra of hers.' 'What about you?' he asked me. 'One of the—' Mooses . . . moosers . . . meese . . . ?"

"Lodge members," I suggested.

"Yeah, one of them. They'd told him I'd gone off with Will Pennington. At first, Carl figured I'd just gone out into the parking lot to spite him—although he'd known me plenty long enough to know I can spite a whole lot better than that—so he came outside and looked around for a while. Then he drove around town looking for us. He even drove over to Will Pennington's house!"

"Did you tell Carl where you'd been?" I asked.

"Yeah," Myra said. "I didn't want him to beat the tar out of poor old Will. Didn't want him to divorce me either. I even showed him the tickets to convince him we'd been at the movies and that nothing had happened. He pouted around at me for a day or two, but he never danced with another woman again. And if he was ever eyeing one, he never let me catch him at it."

I laughed. "At least Mary Breedlove didn't kiss Carl on a stage in front of a room full of people."

"If she had, I'd have ripped her lips off," Myra said. "But that just goes to show you, honey, jealousy is a powerful thing. Once Ben calms down a little, he'll be back."

"I hope you're right," I said. "He and I had been dating when I met Todd—the guy I eventually married. So I guess he has reason to be jealous."

"The killer?" she asked. "You were dating Ben when you met the killer?"

"Well, Todd didn't *kill* me. I'm still here."

"You know what I meant. By the way," she said in a singsong voice. "I could've sworn I saw a pink Cadillac in your driveway last night."

"Does nothing get by you?"

"Not a thing," she said smugly.

"Scottie stopped by to apologize."

"Did he now? I knew it! That Elvis has the hots for you!" She chuckled. "If Ben doesn't come around, I'll let you borrow my Ann-Margret wig . . . only not until after lunch today."

"Are you wearing it to lunch with Cecil?" I asked.

"Of course I am. How many times in my life am I going to get the opportunity to be Ann-Margret? Especially if I have to go to prison. I don't want to be Ann-Margret there," she said. "I'd rather look like Sister Mary Margret in prison."

"Speaking of prison," I said, "let's get together this afternoon and decide how we can figure out who really knocked Dr. Bainsworth in the head."

"Will do, honey. Talk with you later."

With that, she was gone. She was probably off to put on her wig and wait for Cecil to call . . . unless she'd already called him. Ann-Margret is feisty, you know.

I mixed up the brownies and had them baking by the time I got another phone call. "Daphne's Delectable Cakes," I said.

"Hey there, delectable Daphne."

"Hi, Scottie."

"How are you this morning?" he asked.

"I'm fine. How are you?" I asked.

"The boys and I are getting a little hungry and restless for some home cooking, and we were wondering if you could put together a nice lunch for us," he said.

"Um . . . you want me to make you lunch? Today?" I gulped. "As in, within a few hours?"

"Yeah. We're paying. We're not a bunch of freeloaders, you know."

"I know, but I don't run a diner, Scottie. I don't even have enough food here to make a decent snack for the EIEIO."

"You don't have to feed all of us, just about ten of us, and Cecil is bringing that friend of yours, the one who thinks she's Ann-Margret," he said. "We thought you could maybe make us some steaks and some steak fries . . . and a little dessert would be good. Could you whip us up a banana pudding?"

"You love your bananas, don't you?"

"Maybe I'm part monkey." He laughed. "Anyhow, what do you say?"

"Scottie, they have fantastic steaks at Dakota's."

"So? Dakota's is really crowded at lunchtime," he said. "You can hardly hear yourself think, much less talk. Come on. Be a sport. Please."

I sighed. "I have a lot of work to do. On your cake, for one thing."

"Did I mention we're paying?" he asked.

I mentally calculated whether or not I had time to work this unexpected luncheon into my day.

"Top dollar," he said. "No missionary discount."

"Fine," I said. "What time will you be here?"

"Is twelve thirty all right?"

"That'll work." Twelve thirty would give me time to get my brownies out of the oven and then hurry to the Save-A-Buck for steaks, steak fries (yes, the Elvises would have to settle for frozen), rolls, and the ingredients for a chef's salad and a banana pudding.

As I walked the aisles of the Save-A-Buck, I wondered if Myra knew her lunch date with Cecil was going to include nine other Elvises and me. On the one hand, I thought maybe

I should call Myra and warn her. On the other hand, I didn't want to be responsible for sticking a pin in her balloon. She'd already illustrated this morning how spiteful she can be when you get her riled up. Let Elvis/Cecil bear the brunt of that burden himself. Besides, there was still a chance that after talking with Myra, Cecil would change his mind and tell Scottie that he and Myra were having a cozy meal alone somewhere . . . somewhere like Dakota's.

There were a couple soccer moms—although, this time of year, I supposed they were basketball moms—whispering in the produce aisle. I heard Dr. Bainsworth's name mentioned, and then one of the women nodded in my direction.

I listened more closely as I examined the lettuce.

". . . the one who found him," one said.

"What was she doing there that time of night?" the other asked.

"Probably having a fling with him. They say she moved back here after living in Tennessee for about fifteen years. I heard her husband tried to kill her."

"Wonder if he caught her cheating on him?"

I placed the lettuce into my basket and quickly left the aisle. Although tears were threatening, I felt the desire to tell the women exactly why Todd had fired a shot at me. I wanted to yell at them that I'd never been unfaithful to Todd and that I'd never even *met* Dr. Bainsworth. How dare they speculate about me like that! They didn't know me!

By the time I'd finished shopping, I had my emotions under control. I realized this was the big drawback to living in a small town, and it was something I'd simply have to deal with if I wanted to stay here in Brea Ridge. And I did . . . at least, for now.

Juanita was surprised to see me come through her line with a dozen steaks, two bags of steak fries, rolls, and enough salad fixings to feed a small army. Not to mention more bananas.

"You must be hosting a dinner party," she said.

I explained about Scottie's phone call asking me to make lunch for a group of the Elvises. "I tried to tell him that I don't run a restaurant, but he was so insistent . . . and he said they'd pay me well."

"I understand their need for some privacy," said Juanita. "Aaron told me that when they go out, the people in town keep asking for their autographs or to have their pictures made with them—especially the women."

"That makes sense," I said. "I hadn't looked at it that way, but I suppose they do enjoy a bit of celebrity status. Will Aaron be at the lunch today?"

"No, he is working. He is planning to go on the next mission trip, though, so he'll need to get together with some of the EIEIO members to discuss that before they leave at the end of the week." She leaned over and touched my wrist. "I hope things work out however you want them to between you and Scottie, but guard your heart, Daphne. He will be gone in a few days, and you don't know for sure that you will ever see him again."

"I know. I have no interest in Scottie," I said.

"And did you and Ben make up?" she asked.

Someone came up behind me in the line with her cart full of groceries, so I simply gave Juanita a slight shake of my head and made a banal comment about the drizzly weather we were having today.

Juanita finished ringing up my groceries, and I paid her and left. Something she'd said lingered in my thoughts. The Elvises would be gone in a matter of days. If the woman at the Sunoco *had* seen an Elvis with blood on his sleeve, Myra and I had better be talking with her and pursuing that angle before those suspects left town.

BY THE TIME Scottie and four of the Elvises showed up at my door, the steaks were almost done and I'd just taken the fries out of the oven. The chef's salad, complete with hard-boiled egg slices, ham, cheese, and bacon, was sitting in the center of the table. The banana pudding was in the refrigerator.

It was going to be a tight fit, but I had five Elvises and Myra seated at the kitchen table and four set up at the island. I had also set up a card table to accommodate two other people. It wasn't the perfect seating arrangement, but it was the best I could come up with.

"This house smells like a slice of heaven," Scottie said as he came into the kitchen, gave me a peck on the cheek, and hung up his black leather jacket. "Daphne, I want you to meet Craig, Mike, Sam, and John."

I shook each of the Elvises' hands. I told them to make themselves comfortable at the kitchen table and that I had iced tea, soda, or coffee to drink. Not surprisingly, all five Elvises— Scottie included—requested iced tea.

While the other four men sat around the kitchen table, Scottie asked me if there was anything he could help me with.

"No," I said with a smile. "Everything is fine."

"Do you have an invoice for me?" he asked.

"I do. I'll get it for you before you leave," I said. "But for now, go ahead and enjoy the meal. Are the others on their way?"

"They're supposed to be," he said. "They're in the van with Cecil."

My eyes widened. "Myra is not going to be a happy camper."

"Why not?" Scottie asked. "If she was expecting one Elvis to show up at her door, five is five times better, right?"

"If you say so." I poured tea into the men's glasses and directed my next comment to the table in general. "Tell me, what made you decide to become members of EIEIO?"

Craig, a tall Elvis with neatly trimmed blond hair and a mustache, spoke first. "I've always enjoyed working with children, Daphne. When you go on these trips and see those little faces light up, it makes it all worthwhile."

"I imagine it does," I said.

John—a skinny redhead who appeared to be in his midthirties—smiled shyly. "I'm just a small-town southern boy, ma'am. Craig heard me singing in church one Sunday a few years ago when the group was in our town, and he told me I ought to sign up for the EIEIO. I hadn't ever been too many places before, and I thought the EIEIO might be a way for me to get out of Shady Springs, Georgia, and see the world."

I laughed. "I guess it was at that."

"It sure was," he said, "and opened other doors for me too. Doors I never would have imagined opening."

"I like the kids and the travel too," said Sam, a beefy Elvis who wore a thick gold chain around his neck. "But mainly I joined up because I love to perform."

"We all enjoy being onstage," Scottie said with a wink in my direction, "but I think we all appreciate the fact that we're giving something back too."

There came a knock at the door. It had to be Myra and the other five Elvises.

Myra/Ann-Margret strode in first. Her wig was a little skewed, and her mouth was flatter than a breast implant during a mammogram.

I greeted the newcomers and then pulled Myra aside. "Are you okay?"

"I've never been so humiliated in all my life . . . except for that time—oh, never mind, I'll tell you later. I had no idea I was being brought all the way *next door* for a romantic lunch *with a dozen other people!*" Her eyes narrowed. "Did you?"

"No . . . not until a little bit ago. Scottie called and asked if I could make lunch, but he said not all the Elvises would be here." I shrugged and offered up a silent prayer for my version of the truth that was only slightly more skewed than Myra's wig. I reached and adjusted the wig as if that would help—and to ease my conscience. I probably should have called and warned her. "Maybe Cecil is planning on taking you somewhere—just the two of you—after lunch."

"In the stupid EIEIO van? What're we gonna do with the other four? Strap them to the luggage rack?" She sighed. "I'm going home."

"Please don't. I've made a really nice lunch," I said, "and the EIEIO is paying for it, so it would be a shame for your rib eye to go to waste."

"Rib eye?"

I nodded. "And chef's salad, steak fries, rolls, and banana pudding."

"I'll stay . . . but only because you've gone to so much trouble, and I don't want to make a scene in front of this bunch of buffoons," she said. "They've besmirched the good name of Elvis Presley is what they've done—the whole lot of them. And don't you get involved with that slimy little Scottie. He's probably the worst one of the bunch—other than Cecil."

"I'm sure you're right," I said.

Myra and I walked into the kitchen, where Scottie asked us all to gather in the middle of the floor, join hands, and bow our heads. I was standing between him and Myra, so I took one of each of their hands.

"Dear Lord," he prayed, "we thank You for bringing us here today and providing this opportunity for us."

Some of the other EIEIO members chimed in with "Amen" or "Yes, Lord."

"We thank You for the food we're about to receive," Scottie said, continuing, "and we thank You for Daphne."

I raised my head in surprise, looked at Scottie—who, like everyone else, still had his head bowed—and then lowered my head again.

"She's been good to us, Lord," he said. "And we ask You to bless her and to reward her for her hospitality and warmth. She has a heart for others—as You well know—and we appreciate her. Amen." He gave my hand a squeeze before releasing it. Then he raised his head, grinned at the group as a whole, and said, "Let's eat!"

Myra seated herself with the five Elvises at the kitchen table.

"Thank you for joining us, ma'am," John said. "You give the rest of us a pretty view."

She giggled like a schoolgirl.

Three of the Elvises sat at the island. Scottie insisted on joining me at the card table. He pulled out one of the folding chairs for me, moved the other to my right instead of across the table where I'd positioned it, and sat down.

I looked around to make sure all the condiments were available. Fortunately, I had enough steak sauce and ketchup to go around. Salad dressing wasn't as much in demand since the chef's salad was dismissed by most of the EIEIO members. I'd have thought they'd have at least been interested in the meats and cheeses, but I suppose they wanted to save enough room for that banana pudding.

CHAPTER Seven

EVERYONE HAD finished eating, and Scottie was helping me carry the dishes to the dishwasher when the doorbell rang. It was Juanita.

"I'm sorry to interrupt," she said, "but I only had to work half of the day today so I went to get the fountain and the dolls for Isabel's cake."

"Terrific," I said. "Come on in."

"Yeah," Scottie said. "We were getting ready to clear out of here anyway. You guys do whatever you need to do."

Juanita had stiffened. Her mouth was slightly agape, and her eyes were wide. "No," she said. She shoved the bag she was carrying into my hands and backed away. "I must go." She turned and practically ran to her car.

I frowned at Scottie, Myra, and the EIEIO members, who were in various stages of putting on jackets, saying their good-byes, and getting ready to leave. "Wonder what's up with Juanita?"

"Hard to say," Myra said. "She looked rather sick to me."

"Yes, she did. I'll call and check on her later." I sat the bag on the counter and retrieved the invoice for the EIEIO lunch.

"Thank you," Scottie said, glancing at the invoice before putting it in his pocket. "I'll drop your check off later."

"You can simply combine it with the cake invoice if you'd like," I said. "That way you wouldn't have to write but one check."

"We'll see." He kissed my cheek. "Thank you for a delicious meal."

"And thank you for the charming company," John—the Elvis who'd been seated to Myra's left—said with a nod in her direction.

She laughed.

"Before you go, could I see you for one second, Myra?" I asked.

We ducked into the living room.

"I'm going to the Sunoco early this evening," I said quietly. "I want to be there when the clerk who claims she saw some-one acting suspiciously comes in to start her shift." I didn't dare say "the clerk who saw a suspicious Elvis" with ten suspicious Elvises within such close proximity.

"Can I go with you?" she asked. "My butt is on the line here too, you know. I'm going to a matinee with Cecil, but I'll be back in plenty of time to go with you to the Sunoco."

"Okay. But for now, just have fun at the movie," I said.

She gave me a weak smile. "We'll see."

"Give Cecil a chance to make things up to you," I said. "He probably didn't know he wasn't taking you to a romantic lunch alone until Scottie told him all the EIEIO members who could make it needed to meet here for lunch."

"You could be right." She frowned. "But I don't see what they had to discuss that was so all-fired important. John kept getting the details mixed up about when and where the next mission trip was going to be, and Sam only cared about how many people were expected to turn out at the next event. It didn't appear to me the EIEIOs got anything accomplished besides getting their bellies full."

I laughed. "Yeah, I didn't see much point to this so-called meeting myself. Maybe it's like Juanita said this morning—they simply wanted to eat lunch somewhere private."

"Oh, please. They're here because Scottie wanted an excuse to be here," she said.

Cecil stepped into the doorway of the living room. "Myra, darlin', are you ready to go?"

"Sure." She turned to me. "I'll see you later."

As soon as everyone had left and I'd put away the extra food—mainly the chef's salad—and finished loading the dishwasher, I called Juanita's cell phone. My call went straight to voice mail.

"Hi, Juanita. It's Daphne Martin. I was just concerned about you. When you were here earlier, you didn't seem to be feeling well. I hope everything is all right. Please give me a call, okay?"

As I made the call, I noticed the postal worker leaving my mail. I put on a jacket and went outside to the mailbox. Sparrow darted between my feet as soon as I opened the door, but fortunately she didn't run in the direction of the road. Having been a stray, I suppose she was used to the freedom the outdoors afforded her. But she liked her regular meals and comfy bed too much to wander around outside for long.

I opened the mailbox and took out the stack of mail. A small box was included—the sample of fabric softener I'd requested a couple weeks ago. I could already smell the fragrance through the box and was looking forward to giving the product a try.

I flipped through the other pieces of correspondence as I walked back toward the house. There was a letter marked "Urgent" from the bank. I groaned. An urgent letter from the bank couldn't be good. How often does the bank send you a letter marked "Urgent" to tell you that everything is going great and that you have plenty of money?

I tucked the rest of the mail under my arm and opened the envelope. They were saying my checking account was overdrawn.

I hurried inside, deposited the other mail on the kitchen counter, grabbed my purse, and headed for the bank. This had to be mistake. I was diligent in my record keeping.

I found a parking spot as soon as I arrived and got out of the car. As I went into the building, Steve Franklin was leaving it.

"Good afternoon, Daphne," he said.

"Hi, Steve." Remembering the Maureen/Dr. Bainsworth/Steve Franklin connection, I added, "I realize you're probably in a hurry, but may I ask you a quick question?"

"Shoot."

"I'm sure you've heard by now that Myra Jenkins and I found Dr. Bainsworth's body," I said. "Do you know of anyone who might've disliked Dr. Bainsworth?"

"Only every man with a wife, fiancée, or significant other," he said matter-of-factly. "The man was a ruthless womanizer."

"I'd heard that about him," I said. "Did you know him well? Was he your dentist?"

"No," he said. "My dentist is in Kingsport."

"What about Maureen?" I asked.

His lips tightened. "Why do you ask?"

I shrugged. "I'm simply trying to find anyone who knew him well enough to have more information about him."

"Maureen once patronized Dr. Bainsworth's office, but he behaved abominably to her and she transferred to Dr. Farmer," Mr. Franklin said. "I don't think she'd care to discuss Dr. Bainsworth with anyone."

"I understand. Thank you for your time."

His face softened slightly. "Dr. Bainsworth was a jerk, Daphne. The police won't have to look very hard to find a likely suspect in his murder. Don't worry about that."

I nodded and went on inside the bank. All the tellers were busy, so I got in line.

"We meet again. Twice in one day."

I turned and saw that John, the skinny red-haired EIEIO member, had come to stand behind me. I smiled. "Didn't you say you're from Georgia?"

"Yep," he said.

"I didn't realize our little bank had branches that far afield," I said.

"Aw, this trip ain't for me. It's for the EIEIO. They have bank accounts all over the country so that wherever we go, we can get what we need," John said.

"That's cool."

He nodded. "Real cool. By the way, who was that girl who was at your house earlier . . . you know, just before we left? She looked a little green around the gills."

"That was Juanita. She works at the Save-A-Buck. She didn't appear to be feeling well, did she?"

"Nope. Did she say what was the matter?"

"No, she didn't," I said.

"Hope she ain't contagious."

A teller called, "Next!"

I stepped up to her window and explained my situation. She called someone else and then asked me to wait in the lobby. I sat down on a blue sofa that faced two leather wingback chairs and watched John take my place at the teller's window. Juanita had seemed fine when she first arrived. It was only after seeing the EIEIO members in my kitchen that she felt the need to bolt. What was it about those Elvises that had spooked her?

The man I was to meet with promptly arrived and ushered me into a private office. Twenty-five minutes later, I left, relieved by the knowledge that it was the bank—not I—that had made the erroneous calculation and that my account was not overdrawn after all.

I got home, and Sparrow came running. She was ready to have some food before curling up in her bed under my desk. If only all of life's problems could be solved as easily as taking care of Sparrow and keeping my bank records straight.

I had a message from Ben, and I tried to return his call but

I was directed to his voice mail. I let him know I'd phoned, but I didn't say much more than that.

The dishwasher had run its cycle, so I opened it and began putting the dishes away. I'd almost finished my task when Officers Halligan and Kendall came to my door.

"Gentlemen," I said, "what can I do for you?"

"May we come in, Ms. Martin?" Officer Kendall asked.

"Sure. I've got nothing to hide." I gave him a pointed look.

I led them into the living room. I perched on the chair, and Kendall sat on the sofa. Halligan remained standing. He took a small evidence bag from his breast pocket.

"We found this at the crime scene," he said, holding the bag out to me. "Is it yours?"

It was a diamond stud earring, and it appeared to be at least half a carat. "In my dreams."

"I'd prefer a yes or no answer," Halligan said.

"Then no, it isn't mine," I said.

"May we look through your jewelry to ascertain you don't have a matching earring?" Kendall asked.

"Or do we need to come back with a search warrant?" Halligan reached for the evidence bag.

I handed him the earring and told him and Kendall to look wherever they'd like. I led them to the bedroom. "That's my jewelry case there on the chest. I'll stay all the way back here so you can be assured I'm not taking anything out of it."

I watched as Halligan took my jewelry box and dumped its contents onto my bed. Great. That'd take at least an hour to return to some semblance of order. After going through every piece of jewelry I had, they concluded that I did not have the matching diamond earring.

"We're going over to Ms. Jenkins's house now," Halligan said. "If I find out you've called and alerted her that we're on our way, you'll be charged with obstruction of justice. Do I make myself clear?"

"Crystal," I said.

I doubted Myra was even home from the movie yet. And so what if it *was* her earring? The police already knew both she and I had been at the office that night. How could an earring be more damning than our finding the body?

It WAS NEARLY seven P.M. and pitch-dark on that moonless night as I was driving Myra and me to the Sunoco. Both of us were uncharacteristically quiet. I'd been bummed all day because, frankly, it had been a crappy day. Myra had found Cecil a bit boring when stripped of his Elvis persona. Plus, the movie had been a bomb, and she'd come home to find Halligan and Kendall waiting for her. The earring wasn't hers either. Overall, we were both rather lost in our own thoughts.

Suddenly, I glanced up into the sky and, thanks to the streetlights, saw hundreds of crows circling the treetops. I knew they were roosting, as crows are apt to do in winter; but it was still an eerie sight. "Ooh, Myra, look."

I noticed movement to my right and saw that Myra was making the sign of the cross. "What're you doing?" I asked her. "You aren't Catholic."

"So what? I've seen them do it on TV when something bad is fixing to happen and they don't have time to pray."

"What bad is fixing to happen?" I asked.

"I don't know," she said. "But all those crows have gathered to watch whatever it is, and I'm thinking it's got to be something really bad."

"The crows are going to bed," I said. "They know there's safety in numbers."

Myra shook her head. "Haven't you ever seen that Alfred Hitchcock movie *The Birds*?"

"I have. As a matter of fact, the movie is based on a novella written by my namesake, Daphne du Maurier," I said. "Besides, the first bird to peck Tippi Hedren in the head in that movie was a seagull."

"So? The crows didn't waste any time getting in on the revolt," she said. "And you'll think *seagull* when those crows swoop down out of those trees and start pecking your brains out when we get out of this car."

"I'm sorry I mentioned it," I said.

"Me too," she said. "Now I know we're doomed."

"Crows are not portents of doom," I argued.

"Says you," Myra said. "Alfred Hitchcock and Edgar Allan Poe knew different. And you see where they both are now, don't you? They're dead."

"Of course they're dead. Did you expect them to live forever?" I asked.

She huffed. "Let's just go in and talk with this woman for whatever it's worth."

"Myra," I said gently, "we'll get through this. We didn't do anything wrong, and we'll be exonerated."

She nodded. "Sorry. I guess I'm just not used to having run-ins with the law like you are. You know, what with your finding Yodel Watson dead, and then the police checking your cake after Fred died."

"They checked *all* the food at the party where Fred got sick." I sighed, parked the car, and we got out.

"How do we do this?" Myra asked before we entered the convenience store. "We can't flash a badge and tell her we have a few questions for her. . . . Can we? You don't have any sort of badge, do you?"

"No, I don't," I said. "Maybe something from a cake show somewhere at home, but I don't think that kind of badge would convince anyone they have to talk to me."

"I'd talk to you for cake."

"Now that you mention it," I said, "I think that *is* why you talked to me the first time."

"I believe you're right," she said.

When we opened the convenience store door, Myra scrunched up her nose in distaste. "I don't think these people got Governor Kaine's memo about the smoking ban."

"That only applies to restaurants," I whispered.

"Well, maybe so, but Hot Lips over there is gonna need an iron lung if she keeps that up."

"Hot Lips" was, naturally, the woman we needed to speak with, and at the moment, she was using one cigarette to ignite another before stubbing the first into an overflowing ashtray on a stool by her side.

"Hi there," I said, smiling as I approached the counter. "How are you this evening?"

Hot Lips narrowed her eyes. "What do you want?"

"I wanted to ask you about the guy who came in here Saturday night just after the dentist was killed," I said. "You know, the man who had blood on his sleeve."

"And looked like Elvis," Myra added.

Hot Lips blew smoke in my face. "You a cop?"

"No." I looked around the store to make sure Myra and I were the only ones in there. "We're the ones suspected of the crime."

She nodded. "So if you can pin it on this Elvis guy . . ."

"It'd make things a lot simpler for us," Myra said. "So what did you see that night?"

"Just what I told the cops," she said, taking a draw off her cigarette. "Some guy trying to look like he was Elvis came in to buy a Coke. I noticed he had blood on his sleeve. Kinda grossed me out." She blew another breath of smoke at us. "I asked if he'd hurt himself. I especially needed to know if he'd hurt himself on the cooler or something. I'm the night manager here, and if the guy had come in and complained to my boss the next day saying he got hurt here, it could've cost me my job."

"What did he say?" I asked.

"Said he was with a buddy whose nose was bleeding and some must've got on his jacket," she said.

"What type of jacket was it?" I asked. I was thinking that if it would have had to have been professionally dry-cleaned before the next performance, we had a good shot at finding our guy. There were only two or three dry cleaners in Brea Ridge.

"Blue," Hot Lips said. "Dark blue."

"What kind of material?" I asked.

"I don't know. Suede, maybe. Could've been that fake stuff, though," she said.

"Was he a fat Elvis or a skinny Elvis?" Myra asked.

"Uh . . . he leaned more toward skinny, I'd say," said Hot Lips. "Although I don't believe I'd call him bony."

Myra leaned as close as she dared. "Was he wearing a diamond earring?"

"I don't think so . . . not that I remember."

"Old or young?" Myra asked.

"I don't know for sure," she said, taking a draw off the cigarette and expelling smoke through her nose. "He had on those big sunglasses."

"At ten o'clock at night?" I asked.

"Yeah. I thought he looked ridiculous too, but I guess it was part of his costume or whatever." She shrugged. "It was weird. He kept looking out the window. I thought maybe he was watching for his ride. After hearing the dentist was killed, I thought maybe somebody had been driving the getaway car for him."

"The getaway car driver didn't do such a hot job if the Elvis couldn't run right out and jump in the car," I said.

"I heard that," Hot Lips said. "I wouldn't want that guy for *my* wheelman. You know . . . if I ever needed one."

"Me either," I said. "Thanks for your time."

"No problem," she said. "That's really a shame, you know. Dr. Bainsworth was a good guy."

"I guess he came in here a lot?" I asked.

"Yeah. Came in about every day for his Diet Mountain Dew fix." She barked out a husky chuckle. "He was always fussing at me about the smokes." She shook her head. "Oh well. Hope y'all find your guy and stay out of jail."

"Yeah," Myra said. "Us too. Thanks."

We went back outside and got into the car, both of us reeking of smoke.

"Well, now what?" Myra asked.

"I don't know. I'm pretty sure the Elvis who came in here on Saturday night is our guy, which means we have to work quickly to find out which one of the Elvis impersonators killed the dentist before they leave town on Saturday and we're—"

"Screwed?"

"Yeah," I said.

"You're still assuming it was somebody in the EIEIO," Myra said. "Don't forget it could've been somebody who knew they were coming to town and decided it was the perfect disguise."

"Did we ever kid ourselves that this would be easy?" I sighed. "Let's start first thing tomorrow morning by calling every dry cleaner in Brea Ridge. If that jacket was suede, our Elvis would have had to get it professionally cleaned to get the blood out of it, right?"

"I imagine he would."

"And maybe Scottie could tell us if one of the Elvises needed a spare jacket for Sunday's performance," I said.

"Unless *he's* the one who needed it."

I glanced at Myra. "You're right. If none of the local cleaners have the jacket, we'll try every one within a twenty-five-mile radius."

"But don't you need to work on your cakes and stuff?" Myra asked.

"I'll do that tonight," I said. "And after we speak with the dry cleaners, let's talk with some of the people who worked with the dentist."

"But the office is closed," Myra said. "The police are going through the files and records and everything. I don't even know if they'll open the office back up at all without another dentist to come in and take over the practice."

"Still, we can surely find one or two people who worked there, can't we? I mean, you were his patient. You're acquainted with some of the members of his staff, aren't you?"

"Well, sure, but I don't know where they live," she said.

"Do you know anyone who would know where they live or where they hang out so we might be able to meet with them?" I asked.

She thought about it for a second. "Yeah. Tanya. I'll give her a call as soon as I get home." She sniffed her jacket. "Right after I've showered and put my clothes in the washer."

CHAPTER Eight

Like Myra, I was eager to shower. When I got home and washed the day's frustrations—and Hot Lips's smoke—down the drain, I realized I was exhausted. This whole dentist-jail-Elvis-Ben ordeal had left me physically and emotionally empty. I felt as if I could crawl into bed and sleep for a week. But I still had work to do.

I put my hair up and then slipped on clean, crisp cotton pajamas and my slippers. Then I went into the kitchen and tied my apron around my waist. I had made the brownies that morning. Now I needed to get to work on the cookies. I got my recipe box out of the cabinet and found my favorite chocolate chunk cookie recipe. I turned on the oven to 350 degrees and then got out my flour, butter, white and brown sugars, eggs, baking soda, salt, and vanilla. I doubled the recipe so I'd have plenty to put on the party trays.

I mixed up the cookie dough and used a cookie scoop to place it onto the parchment-paper-lined baking sheet. The oven clicked, letting me know it had reached the proper temperature, and I placed the first batch of cookies into the oven. I covered the remaining dough with plastic wrap and set that mixing bowl aside.

I got out another mixing bowl, some cinnamon, and a snickerdoodle recipe. While the chocolate chunk cookies were baking, I stirred up the snickerdoodles. When they were done, I made oatmeal raisin cookies. Finally, I had enough cookies for the party trays. In the morning, I could get up and dip some pretzels in both milk and white chocolate, decorate the sheet cakes, prepare the party trays, and make my delivery to Save-A-Buck.

I TURNED DOWN my bed and eased between the cool sheets. If I didn't doze off right away, I'd watch some TV. Something funny.

I propped my pillows against the headboard, but before I could lay my head back, the phone rang. It was China.

"Hi, Daphne. I'm just calling to check in on you and to see how everything is going. You sound tired."

"I am," I admitted. "So far, it's been a trying week. And it isn't showing signs of getting any better."

"Myra told me that you and she were going to check out the Sunoco," China said. "I take it that visit didn't turn up anything new?"

"No. The Elvis who Hot Lips—I mean, the clerk—spotted could've been old or he could've been young. He had a medium build. He was wearing sunglasses. . . . In short, he could be any one of the EIEIO members, or he might not be any of them." I sighed.

"What's next on your agenda?" she asked.

"We're going to try to get more information about the dentist," I said.

"I'll rack my brain and see what I can come up with," she said. "Have you talked with Ben yet?"

"Not yet. We keep leaving messages but missing each other."

China said, "This spat is weighing on him."

"You think so?" I asked.

"I know so. Millie, a friend of mine who delivers newspapers, said the *Chronicle* folks say he's been grouchy as a bear with a sore paw all day," she told me.

"That's not like Ben," I said quietly.

"I know it's not."

"What do you think, China?" I asked. "Should I apologize again, or should—"

"No indeed, you should not. You've already apologized. It's up to him to accept your first apology. If he doesn't, then that's just too bad for him." She huffed. "You didn't dodge a bullet—literally—from that first man of yours to wind up groveling to another one. You deserve better than to have to do that."

I smiled. "Thank you."

"You're welcome. The right one will come along for you, Daphne. It might be Ben, and it might not. But don't kowtow to anybody."

I digested that in silence for a moment before asking China what she'd thought of Dr. Bainsworth. "I've heard that he was married but that he had one affair after another. Did you know him? Did he strike you as that kind of person?"

"I knew Jim Bainsworth. I'd known him since he was a boy," she said. "He always acted like he was entitled. So, no, I wasn't surprised to learn that he was a skirt chaser."

"What do you mean by entitled?" I asked.

"You know, he acted like he deserved to have more than everybody else did, like he was special, like the world owed him something. A man like that comes across as if he's doing everybody else a big favor just by being there. He probably thought his wife was lucky to have him, no matter how he treated her, and I imagine he felt the same way about his girlfriends."

"Humph. Sounds like Dr. Bainsworth was a real jerk," I said.

"He was, in a lot of ways. But in other ways, he could be sweet and caring," China said. "And he was an excellent dentist. Dr. Farmer will have a hard time measuring up in my book."

"Wait," I said. "You didn't like Dr. Bainsworth, but you continued seeing him as your dentist?"

She chuckled. "I never said I didn't like him. I recognized his faults, but he had some good traits too. One of those good traits was that he was a great dentist. Of course, if I'd been his wife, I'd have killed him."

After speaking with China, I wasn't as sleepy anymore. Her comment about killing Dr. Bainsworth had she been his wife had been said in jest, but I couldn't get it out of my head. I needed to talk with Angela Bainsworth.

I checked the clock and saw that it was still early enough to call Violet. I dialed her number and asked her for Angela's contact information.

"Why do you want to talk with Angela?" she asked.

"Myra and I need to learn everything we can about Dr. Bainsworth and why someone might've wanted him dead," I said. "I figure the man's ex-wife would be the best source of that information."

Vi sighed. "The divorce process has been horrible for her. It really took its toll in the beginning, and she's only now starting to get over it. Or, at least, she was. And now Jim is dead. Isn't there any other way you can find out what you need to know?"

"There might be," I said. "But right now it looks as if Myra and I are the police department's main persons of interest. I'd like to at least be able to point them in another direction. Wouldn't you, if you were in my position?"

"Of course. You know I'd do anything to help you." She blew out another breath. "How about this? I'll call Angela first thing in the morning to see if you and I can talk with her. Maybe we can meet her for lunch or something."

"How did we go from you asking if there was another way to gain insight into Dr. Bainsworth's life to you arranging for the two of us to talk with Angela over lunch?" I asked.

"I don't know," she said. "You reminded me that you're in trouble."

I could hear the unsaid *again* in her tone.

"And I want to help you out," she continued. "Besides, Angela might be more forthcoming if I'm there since she and I are acquainted."

"Are you sure you're not just going with me in order to find out who'll be putting Dr. Bainsworth's house on the market now that he's dead?" I asked.

"Daphne! That's a terrible thing to say! If you don't want me to go with you, I won't."

"I'm sorry, Vi. It was a joke. I didn't mean to be snotty. It's been a rough week and it's only Monday."

"I know, but don't alienate the people who care about you," she said. "I'll call Angela tomorrow morning and then let you know what she says. I'm sure she would like to see this crime solved, too, even if she was divorcing him."

"Thanks," I said.

"And for the record, auction houses usually deal with estate sales."

"I said I'm sorry," I told her, thinking how much she could be like Mom sometimes.

"I'm sorry too," she said. "But you reminded me of Mom when you said that. Sometimes it seems as if she's always looking for an ulterior motive."

My jaw dropped, and I gave an indignant squeak. "Me? *I* sound like her? You're the one who's talking like Mom with that self-righteous attitude that *somebody* has to bail stupid Daphne out *again*."

"She is not self-righteous," she said, "and the only reason any of us would feel like you need to be bailed out of trouble *again* is because you seem to be a magnet for it."

"Apparently, I broke a bunch of mirrors at one time or another," I said. "Please don't worry yourself about any difficulties

I get myself into. I'll find a way to extract myself from them on my own."

"You called me and asked for my help," Vi reminded me. "I offered it, and you got all huffy with me."

I digested this in silence for a full three seconds. Then I started to cry.

"You're really upset," Violet said. "I didn't realize this situation was that serious."

"I guess I'm just weary and fed up." I went on to explain that if I read between the lines in that day's *Chronicle* story, the police didn't have sufficient evidence to charge Myra or me with Dr. Bainsworth's murder—or anything—yet. But they had been following us around and asking questions about us, and we were afraid they'd come up with some sort of motive if we didn't get involved with the investigation.

"That's not your job, Daphne. It's the responsibility of the police department to discover who killed Dr. Bainsworth. Do you think they're too stupid to do their jobs?"

"Of course not," I said. "But people won't talk with them as readily as they'll talk with Myra and me. Police officers are intimidating. They make people nervous."

"That's true enough, I guess. What's Ben saying?" she asked.

I couldn't bring myself to tell Violet that Ben and I had a falling-out. So I said, "Not much, but he confirmed that Myra and I are currently the only suspects in the murder."

"That's ridiculous. There's no way they could seriously suspect either one of you. Try to get some sleep. I'll call you tomorrow as soon as I talk with Angela," Violet said.

"Thank you. I appreciate your help. Really, I do."

I AWOKE TUESDAY morning feeling refreshed, well rested, and a little Doris Day. Not only about the dentist's murder investigation but about Ben too. After all, our high school romance hadn't panned out. Maybe he and I just weren't meant to be. I didn't have the time or the energy to mope. I'd wasted enough time in my life hoping a man I was with would come to care about me. I wouldn't do that anymore.

Que sera sera . . . whatever will be will be.

So now you understand the Doris Day reference and hopefully won't think I had what was referred to as "a nervous breakdown" when I was growing up.

Anyway, I hopped out of bed and straightened it up before I left the bedroom. I took my clothes and went into the bathroom. I peered into the mirror. I looked much better this morning than I had yesterday morning. From now on, self-pity was verboten.

I took a lingering scented bath, and then I dressed in dark denim jeans and a pink cowl-neck sweater. I applied my makeup with care, and I swept my hair up into a ponytail.

I went into the kitchen and removed the sheet cakes from the refrigerator to allow them to warm to room temperature before decorating them. I fed Sparrow and then made my own breakfast. Since I was being especially kind to myself, I opted for a ham and Swiss omelet and a slice of whole wheat toast. I was humming under my breath as I cleaned up my breakfast dishes, strode to the pantry, and took out five party trays.

I placed the trays on the kitchen table and took the brownies out of the refrigerator. I cut the brownies into two-inch squares and arranged them and the cookies on the trays while white and dark chocolate was melting in two double boilers. I'd left a circular space in the middle of each tray for the pretzels. I stirred the now-melted chocolate, opened a bag of pretzels, and dipped the pretzels in the confection.

While the pretzels were cooling on waxed paper, I went to my office to check my e-mail—sadly, no new cake orders or quote requests—and printed off labels for the cakes. Upon returning to the kitchen, I tinted some vanilla buttercream green and iced the cakes smooth. Since these were to be football-themed cakes, I decided to go the simple route and make them all look like football fields. I piped a simple white shell border on the tops and bottoms of all five cakes, and then I piped yard lines with thin white icing. I numbered the yard lines and added plastic goal posts and footballs. When I'd finished, I put the cakes in Daphne's Delectable Cakes boxes with the flavor and ingredient labels on them.

I placed a combination of each type of pretzel on the party trays before putting the lids on the trays. Fait accompli!

I removed my apron, grabbed my jacket, and began loading the party trays and cakes into the backseat of my car. During my last trip into the house, Sparrow made her usual escape out the door. I figured she'd be waiting for me on the porch when I returned.

I noticed a patrol car driving slowly past my house. I recognized Officer Halligan. He was peering at me, so I smiled broadly and waved at him.

It was still early, and there wasn't much traffic on the road. But on my way to the Save-A-Buck, I was stopped at a traffic light and noticed a silver BMW in the parking lot of an abandoned restaurant. I could see that there was a woman in the car and that she was with someone. I couldn't make out anything about the other person but the woman's profile was clearly visible. She leaned toward her passenger, and it appeared they were kissing. I wondered why the couple would be sitting outside a deserted restaurant. It was for sale, so maybe she and the man were planning on buying it or something. Still, it struck me as odd that they would be there alone this early on a Tuesday morning. My imagination was ignited, and I decided they were getting ready to start a new life together. They were going to open this restaurant with the proceeds of the big house they'd sold, or they were getting a small business loan. This had been their dream ever since they'd first married, and now they'd decided to go for it.

The light turned green, and my movie-of-the-week scenario had to end. I drove on to the Save-A-Buck. I went inside and got two shopping carts and a bagger to help me bring in the party trays and cakes. As the bagger and I were bringing the carts back in, Mr. Franklin spotted us.

"Daphne, good job," he said. "Wait just a second and I'll set up a table for those. Josh, will you give me a hand please?"

With a nod, Josh hurried off with Mr. Franklin.

I saw that Juanita was at her usual register and went over. "Good morning," I said. "I left a message for you yesterday."

She smiled slightly. "Yes. I got the message but it was too late to return your call."

"Are you feeling all right?" I asked.

"Yes . . . much better today," she said. "Are the *damas* and the fountain I brought okay?"

"They're terrific," I said.

"Good." She looked down at her hands. "I'm sorry about yesterday, I just . . . I saw . . ." She pressed her lips together and seemed to be weighing her words before she spoke. "I saw that you still had company, and I didn't want to interrupt. And I suddenly felt . . . unwell."

"That's fine, Juanita. I'm just glad you're feeling better."

Mr. Franklin and Josh returned with a white table. They placed the table at the front of the store with a banner proclaiming FRESH BAKED GOODS. I arranged the party platters and cakes on the table, waved good-bye to Juanita, and left.

After I got home from the Save-A-Buck, I decided to mix up the *quinceañera* cakes for Juanita's sister and then cover the Cadillac cake with fondant while they were baking.

Soon the *quinceañera* cakes were in the oven, and my house smelled of vanilla. I got out a tub of white buttercream-flavored fondant and some pink gel color. I put on disposable gloves and worked the tint through a large mound of fondant. When I had it the cotton-candy color I was going for, I placed the mound of fondant on a sheet of waxed paper in the middle of the island. I took off the gloves and laid them aside. Using a rolling pin, I wrestled the fondant into a huge, smooth oval. I gently lifted it off the waxed paper and draped it over the cake. As I was working it into all the creases and crevices that defined the shape of the car, there was a knock at the kitchen door.

"Come on in," I called.

Myra came in, shrugged out of her jacket, and hung it on a peg by the door. "That's as cute as it can be," she said as she sat on one of the stools and watched me finish covering the Cadillac cake. "I can hardly wait to see it finished, and to see everybody's reaction to it at the dinner on Friday."

"Me too." I took a pizza cutter from the utility drawer. "Wait a sec. I thought you said Cecil was boring when he wasn't performing as Elvis."

"Oh, he is, honey. Duller than dirty laundry," she said. "The literal kind, not the gossip kind. But Cecil's not the only Elvis in town, you know." She grinned. "Last night I got a call from John. You remember him from yesterday?"

"I remember. He was the *young* redhead who couldn't seem to keep the dates straight, right?"

"That's him." She lifted one shoulder. "And he's not that young. He's older than he looks . . . a little skinny for my tastes, but he was awfully sweet over the phone."

"Won't that be uncomfortable?" I asked. "Going to a party on Friday with your new Elvis when you know your old one will be there too?"

"It might be," she said. "But Cecil had his chance. He can't imagine a tomato like me would linger long on the vine without getting plucked."

"I guess not."

"Besides," she said, "they'll both be gone in a few days. I need to make a little hay while the sun shines. Why *are* they hanging around so long anyway?"

"From what I can gather, they have this convention somewhere every year to plan the following year's missions and go over the budget, fund-raising ideas, and whatever else Elvis missionaries do," I said. "But speaking of the *suspects* being gone in a few days, were you able to find out anything?"

"Yep. I called both our dry cleaners, but neither of them took in a blue suede jacket over the past couple days."

"So we need to check with out-of-town cleaners," I said.

"I called a few of them, too. One was closed on Tuesdays, but I left a message. I'm thinking that coat is gonna be a dead end," she said. "Not even the real Elvis would've hung on to a costume with a murder victim's blood on the sleeve."

Nodding, I cut the excess fondant from around the cake with the pizza cutter.

"Besides," she said, "what idiot would take a bloody jacket to the dry cleaner when he had to know the police would be looking for it?"

"Excellent point," I said. "Were you able to get anything from talking with Tanya?"

"Oh, honey."

I closed my eyes, thinking that on the one hand I didn't have time for one of Myra's long, drawn-out stories. But, on the other hand, she might have valuable information. "Would you like some coffee before you begin?"

"Oh, no, thanks. Looks like you've got your hands full anyway." She folded her arms. "Do you know Bunni Wilson? She's Jobab Harris's sister. Their mother insisted on giving them Bible names, but she didn't want to pick the same ones most other people do, so she chose a couple of names that were way out there."

I tried not to ask, but it was like trying to stifle a sneeze. I simply couldn't stop myself. "Joe Bob and Bunny are Bible names?"

"Yeah. They're in the Old Testament. Only Jobab is one word, and Bunni is spelled with an *i*. That's why Ms. Harris felt it would be a good girl's name." She nodded. "Of course, *jobab* means 'desert' . . . which might explain the man's personality. He's as dry as the Sahara during a heat wave."

"But what about Bunni?" I asked.

"I don't think too awful much is known about Bunni. You just see the name mentioned a few times in Nehemiah," she said.

I took a breath. "Not Bible Bunni, Dr. Bainsworth's Bunni."

"Oh, yeah. She's worked for Dr. Bainsworth since he opened the practice twelve years ago. She's our go-to gal on this one," Myra said.

"Will she talk with us?" I asked.

"Hard to say." She raised her eyes tentatively. "I figure we ought to play it cool so as not to put her on her guard."

"And how do we do that?"

"Easy. She's got an appointment to get her hair done at three today at Tanya's." Myra grinned. "And so do we."

My eyes bulged and I gulped. "I don't want to change my hairstyle." My left hand flew instinctively to my ponytail brushing against the back of my neck and shoulders. "I refuse to have my hair cut, dyed, permed, or teased to the point of tears."

"I know, sweetie. That's why you and I are only getting a wash and style," she said.

"A . . . a wash and . . . and style?" I gulped again.

"Yeah." She did a wink-nod combo that was meant to reassure me. "You need a little pampering. We both do. It'll make us feel better."

I simply stared at her.

"Plus, we can feel out Bunni and see how willing she is to talk with us. Some of those secretaries take that confidentiality stuff way too seriously, you know," Myra said. She grabbed her jacket. "It's nearly twelve thirty and my soap is getting ready to come on, so I'll let you get back to your work for now. Pick you up around two thirty!"

After Myra left, I washed my hands and went back to work on the Cadillac. I tried not to wonder how much damage Tanya could do to my head with a mere wash and style. Surely she wouldn't do anything I couldn't come straight home and undo. Right?

CHAPTER Nine

By the time Myra had returned for me, I'd gotten quite a bit accomplished. I'd tinted some fondant silver and had made the "chrome" hubcaps, bumpers, and trim. Juanita's sister's cakes had been crumb coated and were in the refrigerator awaiting a second frosting. And, last but not least, Violet had called and said that although Angela hadn't been available for lunch, she'd answer my questions at around four thirty that afternoon.

I'd just finished cleaning up the kitchen when Myra tapped on the door. Other than dreading the hair appointment, I was happy about how my day was shaping up. I motioned Myra inside.

"You ready?" she asked.

"Let me grab a coat," I said. I hurried to the bedroom and took out a navy peacoat to put on over my jeans and pink sweater. I thought for a second about opting for a hooded jacket in case I didn't want to be seen with my head uncovered after the salon visit, but I decided to go with what I had on.

I know you probably think I'm exaggerating and being awfully mean about Tanya's Tremendous Tress-Taming Salon. But, trust me, you'd be nervous too. The salon has catered to the same clientele for decades. Even before Tanya took over the shop and changed its name, it was the only hair salon in Brea Ridge. Tanya's patrons were pretty set in their ways, and they typically believed that hair should be large and immobile. If it could be used as a means of self-defense, then all the better. Tanya naturally had to defer to the wishes of her clientele.

I still recall that about thirty years ago, Ray McGinley used to regale everyone at church picnics with the story of the time his wife Louisa was being chased by a vicious dog. Louisa ran under a maple tree, her stiff coif knocked a branch loose, and the tree limb—along with a fully inhabited wasp nest—was knocked onto the dog. Louisa vowed that the branch was already broken and that she'd only jarred it out of the tree, but even as a little girl I thought that was some pretty serious helmet head. I've had a phobia about that particular salon ever since.

Yet, within minutes, Myra and I were standing on the sidewalk in front of Tanya's Tremendous Tress-Taming Salon with its curlicue *T*s and Ss. Myra flashed me another of her wink-nod combos before we went inside.

The smells of perm solution, shampoo, and hair spray were

punctuated by Tanya's cheery "Hey, darlings! Be with you in a jiffy!" She stood behind a diminutive elderly lady with cottony white hair. One strand of the woman's hair was standing straight up on her head . . . on its own. Tanya went back to teasing the strand of hair until it was even stiffer than before, and then she smoothed it over the rest of the fluffy mass. I nearly took off right then, but a desire to stay out of jail and not have Butter Huffington as my emergency dentist kept my feet glued to the salon's linoleum. That or hair spray residue—I'm not entirely certain which was stronger.

Tanya then hurried over to us, teasing comb still in hand. She waved it at us like it was a long, skinny derringer. "Myra, Peggy Sue will be doing your hair, and Sienna will be doing yours, Daphne. Sienna is new, so just tell her exactly what you want."

"Okay," I said, not sure whether Sienna being new was a good thing or a bad thing. I mean, she'd likely just got out of cosmetology school, which meant she hadn't had time to hone her teasing and big-haired-old-lady styling skills. On the other hand, she'd likely just got out of cosmetology school and hadn't had time to hone any other skills either.

Sienna stepped out from behind a shampoo station and motioned me over. "Hi," she said, her gum a-snapping. "I'm Sienna." She reminded me of Abby from *NCIS*: Goth, dark hair, dark clothes, dark-rimmed eyes, and dark lipstick. And yet, cute. For her, it all worked. Like Abby from *NCIS*. Her own hair had been pulled into a ponytail like mine. Suddenly I felt that everything might be okay with this visit. I thought I might leave looking like Joan Jett but certainly not like one of the Golden Girls.

"Let's get you shampooed," Sienna said.

I slipped off my coat and put it and my purse on a nearby chair. I sat down in the shampoo chair and leaned my head back into the sink. Sienna took the elastic band from my hair and handed it to me. She turned on the water. The blast of warm water on my scalp was nice, and when Sienna massaged shampoo and conditioner into my hair, I have to admit, it was relaxing.

In the chair next to mine, Myra was talking just as fast as Peggy Sue was shampooing. "I know she was nervous about coming in. She's the type of person who hates to try anything new, you know. But I said, 'Daphne, you and I need some pampering.' And we do too. By the way, is Bunni Wilson here yet?"

"Not yet," Peggy Sue answered. "But she's usually ten or fifteen minutes late for her appointments. Why?"

"Oh, just curious," Myra said. "Tanya said Bunni has a standing Tuesday afternoon appointment, and I wanted to ask her what she thinks happened to Dr. Bainsworth."

"Wasn't that just awful?" Peggy Sue asked. "And I heard you and Daphne were the ones who found him."

"We were," Myra said. "It was a terrible ordeal. I can't imagine anyone wanting to hurt Dr. Bainsworth. Can you?"

As Peggy Sue was answering Myra, Sienna posed the same question to me about the dentist's demise.

"I don't know," I answered. "Do you have any theories?"

"I do," she said dramatically. "See, I think one of his patients was a werewolf—you know, like in that movie *The Werewolf*? And that night, he broke into Dr. Bainsworth's office to steal something—you know, like maybe nitrous oxide so he could get woozy and forget his obsession. And then the dentist came in and caught him by surprise, and so he had to devour him."

"But Dr. Bainsworth wasn't devoured," I said.

"Right, because someone scared the werewolf away." Sienna smiled triumphantly.

"You might be on to something," I said. I didn't believe her werewolf theory, but what if someone *had* come into Dr. Bainsworth's office to steal something? I'd been going on the belief that someone had tracked him to the office with the intention of killing him. But if murder was the intent, someone could have just as easily killed him in his home or somewhere else. Why follow him to a public place in order to kill him? "Seriously, Sienna, you might be on the right track."

Ten minutes later, Myra and I were sitting one seat apart getting our hair done. The seat between us was empty. Peggy Sue sported a fairly large bob sprayed into submission by some type of hair spray that even at a distance was making my nose itch. Pictures of children of various ages were taped to either side of her mirror, and she had a princess crown perpetual calendar on the counter of her workstation.

Sienna had little skulls with pink bows on their heads attached to the top corners of her mirror. On her counter was a white teddy bear in a black leather vest and a framed photo of her and a guy with heavily tattooed arms standing outside what looked like a concert venue.

"So, what're we doing?" Sienna asked me.

"I'm thinking just your most basic blow-dry and comb-out," I said. "Nothing fancy."

She smiled and snapped her gum. "Gotcha." She grabbed the blow-dryer and a thick-barreled round brush.

At that moment, Myra gave the most exaggerated throat clearing I'd ever heard. I glanced over, and she jerked her head in the direction of the door—no easy task with Peggy Sue's comb buried in her hair. I saw that a middle-aged, square-shaped woman with a lacquered light-brown bouffant had walked into the salon. Myra placed her front teeth over her bottom lip and twitched her nose before rolling her eyes toward the door.

Did she think her *ahem!* hadn't been enough to clue me in that the lady was Bunni Wilson? Still, I nodded, afraid Myra might get up and begin hopping around.

"Hi, Bunni!" Tanya called. "Go on over to the shampoo chair, and I'll be there as soon as I finish up with Rosa."

Bunni strolled over to the shampoo area and picked up a tabloid magazine.

Sienna had my hair almost dry by the time Tanya brought Bunni over to occupy the chair between Myra and me. As Sienna turned off the hair dryer, I asked, "Did you see on TV where that actor was caught cheating on his wife? She appeared to be heartbroken." I was hoping this would give us a segue into Dr. Bainsworth cheating on *his* wife.

"I know," Sienna said. "And the wife was so much prettier than that sleazy record producer."

"*She* wasn't the producer," Tanya chimed in. "The record company belonged to her husband. *He* was the producer."

"Then what does that make her?" Peggy Sue asked.

Everyone else—Myra included, to my surprise—averted her eyes and let that question hang.

"I don't know what makes men behave that way," Myra said. "It's not just a Hollywood or big-city problem either. Why,

I heard our very own Dr. Bainsworth—rest his soul—cheated on his wife, Angela."

Myra was at the top of her sleuthing game today.

"I heard that myself," Tanya said. "And I heard that because Dr. Bainsworth had been caught cheating, Angela was able to wipe him out financially."

"She did wipe him out," Bunni said softly. "It's true that he and one of the hygienists had taken to meeting in Bristol or Kingsport now and then for drinks or for dinner, but the poor man had no one else. I'd have helped him work out his problems, of course, but he refused to burden me with them." She shook her head sadly. "He needed someone to talk to, that's all."

"Couldn't he talk to his wife?" Myra asked.

Bunni scoffed. "His wife was the reason he needed someone to talk with. According to Jill, the hygienist, Angela was dreadfully mean to Dr. Bainsworth."

"In what way?" Peggy Sue asked.

"She spent money faster than he could bring it home," Bunni said. "She seldom cooked for him, and she wasted the majority of her time at the country club. Jill said Dr. Bainsworth was afraid Angela was the one having an affair."

"Well, it's good Dr. Bainsworth had Jill there to help him pick up the pieces after his divorce, right?" I asked. "Didn't she leave her husband for Dr. Bainsworth?"

"She did," Bunni said, "because she completely misunderstood the nature of their relationship. She wanted more than friendship, and Dr. Bainsworth didn't."

"How did Jill get such a *wrong* idea?" Myra asked.

"She was delusional." Bunni nodded. "That's why Dr. Bainsworth had to let her go."

"He broke her heart and then he fired her?" Sienna asked incredulously. "How cold was that?"

"It wasn't like that," Bunni said heatedly. "It wasn't Dr. Bainsworth's fault that Jill mistook his attention for something more than friendship. Jill had mental problems."

"Poor Jill," Tanya said as she combed through Bunni's wet hair. "It's a shame that her mistake cost her everything."

"It was a sad situation." Bunni looked down at her clasped hands. "At least Dr. Bainsworth was good enough to give her some severance pay and a letter of recommendation." She dabbed a tear from the corner of her eye. "He was a kind, kind man."

And this woman called *Jill* delusional?

Peggy Sue finished with Myra. Her hair wasn't too big or too stiff. It looked pretty much like it usually did. Maybe there was hope for me after all.

Sienna finished with my hair and turned the chair to face the mirror. I didn't look like Joan Jett or any of the Golden Girls.

The phone rang, and Tanya picked the cordless up off her workstation. I was guessing it was Priscilla Presley circa 1960 calling to say she wanted her hair back.

CHAPTER Ten

I ASKED MYRA if she'd mind dropping me off at Violet's office since Vi and I were to meet Angela at four thirty.

"No, I don't mind. That won't be a bit of trouble," she said.

"I wish I had time to go home and wash my hair," I said glumly, "but I'm cutting it close as it is."

"Wash your hair?" Myra asked. "You just had your hair washed. And it looks great."

I shot her a glance before pulling down the sun visor and peering at my hair in the vanity mirror. "Well, I'll give Sienna credit. She didn't tease my hair. She completely outraged it. It's incensed. It wants to march on Capitol Hill in support of hair rights."

"I've never known you to be so dramatic," Myra said. "Your hair is fine. It's your brain I'm worried about. Why in the world did you go along with Sienna's crazy werewolf theory? Are you seriously contemplating the fact that one of our Elvises might be a werewolf?"

"Of course not. When I said she might be on to something, I was talking about her theory that the killer was in Dr. Bainsworth's office when the dentist arrived that night," I said.

"You mean, he could've been there robbing the place and didn't go to the office with the intention of killing Dr. Bainsworth?" she asked.

"It's possible." I flipped the sun visor back up. "If you think about it, it's much more plausible. If the killer had been out to get Dr. Bainsworth, there are much more convenient places to kill him than in his office."

"But if the killer was after something in Dr. Bainsworth's office," Myra said, "he might've only killed Dr. Bainsworth because he got caught."

"Right."

Myra pulled into the Armstrong Realty parking lot. "What we need to know now is what is—or was—in that office that's so all-fired important."

"Let's hope Angela knows—and that she'll tell me," I said.

I was walking up the steps to Violet's office when she stepped out the door.

"I'll lock up and then—"

She stopped. Just like that, with her key in midair and her mouth hanging open, eyes as wide as cupcake tops.

I plucked the key from her hand and locked the door. "You wouldn't happen to have a hat I could borrow, would you?"

Violet shook her perfectly adorable blond curls. "No, but I wish I did. What . . . ? Who did this to you?"

"Sienna at Tanya's place. Myra and I went there to talk with Bunni Wilson, who worked for Dr. Bainsworth."

She tentatively raised her hand to my hair. "It feels like fiberglass insulation," she whispered. "Honest to goodness, it does. Jason had insulation of this exact consistency blown into our attic last year."

"I know, Vi. It's hideous. But it'll wash out. Right? No real harm done?"

"Sure." She nodded slowly. "Of course it will."

"You can tell Angela I'm stressed about the investigation if that'll suffice as an explanation for my hair being an equivalent to Edvard Munch's *The Scream*," I said.

"No, I'm afraid that wouldn't work. I think the little guy in that painting is bald. This is more like an Einstein sort of thing. Want me to casually mention to her that you're a genius?" She brightened. "Hey, I could say you're a genius in the kitchen."

I sighed. "No, I just want to go on to her house and get this over with."

We got into Violet's silver Volvo. She looked over at me. "It's not that bad once you get used to it. You . . . .it took me by surprise when I first saw you. That's all."

"That was very convincing, Vi. Now drive."

She started the engine. "Did you learn anything valuable from the woman who worked for Dr. Bainsworth?"

"Besides the fact that she believed the dentist hung the moon and stars?" I asked. "Not much. I did get the first name of the hygienist who left her husband for Dr. Bainsworth, though. It was Jill."

"I'm certain Angela can supply you with Jill's last name, and maybe her address. I believe she was named as a third-party defendant in the Bainsworths' divorce. And if it was me, I'd be more than happy to point the police in the direction of the woman who destroyed my marriage."

"Jill didn't do it alone . . . unless you buy Bunni's story of Jill *misunderstanding* her relationship with the dentist," I said.

Angela had a modest home between Brea Ridge and Abingdon. It was far enough out in the country to afford the woman some privacy, but it wasn't so far from civilization—translation, shopping—to be inconvenient. The house itself was a split-level with vaulted ceilings. There was beige carpet throughout—or at least as far as I could see—and the walls were ecru. The neutral color scheme might have been boring if not for the splashes of color and designer touches in evidence. An overstuffed sofa in a bold yellow fabric dominated the living room. Accent chairs in blue damask carried over the hint of blue in an Oriental rug occupying the center of the room.

I might have been mistaken in my estimation of the worth of the home's furnishings, but they appeared expensive to me. And I didn't get the feeling Angela Bainsworth was hurting for money.

Angela, a petite brunette with watchful green eyes, welcomed us into her living room and then went into the kitchen to get a coffee-and-tea tray. She placed the tray on the cherry table in front of the sofa. I had the feeling I'd seen her somewhere before.

"Daphne, would you like coffee or tea?" she asked.

I chose tea, Violet opted for coffee, and Angela didn't take either one, which made me doubly anxious about spilling my tea on her Oriental rug.

I held my white china cup and saucer awkwardly. "I suppose Violet told you why I wanted to talk with you. The police seem to think I'm a person of interest in Dr. Bainsworth's death since I was in his office that night. I'm trying to clear my name."

"She did," Angela said. "I'm sorry you've found yourself in such a predicament. How can I help?"

I glanced at Violet, who gave me a brief nod of encouragement.

"First of all, I'm sorry for your loss," I said. "I know you and Dr. Bainsworth were divorcing, but you were his wife, and I'm sure you loved him once."

Angela blinked. "Thank you. . . . That . . . that's not what I expected you to say. I appreciate your thoughtfulness. It has been a trying few days. While I understand there were many people angry with Jim—including me—I can't imagine anyone killing him."

"I know his death comes as quite a shock. My friend Myra and I were the ones to discover his body. I had just spoken with him less than an hour before and made an emergency appointment with him for Myra, who was a patient of his. You have no idea why anyone would've broken into his office? Did he keep money or any other valuables there?"

She shook her head. "Any money received was deposited at the end of each day."

"What about drugs?" Violet asked. "Dentists often prescribe painkillers, don't they?"

"Naturally," Angela said, "but he never even kept samples in his office. And Jim always kept his prescription pads locked in his desk."

I frowned. "Then what could his attacker have been looking for?"

"I have no idea," Angela said. "Maybe he or she wasn't looking for anything except Jim. I mean I've heard of people breaking into dental offices for the nitrous oxide, but Jim didn't even use gas anymore. His patients who preferred sedation dentistry went over to Dr. Farmer."

I pursed my lips. "I know the police have asked you this already, but can you think of anyone—anyone at all—who might've wanted to harm Dr. Bainsworth?"

She scoffed. "I'll tell you what I told them—interview the husbands of his female patients."

"What about a hygienist named Jill?" I asked. "According to Bunni Wilson, this woman completely misunderstood Dr. Bainsworth's kindness toward her and gave up everything for him. Bunni said Dr. Bainsworth had to fire her to make her leave him alone."

Angela gaped. "Yeah, and if you're looking to unload a piece of oceanfront Tennessee real estate, Bunni's your buyer."

Violet smiled slightly. "I'll keep that in mind."

"Jim was having an affair with Jill. It was nothing serious to him, although I initiated divorce proceedings against him when I found out about it." Angela lifted her shoulders. "I couldn't stand the thought of him ever touching me again after he'd cheated on me." She looked away. "I think Jill was in love with Jim, but the feeling wasn't mutual, and she wound up paying dearly for her mistake."

"I admire your ability to speak of her sympathetically," I

said. "I'm not sure I wouldn't be glad the other woman got the shaft."

"Oh, I never said that." She took a deep breath. "At first, I was absolutely delighted to watch Jill Fisher's life fall apart. But then I began to realize she and I weren't all that different. He conned me, and he conned her." Her eyes filled with tears. "And he devastated us both. In a way, I'll be glad to get the funeral over with on Saturday so I can start getting on with my life . . . again."

I realized where I'd seen Angela Bainsworth. She was the woman who'd been parked outside the restaurant this morning. "At least you have new ventures to look forward to, right?" I asked.

She tilted her head toward me. "What do you mean?"

"I saw you this morning at that abandoned restaurant that's for sale downtown. I thought maybe you were planning to buy it, give it a makeover, and set up shop," I said.

Angela began shaking her head. "No. That wasn't me. I don't know who you saw, but it definitely wasn't me."

"Oh," I murmured. "My mistake."

When Violet and I left, I noticed the silver BMW in the driveway. How likely could it be that the woman parked outside the abandoned restaurant this morning was a dead ringer for Angela Bainsworth *and* she had exactly the same type of car? But then if it had, in fact, been Angela, why would she try to hide the fact that she'd been there? Was it because she'd been with a boyfriend? Perhaps she didn't want anyone to see her with him. I can imagine she'd have hidden her relationship while Dr. Bainsworth was still alive because their divorce wasn't final. That way, as far as the judge was concerned, Angela would be the blameless victim in the divorce right up until the end. But why the secrecy now? Was it because Dr. Bainsworth was so recently deceased? Or was it because Angela had been having an affair as her husband had suspected, and Angela didn't want that fact brought to light now?

"Wonder if the police have spoken with Jill Fisher and her ex-husband," I said to Violet as we got into the car.

"See if Ben knows," Violet said as she backed out of Angela's driveway. "Even if he doesn't, I'll bet he can find out."

I WAS DRYING my freshly washed hair and scanning the *Chronicle*. The only mention of the Bainsworth murder today was the article stating that police had found new evidence—the earring was my guess—and that they were making inroads into finding the killer. Dr. Bainsworth's funeral arrangements were in the obituary section. The autopsy—the results of which were still pending—had delayed the funeral until Saturday, over a week after the man's death. But he was to be memorialized in a graveside service Saturday morning at the cemetery, with the burial taking place immediately afterward.

I mulled over what Violet had said about asking Ben what was going on with the police investigation that wasn't being mentioned in the *Chronicle*. She'd given me the perfect excuse to call him without appearing desperate to make up with him.

I picked up the phone, dialed all but the last number, and hung up. After doing that twice, I finally got up the nerve to complete the call. I half hoped he'd answer, and I half hoped he wouldn't. He answered.

"Ben, hi," I said. "It's Daphne."

"What's up?" His tone seemed guarded.

"I was wondering if the police have spoken with Jill Fisher and her ex-husband about Dr. Bainsworth's death."

"I believe they have," he said.

"Are the Fishers being considered as suspects?" I asked.

"Not that I know of."

"Oh." I sighed. "Well, thanks."

"If I hear anything to the contrary, I'll let you know," he said quickly.

"I'd appreciate that." I paused, giving him a chance to say something else. He didn't. "I'll talk with you later."

"Wait," he said. "What about you and Myra? Are you two still investigating?"

"Oh, yeah, we're on the case, all right. Today Myra made appointments for us at Tanya's so we could talk with Bunni Wilson." I huffed. "By the way, that wasn't a solar eclipse this afternoon. It was my hair blocking out the sun."

He laughed. "I'd like to have seen that. Hey, I'm sorry about the other night."

"Me too. I miss you."

"May I come over?" He paused. "I can be there in ten min-utes."

"I'll be waiting."

The line went dead. I hung up the receiver and hurried to the bathroom. I wasn't wearing any makeup, and my hair was a fuzzy mess. I brushed and sprayed my hair. Then I applied a tinted moisturizer, mascara, and lip gloss. I didn't want it to be obvious to Ben that I'd rushed to the bathroom to try to make myself pretty for him, so I quickly went to the living room and sat on the edge of the sofa.

I looked around to see if there was any clutter to be picked up. There wasn't. I'd been spending so much time baking, I hadn't had the chance to mess up the living room. There came a knock at the kitchen door. As I expected, it was Ben. I unlocked the door and started to open it, but Ben pushed the door on open. Closing the door with his foot, he took me in his arms and backed me up against the wall. He was kissing me like he'd been dehydrated for days and I was a cool, clear mountain stream. I don't think Ben had ever kissed me like this before, with such passion, such purpose, such . . . *Oh, my . . .*

I wrapped my arms around him. I was so lost in our kiss, I didn't even realize he'd picked me up until he was lowering me onto the living room sofa.

He dragged his mouth away from mine and slid his lips up my neck toward my ear. "I've missed you like crazy."

"I've missed you too."

"When I saw you onstage kissing that jerk, it made me sick," Ben said. "I know you didn't initiate the kiss, but it was Todd all over again. I was afraid you were ditching me for somebody . . . cooler."

My eyes flew open. Of course, Ben would equate Scottie with Todd. When I was in college, I broke up with Ben and started dating Todd. Not my wisest move . . . and very probably my dumbest.

"Oh, Ben . . ." I took his face in my hands. "It's you I want. Only you."

I WAS AWAKENED on Wednesday morning by the shrill ring of the telephone on my nightstand. I fumbled for the phone, pressed *answer,* and said a groggy hello.

"Good morning," Myra said, all chipper and excited. "First off, congratulations. I saw Ben's Jeep parked at your house last night, so I'm guessing y'all worked everything out."

"We did," I said. "Or, at least, I felt pretty good about everything when he left."

"Great. I'm really glad. I do believe the two of you are meant for each other," Myra said. "Now, I ain't got a thing against Scottie, and he's as cute as can be. I just don't know that he's right for you."

I stifled a yawn. "I agree, Myra. If you'll give me thirty minutes, I'll get dressed and make us some breakfast. We can discuss my meeting with Angela while we eat."

"Well, that's the thing, hon. You'll have to tell me about Angela on the way," she said.

"On the way where?" I asked, raising up on my elbow.

"On the way to Dr. Bainsworth's office," Myra said, as if it should've been obvious. "I was aiming to call you yesterday evening when I found out, but I saw that Ben was there and decided to wait until this morning."

"But why are we going to Bainsworth's office?" I asked. "Isn't it shut down?"

"Not to us. We're part of the cleaning crew."

I sat all the way up. "Myra, we're as good as suspects. The police aren't going to allow us within a hundred yards of that place."

"That's why they don't know about it. Hurry and get ready, and I'll be over to get you in about fifteen minutes. I'll fill you in on the way."

Myra hung up, and I turned off my phone and placed it back on the nightstand. It was a good thing I'd showered and washed my hair last night. By the time I'd fed Sparrow and grabbed an English muffin, Myra was pulling into the driveway. I wrapped the muffin in a napkin and went out to the car.

"Buckle up quick," she said, backing her enormous white car into the street. "We're running behind."

"Explain to me how you plan to pull this off," I said.

"Oh, honey, this fell together like a fat man with an umbrella."

I frowned, trying unsuccessfully to figure out the analogy. Myra continued talking, and I decided her analogy didn't have to make sense. Most of her analogies don't.

"You see, China called me late yesterday afternoon," she said. "She'd talked with her cousin Pat who lives over in Lebanon—the town, not that foreign country they're always fighting in, and Virginia, not Tennessee."

"Keep going," I said, unwrapping my breakfast. "Want half of this muffin?"

"No, thanks."

I took a bite as Myra stopped for a red light. "And?"

"Well, China's cousin has been hired to clean Dr. Bainsworth's office," Myra said. "That's what she does—China's cousin Pat; she has her own cleaning business."

I hated to be redundant, but I was compelled to again ask, "And?"

The light turned green, and Myra pressed the gas with such gusto I was afraid I'd wind up in the backseat.

Myra scoffed at my inability to appreciate our good fortune. "*And* China arranged for us to get in there and snoop around."

"Okay, but what is there to snoop around in?" I asked. "Haven't the police already confiscated the files and appointment books?"

Myra rolled her eyes. "Maybe, but that doesn't mean there still aren't things to find."

"You've got a point," I said. "But what if the police show up?"

"We'll hide."

"Well, we have to be sure that we don't leave any fingerprints that would further implicate us," I said.

"That's why I brought us each a pair of rubber gloves." She pulled into the parking lot of a building across the street from Dr. Bainsworth's office. She looked all around the area and then pulled out two pair of gloves from her bag and flipped up the collar of her tan coat. She reached into the back floor and got a man's gray felt hat and tortoiseshell sunglasses to complete her disguise.

"Nice fedora," I said.

She grinned. "Thanks. It was Carl's. It's one of the few things I didn't send to the Salvation Army after he died. I actually hung on to it in case something like this ever happened." All traces of her smile disappeared as Myra quickly surveilled the area again. "Let's go."

Myra Jenkins was born for intrigue. Or maybe just born to be wild.

CHAPTER Eleven

WHEN WE arrived at the back door of Dr. Bainsworth's office, Myra gave two sharp taps. All the while, she was looking furtively from side to side. It was comical, but I didn't dare laugh. I was afraid she'd give *me* two sharp taps and say something Edward G. Robinson–y like "Schnap out of it, cookie. You're fallin' apart on me, schee."

The door was opened by a withered little soul who looked as if she might've been born sometime after the Battle of Vicksburg but before the swearing in of President Johnson—the first one.

"You Myra?" she asked gruffly.

Myra gave a single solemn nod.

The woman indicated with a jerk of her head that Myra and I should come inside. We stepped through the door, and she locked it before turning to speak with us.

"I'm Pat."

"Hi, Pat," I said, extending my hand. "I'm Daphne—"

"No names," Pat said, ignoring my gesture of a handshake and making me wonder if I was the only one who didn't get a spy movie script the night before. "It's bad enough I know hers. And I don't know her last name."

"Jenkins," Myra said.

Pat huffed and rolled her eyes. "What'd you have to go and tell me that for? I'm trying to remain ignorant of the facts here." She blew out another breath. This time I was unfortunate enough to catch a whiff of Pall Mall and sausage.

"Now, here's how we're gonna do this," Pat said. "As far as I'm concerned, you two are just volunteers who're helping me clean this office today. And you *will* help me clean because you're here in place of the rest of my crew. So you'd best get to your prying."

"Yes, ma'am," I said.

Myra tried to play it cooler, giving Pat her patented wink-nod combo.

"You've got thirty minutes before I come after you and put your butts to work," Pat said. "Thirty minutes."

As soon as Pat scurried away, Myra turned to me with a scowl. "Who died and made that freakin' hobbit queen of the world?"

"I don't know," I said. "I didn't realize we'd signed on for cleaning duty."

"I sort of did, but I didn't know she'd be so hard-core."

I sighed. "We'd better snoop quickly."

"Where do we start?" Myra asked.

"Who knows?" I asked with a shrug. "But to make better time, let's start at opposite ends and work toward the middle of the office. Does your phone have a camera?"

"Yeah," she said, digging in her purse for her cell phone. "I've never used it before, but it's got one."

Fear of being compared to *that freakin' hobbit* was all that kept me from rolling my eyes. "Can you figure it out and take pictures of anything suspicious?"

"Of course," she said with a huff in her voice.

"Great," I said. "I'll do the same and see you back here in thirty minutes."

"Twenty-nine!" Pat called.

The hobbit must have had ears like an elephant. Myra and I went in our separate directions. I headed toward the back, where Dr. Bainsworth's office was located, and Myra began with the waiting room. There wasn't much on Dr. Bainsworth's desk—just a couple photos, even one of him with Angela; a clock; an empty in-box; a telephone; and a crystal paperweight. His appointment book and desk calendar were gone. I figured they, like the files, had been taken to police headquarters.

I opened the middle desk drawer. Not really having time to rifle through its contents, I snapped a photo. Basically, it contained some change, paper clips, notepads, a woman's gold bracelet, the blank prescription pads Angela had mentioned, and some miscellaneous clutter. Some of the coins appeared to be foreign currency, so I took a close-up photo of them so I could reference them on the Internet later. Maybe they were from the country where Dr. Bainsworth had gone on his mission trip. I supposed maybe they could be from some other country, though. What if Dr. Bainsworth had taken a trip no one else knew about? A place where he'd met the murderous Elvis?

I also took a picture of the bracelet. Maybe it had belonged to some girlfriend we—and maybe even the police—hadn't discovered yet. Maybe this woman—or her husband—was the killer. There didn't appear to be any engravings on the bracelet, but it could still be a valuable clue.

The other two desk drawers were completely empty. On a wild hunch, I took the photos out of their frames and looked at the backs of the pictures for any notations. There wasn't any writing, but the frame holding the photo of him and Angela contained a hotel key card. I snapped pics of both sides of the key and then put it back where I'd found it.

I turned my attention to the trash can. I imagined the police had already gone through the wastebasket and taken anything they had considered noteworthy, but they could've overlooked something. I sat on the floor and dumped the contents out in front of me. I unfolded wadded paper receipts, messages, and correspondence. There were several messages from "Mark." I took photos of everything and then put it all back in the trash can.

I got up and strode over to Dr. Bainsworth's bookshelves. Besides your normal, everyday healthy-tooth tomes, I didn't see much of interest. I took pictures of the shelves anyway on the off chance that we'd either need to revisit the shelves later on or that I'd someday find myself responsible for another of Myra's tooth emergencies and need the title of a good dental reference book. I'm sorry, but that's how my brain works on half a cup of coffee before eight A.M.

"Nineteen minutes!" Pat called.

I had a vision of the taskmaster in that famous *I Love Lucy* candy factory episode yelling, "Speed 'er up!" while Myra and I stuffed chocolates in our mouths, under our chef's hats, and down the front of our aprons.

After looking under Dr. Bainsworth's desk and the other furniture in the office for some vague clue and finding nothing, I moved on to an exam room. It gave me the willies. All those nasty tooth and gum pictures, the smell of dental stuff, the drill, remembering the sound made by the drill. . . . A quick check of the cabinets assured me there was nothing to see in there. Nope, nothing at all. I didn't even take any pictures. I mean, who'd hide whatever it was we were looking for in a dental exam room? We didn't even know for sure that the Elvis—or the hygienist's ex, or the hygienist, or Bunni, or one of Dr. Bainsworth's many other women—had even been looking for anything that night.

I stepped outside the exam room and tried to get control of my breathing. I'd always heard you're supposed to breathe into a paper bag when you're hyperventilating. But most people use plastic bags these days, or those eco-friendly totes. Could you stop hyperventilating by breathing into an eco-friendly tote?

"Fourteen!" Pat shouted.

"Coffee!" I yelled back. "Is there any fresh coffee here?"

"No. We're here to clean the place, not dirty it up," Pat responded from somewhere in the bowels of the building.

"Is there a soda machine?" I asked.

"Don't know. You're the one snooping around," she said. "See for yourself."

Across from Dr. Bainsworth's office, there was a small

kitchenette. Given my fear of dentist drills, I should've explored the kitchenette before venturing into an exam room. But I doubted there was anything in the tiny space except a refrigerator full of rotten food and half a pot of almost week-old coffee. And, unfortunately, I also have a fear of rotten food. Okay, that's not so much a fear as a strong gag reflex.

As desperate as I was for caffeine, I decided to hold my nose and my breath and open the refrigerator door. I could almost hear the hallelujah chorus when I saw a single, unopened can of Diet Coke sitting there amidst the take-out containers and coffee creamer.

My eyes zeroed in on that refreshing, energizing goodness. I continued to hold my breath but let go of my nose in order to claim my prize. I snatched the soda can off that wire shelf and shut the door. I expelled a breath of victory and popped the top on the can. With the first drink, my eyes burned and I could feel the cold liquid coursing down my esophagus. Sweet, sweet nectar.

"Why're you lollygagging?" Pat barked from behind me.

I started and dropped . . . the . . . can.

"Humph. Now you can clean *that* up too," Pat said.

The insult was nearly as bad as the injury. Nearly.

"WANT TO STOP somewhere and grab a bite to eat?" Myra asked on the drive home.

I shook my head. "I need to get cleaned up and work on the *quinceañera* cake for Juanita's sister."

"Yeah. I need to get cleaned up too . . . and rest awhile."

Her voice broke, and I turned sharply to look at her. "Myra, what is it?"

"I'm sorry I dragged you into this."

"No," I said. "It was good we were able to do some snooping in the dental office. We'll upload our photos later and see what we've got."

She sniffled. "N-not just today. I'm sorry I got you into this entire mess."

"It's not your fault. If it's anybody's fault, it's mine." She was crying now, and I felt horrible. "Do you need to pull over?"

"I'm okay," she said. "I don't know how you can try to take the blame for all this, though."

"Hello? The cashew brittle? Had I made a softer snack, we wouldn't be in this predicament," I reminded her.

"Would you hand me a tissue from the glove box?" she asked.

"Sure." I opened the glove box, retrieved a travel pack of tissues, and handed her one. "Why don't I fix us some lunch? That'll make us both feel better."

"No, thanks. I ought to go home."

"If you do, you'll wind up giving yourself a pity party," I said. "And so will I."

She sighed.

"We can have ham sandwiches on rye bread, and I can heat up some pumpkin roll I have in the freezer," I suggested. "What do you say?"

"Are you certain it won't be any trouble?" she asked, her voice a mixture of self-pity and hope.

"No trouble at all," I said.

"That pumpkin roll does sound awfully good." She smiled resolutely. "All right then."

Even though I had a lot of work to do after lunch, I suggested to Myra that we look at the photos we'd taken in Dr. Bainsworth's office. I do some of my best thinking while I'm working on cakes. I hoped the photos would give me something to work with so I could make better sense of what had happened to the dentist and why.

We went into my office and I booted up the computer. I sat down at the desk, and Myra dropped onto the sofa.

"Did you see anything in the office to make you suspect why Dr. Bainsworth might've been killed?" I asked.

"No, honey, I didn't. I just figure it had to be something personal," she said. "Unless there had been cash or drugs stashed somewhere in the office, and the police found and confiscated them, I don't know what else it could be."

I plugged the USB cable into my phone and the computer and began uploading the photos I'd taken. "I agree that it was personal. At least, it looked personal to me when we found Dr. Bainsworth lying there on his floor Friday night."

"He had the nicest smile," Myra mused. "Of course, he would, being a dentist and all. Who'd go to a dentist with bad teeth?"

"The same people who get their hair done by people with bad haircuts, I guess," I responded.

"I suppose," she said. "Some of those male hairdressers have especially weird hairdos—Mohawks and such. I heard somewhere it's like seven hundred dollars for an appointment with that one French guy who has a salon in New York. He has nice hair, though . . . and a nice smile . . . nice eyes. I might start saving up. Think I could get in?"

I smiled. "He'd be lucky to have you as a client." I nodded toward the computer screen. "Here. See if you find anything weird about the pictures I took." I stood and offered her the chair. She sat down, and I stood behind her, reaching around and using the mouse to begin a slideshow of the photos I'd downloaded.

The first photo was of the desk drawer contents.

"Oooh," Myra said, "can you zoom in on that bracelet?"

I did as she instructed.

"Eh." She grimaced. "It's fake."

"Are you sure?" I asked.

"Yep. They used to sell those at the mall for ten bucks apiece. It was probably a gift for one of his girlfriends. Or maybe he gave it to one of them, and she threw it back at him." She chuckled. "Maybe that's why he wanted to upgrade his jewelry stash."

"Upgrade his jewelry stash?" I asked.

"Yeah. I found photos of some really nice pieces of jewelry tucked into a book on a shelf in the waiting area," Myra said. "I took pictures of them. I wanted to show them to you, but I also wanted to find out where I could get a couple of the things. They're gorgeous."

"Great," I said. "Maybe the jewelry is what the killer was looking for. I'll upload your photos as soon as we've gone through these." Having the photo of the desk drawer enlarged in order to get a better look at the bracelet made me notice something else I hadn't seen before. I squinted at the screen. "Do you see that?" I pointed at the corner of a flier or brochure barely visible in the photograph.

"I do see it," she said. "I can't make out much of it, but I can see *EIE*." She turned to look at me. "EIEIO?"

"That's what I'm thinking," I said. "Of course, from this

photo we can't be certain, but it does make some sense . . . especially combined with the Elvis that Hot Lips from the Sunoco saw. But what could the connection be?" I wrinkled my forehead. "I wish I'd noticed this earlier today."

"Wonder if we could get back into the office," Myra said.

I shook my head. "Too risky." I thought a second. "But maybe I could ask Scottie for a brochure. I could tell him I want to put their information on my website with a photograph of the finished Cadillac cake—you know, both to show off the cake and to promote their organization."

"That's not a bad idea," Myra said. "Then we could compare the brochure with this image and see if they match."

"Exactly," I said.

We flipped through the photographs of the coins—I made a note to try to look up their country of origin later—the books, and the contents of Dr. Bainsworth's wastepaper basket.

"Do any of those names jump out at you?" I asked Myra.

She shook her head. "No, and none of the messages look all that important either. By the looks of his office, you'd have thought Dr. Bainsworth was boring."

"Right. Only we know better, thanks to Bunni and Angela," I said. "There are several messages here from someone named Mark—just asking Dr. Bainsworth to call him back. Wonder what that was about? If it was a tooth emergency, wouldn't Bunni have simply made the man an appointment to come into the office?"

"Yeah." Myra chewed her bottom lip for a moment. "We need to talk with that Jill—the hygienist who left her husband and then got dumped. I'll bet she was ready to kill Dr. Bainsworth after the way he treated her."

"I agree. Maybe we can look her up." I frowned. "But how do we go about doing that? 'Hi, we're calling to see if you've murdered any dentists lately.' That would be subtle."

"We'll come up with something."

The last photographs on my phone were the ones of the hotel key.

"Where's this from?" Myra asked.

"I don't know. There isn't a hotel name on the card." I zoomed in on the image. "It must be important, though. The card was hidden in a photo of Dr. Bainsworth and Angela."

"Weird. Maybe it's where he had all his flings." She stood. "Let me get my phone so we can look at my pictures."

As Myra hurried into the kitchen to retrieve her phone, I sat and looked back through the photos. The bracelet was nice, but it was obvious Myra was right—this was a piece of costume jewelry, not something a supposedly well-to-do man would choose to give a woman he was trying to impress. Granted, the dentist had fallen on some tough times financially after his divorce, but I would have thought he'd either do better than this bracelet or would be better off not buying the woman any jewelry at all.

Myra returned with her phone. I disconnected mine from the computer and plugged hers in. As I downloaded her photos, she paced behind me.

"Didn't you tell me that Dr. Bainsworth had dated Maureen Fremont at some point?" Myra asked.

"Yes. Why?" I asked.

"I was just imagining how insulted she'd be with that bracelet you saw in his desk drawer," Myra said.

I tilted my head. "You're probably right. But just because

the Fremonts have money doesn't mean she wouldn't understand that the dentist couldn't afford a pricier piece of jewelry, does it?" I asked. "After all, she's dating Steve Franklin now. I can't imagine he can afford to give her many luxuries."

"Don't write Steve off that quickly. He lives in the house he grew up in, has a steady job. . . . I'd say he does all right," Myra said. "Not *Fremont* all right, but then who does?"

"Maybe I can talk with Maureen. Mr. Franklin made it clear to me that she wouldn't want to discuss Dr. Bainsworth, but we need to follow up with every lead."

Myra agreed. Her photos finished uploading, and I started the slideshow. The first photographs Myra had taken were terrible. They were blurry, and her fingers were in the way. Thankfully, she'd finally gotten the hang of using her camera phone, and the rest of the photographs were viewable. Some were just shots of the interior of the waiting room. Then she had photographed shelves. Finally, we came to the photographs of the jewelry she'd mentioned earlier.

"Wow, these *are* beautiful pieces, Myra," I said. "But what makes you think they're real when the one in the desk wasn't?"

"Well, for one thing, there's a *24K* on the lobster claw of that necklace," she said.

I leaned in closer. "Oh, yeah. I can make it out now. You've got good eyes."

"And I saw the original photo," Myra said. "Who carries around pictures of jewelry anyway? A salesperson? Do you think Dr. Bainsworth was planning to start a side business selling upscale jewelry?"

"You never know," I said. "Were the photos loose or in some sort of binder?"

"They were just loose, individual pictures." Myra studied the photographs for a moment in silence. "Maybe they're pieces from an estate sale or something. A few of the pieces look old. Wonder if that earring the police found had anything to do with this jewelry?"

"I don't know. Maybe the jewelry is Angela's," I said, "and she and Dr. Bainsworth had photographed them for insurance purposes. Maybe they kept one set of the photos at home and one set at the office just in case anything happened. It makes sense." I shrugged. "I'll try to follow up on that with Angela later this afternoon."

"You do that," Myra said. "I'm going to try to track down Jill, the dumped hygienist."

CHAPTER

Twelve

After Myra left, I began working on the largest tier of the *quinceañera* cake. I frosted the cake with rose-tinted buttercream and allowed it to set for fifteen minutes. Once it had, I used a plain white paper towel to further smooth the buttercream in preparation for decorating. I filled a decorator bag with thin white frosting and used a tiny writing tip to pipe scrollwork onto the sides of the cake. I find scrollwork easy and repetitive, and it affords me the opportunity to let my mind wander while I work.

Since I was wearing my telephone headset, I went ahead and called Angela Bainsworth to ask about the photographs Myra had found. Angela answered on the first ring and sounded a bit antsy.

"Hi, Angela. It's Daphne Martin."

No response.

"I'm Violet Armstrong's sister," I said. "We spoke yesterday afternoon?"

"Yes, of course, Daphne. What can I do for you?"

"There were photographs of jewelry on a shelf in your ex-husband's office. I thought maybe the jewelry was yours and that Dr. Bainsworth might've stored them in his office for insurance purposes."

"Well, I don't know about any photos," said Angela, "but I can assure you the pieces aren't mine. I'm not big on jewelry and prefer to invest my money in ways that will return a profit."

"You didn't happen to lose a diamond earring in the office, did you?"

"No."

"I see. Well, thanks for your time," I said. "Sorry to have bothered you."

"No bother, Daphne. My suggestion is to simply forget the photographs."

"You don't think they have anything to do with the reason Dr. Bainsworth was killed?" I asked. "I mean, what if he'd been trying to sell the jewelry or something, and the buyer decided to steal them rather than pay for them?"

"I think his murderer was either a woman scorned, a jilted husband or boyfriend, or some homeless junkie who'd hoped the office would provide a warm place to sleep that night. That makes the most sense to me," Angela said.

I stopped making scrolls to rest my hand for a second. "You really think it's that simple?"

"I do," she said firmly. "The police couldn't seriously suspect you or that Jenkins woman of killing Jim. Don't let this situation stress you out."

"I'd love to believe you're right about that, but this isn't the first dead body I've stumbled across since I've been back in town," I said. "The police have been asking around, slowly driving past my house, following me. Without another suspect, Myra and I are all they have."

We said our good-byes, and I went back to piping tiny scrolls on the sides of the twelve-inch round cake.

The *Chronicle*'s original article stated police had confirmed that there had been no forced entry into Dr. Bainsworth's office that night. That fact alone would pretty much negate the idea of a homeless junkie wandering into the building, wouldn't it? I couldn't imagine Dr. Bainsworth or the fastidious Bunni forgetting to lock the doors. So wouldn't Dr. Bainsworth's killer have to have been either someone Dr. Bainsworth knew and allowed into the office or someone who had a key?

I set my decorator bag on the island and retrieved the phone book from the table in the living room. I was going to call Bunni Wilson. If I played my cards right, she just might tell me what I wanted to know.

I dialed in Bunni's number before returning to the kitchen, washing my hands, and resuming the scrollwork on the *quinceañera* cake. Bunni answered on the first ring.

"Good afternoon. Dr. Bainsworth's office," she said. "Oh . . . sorry . . . force of habit."

"I understand completely," I said. I introduced myself and reminded her that we'd met at Tanya's Tremendous Tress-Taming Salon the day before.

"Oh, yes," Bunni said. "How can I help you, Daphne?"

"Myra Jenkins—she's the other lady who was in the salon yesterday—"

"I know Myra," she said, interrupting. "She's one of our patients. I know all our patients."

"Of course," I said. "Well, she and I are in a bit of a pickle."

"Because you found Dr. Bainsworth?" she asked.

"Yes." I sighed. "Bunni, I'm afraid that if she and I don't figure out who did this, the police will try to blame us."

"I still don't know how I can help you," she said.

"First of all, I want you to know that I realize how very valuable you were to Dr. Bainsworth," I said, "and I don't want you to betray any confidences. But, on the other hand, I don't want his killer to get away either. How well did you know his wife?"

"You think it was her too?" Bunni asked, a note of excitement creeping into her voice.

"I'm not sure, but I recall you saying yesterday that Dr. Bainsworth thought maybe she was having an affair," I said. "I'm thinking he might have been right."

"I knew it," she said vehemently. "I knew that piranha was cheating on poor Dr. Bainsworth. Then she used his friendship with Jill to give her the excuse she needed to divorce him and take everything he had."

"But it worked," I said. "Everything in the divorce was going her way. Why would she want to kill Dr. Bainsworth?"

"Because he was about to uncover her deception," Bunni said. "His private investigator had been tailing Angela for weeks."

"Private investigator? He'd hired a private investigator?"

"That's right," Bunni said. "Dr. Bainsworth thought Angela

had been cheating since before she accused him of having an affair with Jill, and he hired this man to prove it."

"What was the detective's name?" I asked.

"Mark Thompson," she said.

That's why there were so many messages from Mark in the trash can, I mused. "Mark had found out something, hadn't he?"

"Yes, he had. He and Dr. Bainsworth were trying to figure it all out and decide how to best use whatever information Mark had uncovered."

"You don't know what information Mark had found?" I asked.

"Oh, no," Bunni said. "That wouldn't be appropriate. Dr. Bainsworth never burdened me with his personal problems. Our relationship rose above that."

"Of course," I said. "Who besides Dr. Bainsworth had a key to his office?"

"I'm the only other person Dr. Bainsworth trusted with a key to the building."

"What about Angela?" I asked. "Did Dr. Bainsworth change the locks after the two of them separated?"

"No. . . . So I suppose it's possible she had a key . . . and the police said there was no forced entry into the building. . . ." Her voice trailed away.

I hurried to undo whatever damage I might have done. "Please know I'm not accusing Angela in any way. I simply wondered if she had a key."

"I'm accusing her," Bunni said. "Mark Thompson found something that would turn the tide of the divorce back in Dr. Bainsworth's favor, and she killed him because of it."

"Maybe not," I said. "There were photographs of jewelry in Dr. Bainsworth's waiting room, and the police found a diamond earring. Was he looking into a side business?"

"No," she said. "I don't know anything about any jewelry. I just know that Angela Bainsworth killed my—killed her husband. Thank you for calling, Daphne. Good-bye."

And she hung up. Okay. So I had successfully turned the secretary's—if not the police department's—suspicions to someone other than Myra and me for the murder of Dr. Bainsworth. That was good, right?

I dialed Myra. She didn't answer, and I left her a message.

Next, I called directory assistance and got the phone number of the private investigator, Mark Thompson. He wasn't available to take my call either, so I asked his secretary to have him give me a call.

A sharp rap on my kitchen door startled me, and I flubbed the scroll I'd been working on. I removed my plastic gloves and stepped over to peep out the window. It was Scottie. He was dressed in a Loyola sweatshirt and jeans, so he didn't look as Elvis-like as usual.

"Hey," I said, opening the door. "Are you here to make sure the cake looks all right before Friday? I still have a couple of last-minute—"

"I'm not worried about the cake," Scottie interrupted, and brushed past me and into the kitchen. "I don't have a doubt in the world that the cake looks fantastic. I just came by to ask you out."

"I appreciate the offer," I said, "but I have a lot of work to do this evening."

"Aw, come on," Scottie said. "I'm only here for a couple more days, you know."

"I do know."

"But that doesn't mean I have to walk out of your life completely, though." He stepped closer to me.

"I think it's great that we can still be friends after you leave. In fact, do you have any brochures with you? I'd love to mention the EIEIO on my website with a photo of the Cadillac cake so visitors to my site could contribute to your cause." I heard a car door slam. "Let me see who that is." I flung open the door. "What do you know? It's Ben! Hi, Ben! Look who's here."

Ben gave Scottie an icy stare. "Does your cake look all right?"

"Flawless," Scottie said, folding his arms. "Daphne is a woman of many extraordinary talents. Wouldn't you agree?"

Ben narrowed his eyes but didn't say anything.

"Okay," I said. "I'll deliver the cake and begin setting everything up at five thirty Friday."

Scottie smiled. "Thank you."

"You're welcome," I said.

"If I told you I have a stack of brochures back at the hotel, would you come with me to get one?" he asked.

"Nope. I have plans with my niece and nephew tonight," I said. "Could I stop by and pick up a brochure from you tomorrow? You could simply leave it at the front desk for me."

"Sorry," Scottie said. "We ran out of brochures at the concert Sunday night. But I'll bring you by the information."

"Thanks." I gave him what I hoped was a very professional smile. "Is there anything else I need to know about setting up the cake on Friday?"

"Just remember what I told you." He nodded at Ben and left.

"This is a nice surprise," I said after the door closed behind Scottie. "What brings you by?"

"Him. I saw the car and decided to stop," Ben said. "I don't like that guy in the least."

"Well, he and all the rest of the Elvises will be gone in two or three days," I said with a smile.

"What did he mean when he told you to remember what he said?" Ben asked.

I looked into Ben's fathomless blue eyes and debated about lying. No dice. Ben has always been able to tell when I was lying. "He told me that when he leaves, it doesn't have to be permanent. I let him know I'm not interested in anything but friendship." I slid my arms around Ben's neck. "You're the only one I want hanging around here."

Ben kissed me softly. "I'm glad."

"You know, I have to wonder about Scottie's motives. Maybe he killed the dentist, and he wants to hang around me to find out what Myra and I know."

"Or it could just be that you're beautiful." He frowned. "Still, don't dismiss that thought about him being the killer. It pays to be cautious."

I took his hand and led him into the living room. "You look a little worn-out," I said as we sat on the sofa. "Did you have a busy day?"

"Busy, but productive," he said. "You?"

"Busy, but I don't know how productive it was." I went on to tell Ben about going with Myra to snoop around—and ultimately help clean—Dr. Bainsworth's office. I explained about the brochure and coins. "Plus Myra found photographs of jewelry, but Angela says the pieces aren't hers."

"Maybe they're pieces passed down through Dr. Bainsworth's family," Ben said. "He could've had the pieces stashed in a safe-deposit box somewhere and chose not to tell Angela about them."

"She did tell me she wasn't into jewelry."

Ben shrugged. "Then it's possible he knew Angela wouldn't want them and kept them either for posterity or in case he ever needed to sell them."

"Good point," I said. "It appears to be common knowledge the guy was having financial difficulties since his wife initiated divorce proceedings. He could've intended to sell some of the jewelry."

"That would be my guess." Ben laced his fingers behind his head and closed his eyes. "Check the *Chronicle*'s online classifieds to see if any of the pieces are listed there."

"I'll do that. Bunni, Dr. Bainsworth's secretary, didn't know about the jewelry either. Of course, jewelry wasn't the only thing I think he kept her in the dark about. She thought the man was a saint." Before I could comment further, the phone rang and I realized I'd forgotten to remove my headset. I answered, "Daphne's Delectable Cakes."

"Hi, hon," Myra said. "Can't talk but a sec because I've got a date with John. Don't worry about Bunni and Angela. I doubt Bunni will confront her or anything."

"I hope you're right," I said. "Bunni did tell me the name of Dr. Bainsworth's private investigator. I left a message for him to call me back."

"Dr. Bainsworth had hired a private investigator?" Myra asked. "That's interesting. By the way, I found Jill Fisher. You and I are having coffee with her at my house tomorrow morning at nine."

"That's interesting too," I said. "How'd you get her to agree to talk with us?"

"It was easy. I asked and she said yes. See you tomorrow morning."

When I disconnected from the call, I noticed Ben was giving me a bemused frown.

"What?" I asked.

"You *have* been a busy investigator, haven't you?" he asked.

I shrugged. "Did I mention Myra has a date with one of the EIEIO members tonight?"

"Which one?" asked Ben.

"His name is John. He's at least twenty-five years younger than her."

Before I could fully entertain Ben with Myra's romantic ups and downs with the Elvises, Violet, Lucas, and Leslie arrived. The twins were bubbling over with stories about their day at school, but Violet was quiet. Other than exchanging pleasantries with Ben, she didn't have much to say.

"What time would you like me to come back for them?" she asked me.

"I'll bring them home," I said. "Give me a curfew so I won't get them home too late. I realize tomorrow is a school day."

"Is eight o'clock okay?" Vi asked.

"That'll give us plenty of time." I considered her wan face. "Are you feeling okay?"

"I'm just a little tired. Jason has been out of town for the past couple of days, and I never sleep well when he's away," she said.

"Yeah," Leslie said. "You should hear them on the phone when he calls at night. 'I miss you.' 'No, I miss you more!'"

Lucas clutched his throat and made gagging sounds.

"Knock it off, you two," Violet said. She turned to me. "I think I'll go home and soak in the tub until I'm as wrinkly as a raisin."

"You do that. We'll bring you some cake balls," I said.

As Violet left, Lucas grinned slyly at Ben. "Are you helping us make cake balls? It'll be great not being outnumbered by girls for once." He glanced at me. "No offense, Aunt Daphne."

"None taken," I said. "I think it'd be cool to have another man in the kitchen too if you can talk Ben into staying."

"Well, I haven't fed Sally yet," Ben said, but when Lucas's smile faded, he wavered. "But she's in the fenced backyard. I think she'll be fine for a little while longer."

I gave Ben a quick hug and whispered, "Thank you." Turning back to Lucas and Leslie, I said, "All right then. Let's get washed up and started on those cake balls."

The kids raced to the bathroom sink to wash up while Ben and I washed our hands in the kitchen. We then donned aprons and plastic gloves, sat down around the table, and began crumbling the pieces of peanut butter and banana cake I had left over from carving the Cadillac cake.

"That cake is pretty," Leslie said, eying the tier of the *quinceañera* cake I'd left on the island.

"Thanks," I said. "Before we get too far into making cake balls—and as soon as I'm sure the icing has set—I need to box it up and put it in the fridge."

"Is it part of a wedding cake?" she asked, her eyes sliding from me to Ben and back again.

"No, sweetheart," I said with a smile. "It's for a *quinceañera*."

"That's like a sweet sixteen party for Latin American girls, isn't it?" she asked. "I saw it on Selena Gomez's show once."

"You're right," I said, "but *quinceañeras* are for fifteen-year-olds."

"What do the boys have?" Lucas asked. "Do they have big parties with fancy cakes on their fifteenth birthdays too?"

"I . . . I'm not really sure," I said.

"You bet they do," Ben said. "Their aunts who are cake decorators make them enormous cakes shaped like their favorite action heroes—you know, like a life-sized Superman cake."

"No way." Lucas scoffed.

"Oh, yeah," Ben said insistently. "You don't believe me?"

Lucas and Leslie shared a look and then they both laughed.

"Okay," Lucas said. "Keep going."

"Good." Ben's smile broadened as he continued spinning his tale. "They invite all their friends, and they eat gigantic pizzas the size of tractor tires. Then they play video games all night."

Leslie giggled. "If they eat that much pizza, they'll be too full to have any cake."

"Nonsense," Ben said. "Everybody knows they eat the cake for breakfast." He winked at me.

I shook my head. He was gorgeous, and it meant the world to me that he was taking this opportunity to get to know my niece and nephew. But if I wound up having to make a life-sized Superman cake and pizzas as big as tractor tires because of his outlandish story, I might just punch him in the arm. Hard.

CHAPTER
Thirteen

SINCE MYRA and I were having coffee with Jill Fisher at Myra's house at nine A.M., I got there at eight thirty in order to hear about Myra's date with John before Jill arrived. For the life of me, I couldn't picture Myra with the skinny, red-haired Elvis impersonator. Cecil had seemed far more in keeping with what I imagined would be Myra's "type." And he was much closer to her age. Myra, a cougar? I guessed anything was possible. Especially after seeing her the night of the EIEIO concert.

Myra greeted me at the door dressed in jeans and a yellow crewneck sweater but with rollers in her hair. "You're early."

"I came by to see if you need any help," I said.

At her raised brow, I admitted, "And to see how your date with John went."

She grinned. "It went super. He's the sweetest little thing."

"Did you wear the Ann-Margret getup?" I asked.

She shook her head. "No. He asked me to be myself, and I was. Mainly, I was afraid my wig would clash with his hair. His hair is a color that looks like something of a cross between a carrot, a sunset, and a clown wig—but don't tell him I said that. It looks good on him. Anyway, after everything was said and done, it felt pretty nice to be Myra Jenkins instead of Ann-Margret."

"So where'd you go?" I asked.

"We went to one of the steakhouses over there in Bristol. John requested to the hostess that we have a table that was as private as possible." She blushed. Myra actually blushed.

I giggled. "Did he hold your hand?"

She nodded. "And we talked for so long I was afraid the restaurant manager was going to ask us to leave."

She motioned for me to follow her into the bedroom. The bed was neatly made—a floral comforter and shams were further adorned by half a dozen decorative pillows. The room contained a walnut armoire and a matching dresser, vanity, and chest.

Myra sat at the vanity and began taking the rollers out of her hair, and I sat on a pale mauve slipper chair by the window.

"Did John tell you all about his exciting travels with the EIEIO?" I asked.

"We spoke about that some," she said, "but he mostly wanted to talk about me. We talked about my life—my hobbies, my kids, my favorite kinds of music, that sort of thing."

"What about him?" I asked. "Has he ever been married? Does he have any kids?"

"Nope. He said he's been a loner pretty much all his life but that he's always wanted to meet someone like me." She smiled.

"It sounds like this could get serious," I said.

She opened one of the vanity drawers and took out a comb. "I suppose it could. Still, he'll be gone in a couple of days. I really enjoy John's company, but I'm not kidding myself here."

I thought about Scottie telling me he didn't have to walk out of my life permanently when the EIEIO left town. I hadn't realized Myra had been watching my expression in the mirror until she spoke.

"What was that look about? All of a sudden you got thoughtful on me."

I shrugged. "I was simply thinking that just because John is leaving doesn't mean you'll never see him again. It doesn't mean you couldn't still have a relationship."

"Is this about me and John or about you and Scottie?" she asked.

"It's about you and John. Granted, Scottie reminded me of that very fact yesterday, but it's Ben I want."

"You're sure?" she asked.

"Positive," I said. "Scottie and the other Elvises have been a lot of fun. But they've caused plenty of trouble too. So, how'd you find Jill?"

"Tanya, of course. I just hope Jill will be able to help us in some way."

"Maybe she'll tell us all the dirt she knows about Dr. Bainsworth," I said. "After all, a woman scorned and all that jazz."

"Yeah," Myra said in agreement. "Unless she's the one who bashed his head in. Then she might try to lead us down a path of falsehoods."

"A path of falsehoods?" I asked. "Have you been watching the BBC again?"

"Maybe."

I sighed. "I don't know, Myra. I think the person Hot Lips from the Sunoco saw is our best bet. I'm not sure a woman could hit a man Dr. Bainsworth's size hard enough to kill him."

"Oh, honey. Some women are pretty strong. I read a story about this woman named Belle Gunness. They called her Lady Bluebeard because she'd put ads in the paper to try to find a husband, and when the men came to answer the ad, she killed them." Myra fluffed her hair and picked up a bottle of hair spray. "Killed them, stole their money, and then hoisted them up on her shoulder to carry to the basement and chop up for burial. Blech!"

"Are you serious?" I asked.

"Yep. True story. She wound up being suspected of over forty murders, including those of her own children. So, you see, some women are not only downright mean but strong enough to kill more than one Southwest Virginia dentist." Myra sprayed her hair. "Besides, whoever it was could've snuck up on him. Still, Hot Lips's seeing an Elvis enter the store with a bloody sleeve right after the murder happened does lead me to believe it was a man."

"Me too. And I'm afraid it's likely one of the EIEIO guys, especially after seeing the corner of that flier in that photo of Dr. Bainsworth's desk drawer," I said.

Myra sprayed her hair again until she seemed certain it

wouldn't dare move. "It probably was one of the Elvises. But it couldn't have been John. Hot Lips said the Elvis she saw wasn't too fat or too skinny, and every time John turned sideways last night, I could've sworn he disappeared."

We both laughed, but I was thinking he could've looked bigger in a heavy winter coat.

"Maybe he could help us," I said. "Would he know if any of the Elvises had it in for Dr. Bainsworth?"

Myra shook her head. "I'm way ahead of you. I asked him that last night. He said he didn't know anyone who'd have it in for a dentist, but he agreed with our theory that he was killed because of his dalliances with all those women." She took a lipstick from the vanity. "Surprisingly enough, Dr. Bainsworth never once made a pass at me."

I suppressed a smile. "Imagine."

The doorbell rang.

"Get that, would you?" Myra asked as she swiped brownish-pink lipstick onto her lips. "I'll be right there."

I hurried to the door and opened it to a woman who was older and plainer than I'd expected her to be. Jill Fisher was bony with thick black glasses, a hawk nose, and a flat mouth. She wore her dark auburn hair in a severe bun, and she was wearing a shapeless ankle-length dress. I couldn't help but compare her to Dr. Bainsworth's ex-wife, Angela, who was beautiful. Why on earth would the dentist have cheated on his wife with this woman?

"Are you Myra?" Jill asked.

"No," I said, smiling as I opened the door. "I'm Daphne Martin. Myra will be right out. Let's go on into the kitchen."

Jill lifted and dropped one shoulder as if she couldn't possibly care less who I was or where we were going, but she did follow me into the kitchen. Myra had made the coffee and set three each of cups, saucers, spoons, and dessert plates out. She had also put some pastries on a platter. As I poured the coffee, Jill pulled out a chair and plopped down. She placed her oversized purse on the floor next to her.

"Good morning," Myra said, breezing into the kitchen and retrieving the plate of pastries. "I'll just pop these into the microwave to warm them." Her smile encompassed both Jill and me, but her eyes widened as they lingered on mine as if she were wondering about the attraction too.

I smiled and nodded, acknowledging that we were indeed thinking the same thing. "Nothing like warm pastries with hot coffee."

Myra set the timer. "Thank you for coming, Jill."

"I'm curious about what you think you can gain from talking with me," Jill said. "I've already told the police everything I know."

"Well, hopefully, you can help us think of a reason someone would have for wanting to hurt Dr. Bainsworth," I said, setting her coffee in front of her.

Jill scoffed. "You want the entire list?"

The microwave dinged, saving Myra or me from having to answer that question just yet. Myra put the pastries on the table while I got our coffee. We joined Jill at the table, and everyone busied herself with stirring cream and sugar into her coffee.

I took a pastry from the platter. "These look delicious, Myra," I said.

"Thank you." Myra took a deep breath. "So, Jill, let's start on that list. Who do you know that might want to hurt Dr. Bainsworth?"

Jill stirred her coffee, looking into its creamy depths. When she spoke, her voice was softer than it had been before. "I don't know. The truth is I loved Jim right up until the end. Most people loved Jim. He was a con man." She placed her spoon in her saucer and took a sip of coffee.

"A con man?" I echoed.

She nodded. "Yeah. He was whoever you wanted him to be, you know? He played a part until he got what he wanted or got tired of you, and then he moved on."

"I'm sorry," I said.

"Yeah, me too," Jill said, sighing and tracing the pattern of the tablecloth with her fingertip. "I thought he loved me. I had a good life until he came along and sweet-talked me out of it."

"Why would he do that?" Myra asked. "Why would he pretend to love you if he didn't?"

Jill gave a half smile, but she still didn't look up. "The thrill of the game. Jim liked to make conquests . . . he liked to win. He didn't think—or care—about consequences."

"Apparently not," I said. "Yet, he seemed to really care about his patients and about helping people."

Jill looked up at that. "Why do you say that?"

"Well, he didn't mind coming into the office after hours to help Myra," I said. "It's why he was there the night he was murdered. And Ben Jacobs told me Dr. Bainsworth took a mission trip to provide dental care for the poor recently."

Jill barked out a laugh. "He'd have charged Myra or her insurance carrier out the nose for that emergency visit, and providing dental care was the only way he could have the mission people pay for his trip to Mexico."

"So it was a vacation?" Myra asked. "He went to Mexico on vacation rather than on some sort of mission of mercy?"

"Exactly," Jill said. "He'd hoped Maureen Fremont would foot the bill, but she wasn't as stupid as the rest of us. She caught on to him fairly quickly. Getting money out of her was like getting blood from a turnip. When she wouldn't pay for the trip, he got the mission people to do it for him." She sipped her coffee again. "I don't doubt he did some pro bono work while he was there, but it wasn't his primary reason for going."

I swallowed. "I've heard some good things about Dr. Bainsworth. How could he have had everyone fooled?"

Jill shook her head. "Because he only let people see what he wanted them to see."

"But what about Bunni?" Myra asked. "She practically worshipped him. Wouldn't someone in her position know what a jerk he really was?"

"Even people who should know better generally see what they want to see. Jim would come in every morning and tell Bunni how beautiful she looked. Throughout the day, he'd mention how he couldn't get along without her . . . how she was a clerical genius . . . how she was his right arm." Jill rolled her eyes. "Bunni ate it up like candy. Then when Jim acted like a jerk or got caught in some indiscretion, she made excuses for him."

"In her eyes, he could do no wrong," Myra said.

"Precisely." Jill took another sip of her coffee.

"Then maybe it was her," Myra said. "Unrequited love makes people do crazy things."

My eyes widened. I glanced at Jill to see how she'd taken Myra's statement.

"It sure does," Jill said in agreement.

"I'm sorry," Myra said. "That didn't come out the way I'd intended."

"No, that's okay." Jill took a scone from the platter. "But it wasn't Bunni. She adored Jim. I truly think she believed that one day he'd look around and realize she was the love of his life."

"Poor Bunni," I said. "What does she have now? No job, no fantasy guy . . ."

"Maybe she'll finally be able to get a life," Myra said.

"I doubt it." Jill took a bite of her scone. "She'll find another job and start dreaming all over again."

"You didn't happen to lose an earring in the office, did you?" I asked.

She shook her head. "Not me. I lost a lot in that office—mainly my dignity—but not an earring."

"A clerk at the Sunoco near Dr. Bainsworth's office said a man came in there around the time of the attack with blood on his sleeve," I said. "Do you know of any man who might have been looking for something in the dental office?"

"Yeah," Myra said, "we're thinking maybe the guy didn't break into the office with the intention of killing Dr. Bainsworth but that he bashed him in the head when Dr. Bainsworth came upon him while he was trying to steal . . . something."

"I can't imagine what anyone would have wanted from Jim's office," Jill said, swallowing. "We didn't keep any drugs there. Jim didn't even use the nitrous anymore." She thought a moment. "But one of the other girls who worked there told me he did act weird after the Mexico trip."

"Where did he go in Mexico?" Myra asked. "Was it Tijuana? I've heard about people messing around in Tijuana and completely going out of their gourds—drinking stuff with worms in it, getting drugged, being put in jail. And they say that if you get thrown in a Mexican jail, it's really hard to get out. He didn't get arrested, did he?"

"No, he didn't get arrested," Jill said. "And he didn't go to Tijuana, as far as I know. He went to Nuevo Laredo."

"I've heard of that place," I said. "It's just across the border from Laredo, Texas, isn't it?"

Jill nodded. "When I found out that's where Jim was going, I did some research on it. Seems to me it's a pretty wild place. It has a red-light district known as La Zona or Boys Town. Not to mention that the drug cartels run the town these days. Every time they appoint a police chief, the person disappears."

"Oh, no, honey!" Myra exclaimed, patting Jill's arm. "Boys Town is that place Father Flanagan came up with. Spencer Tracy did a movie about it and everything. It was an orphanage. Maybe Dr. Bainsworth really did go there to Boys Town to do something noble and worthwhile."

"I think Father Flanagan's orphanage was founded in Nebraska," I said quietly. Besides, I'd read a recent online news article stating that U.S. Secretary of Homeland Security Janet Napolitano was trying to dispel misconceptions about the border towns and had not only said that they were safe for travel, trade, and commerce, but that "the border is better now than it has ever been." It made me wonder whether Jill was given to exaggeration.

"Maybe," Myra said, still talking about Boys Town, "but don't they have branches located all over the place now?"

"Who knows? But even if there are," Jill said, "I don't think that's the type of thing Jim was into. And I'm pretty sure if Spencer Tracy had done a movie about Nuevo Laredo's Boys Town, it wouldn't have been an Oscar winner. They don't give out Oscars for those kinds of movies." She lifted her hands. "Trust me. Or, if you don't want to take my word for it, look it up for yourselves."

Myra simply drank her coffee and looked skeptical.

"But you said Dr. Bainsworth liked the challenge—the thrill of the game, I believe you said," I reminded Jill. "Why would he be interested in prostitutes?"

Jill shrugged. "I don't know. But I don't know of any other reason he might've gone to Nuevo Laredo. I mean, don't most people going to Mexico on vacation go to Acapulco or Cancún?"

I nodded and made a mental note to look into the story of the Nuevo Laredo trip a little deeper. China York believed Dr. Bainsworth was a cad, but she also thought he had good qualities. I doubted many people were able to fool China. Plus, Jill had been terribly hurt by Dr. Bainsworth. She was unlikely to see anything but bad in him. Maybe Scottie would know if there had been any legitimate mission outreaches in Nuevo Laredo.

Jill finished her coffee, dabbed at her mouth with a napkin, and then tossed the napkin onto the plate with her half-eaten scone. "I appreciate the breakfast, ladies, but I really must be on my way. I have a job interview at eleven."

"A job interview?" Myra asked. "Were you still working for Dr. Bainsworth before he died?"

"No," Jill said, pushing back away from the table. "But I've been on unemployment or working for temp agencies since I left his office this past fall. It's hard. No one wants to hire a home wrecker."

"But that's discrimination," I said. "How could they even know about your affair with Dr. Bainsworth anyway? Did he give you a bad recommendation?"

Jill scoffed. "This is Brea Ridge, Daphne. Everybody knows—or thinks they know—everything. Dr. Farmer wouldn't hire me—said he wasn't hiring hygienists at that time but would let me know when he needed someone. But he never called, even though I know one of his hygienists is on maternity leave. And I wasn't able to secure a secretarial position anywhere in this town either."

"What about Bristol or Kingsport?" I asked. "Did you apply for work in dental offices in either of those cities?"

Jill shook her head. "It's too far for me to drive. Besides, I've been in Brea Ridge my whole life."

"Then maybe it's high time to get a fresh start somewhere else," Myra said. "That's what Daphne did."

At my frown, Myra said, "Well . . . you did."

"You did?" Jill asked.

I nodded. "Yeah. My ex-husband is in Tennessee." I left out exactly *where* in Tennessee. A woman doesn't necessarily want *everybody* knowing her ex is in the penitentiary for trying to murder her. "So I came here to start all over."

Jill gave me a half smile, but her eyes filled with tears. "That's where you and I are different, I guess. You wanted to start over. I want to go back to where I was. I want my old life back."

"I hope you get it," I said softly.

CHAPTER
Fourteen

AFTER THE meeting with Jill, I decided to pay the private investigator a visit. He hadn't returned my call yesterday, and I really wanted to talk with him. I recalled his address from the telephone directory, and I plugged it into my GPS. The office was only about a fifteen-minute drive away.

I strode into the office. It was stuffy, so I removed my coat and draped it over my arm. The secretary greeted me, and I asked to see Mr. Thompson.

"I'll check and see if he's in yet," she said. She walked back through the hallway.

While I waited, I looked around the office. It was nicely, although sparsely, furnished. The secretary had a neatly kept desk, the wooden chairs and tables in the waiting area were highly polished, and there were large peace lilies on either side of the door. Magazines were fanned out on the coffee table. Security cameras were evident in the right and left corners of the room. I wondered how the secretary felt about the constant scrutiny.

She returned and told me Mr. Thompson would see me. I guessed he'd already seen me from the security feed, but I didn't say so. She ushered me into his office.

A broad, older man with a gray buzz cut and gray eyes, he stood when his secretary and I walked into the room. I was guessing he was ex-military.

"Ms. Martin, it's a pleasure to meet you." He had a gravelly voice that sounded as if it might be coming from the bottom of a tin can. "I received your message and was planning on calling you back today."

"Now you won't have to," I said with a smile.

The secretary discreetly left the room.

"As you may be aware," I said, continuing, "my friend Myra Jenkins and I found Dr. Bainsworth's body on Friday night."

"I am aware of that," he said, sitting back down and indicating that I should do the same.

I took a seat on one of the chairs in front of his desk. "I understand from Bunni Wilson that Dr. Bainsworth hired you to find out if his soon-to-be ex-wife was having an affair."

He emitted a chuckle that sounded more like a wheeze. "You don't pull any punches, do you, Ms. Martin?"

"I don't feel I have the time for that luxury," I said. "I need to find out who killed Dr. Bainsworth, especially since Myra and I are currently the only suspects. Was Angela having an affair? And had she been prior to her discovery that Dr. Bainsworth was cheating with Jill?"

"You do realize I'm in the business of handling delicate matters," Mr. Thompson said. "Why should I disclose my client's information to you? After all, there are legitimate reasons why you're a suspect in this murder."

"Such as?"

He arched a bushy gray brow. "My client was a known womanizer. You're stunning, and you haven't been in town all that long. Maybe you went in for a cleaning, Jim liked what he saw, and the two of you hooked up."

"You can check his client records. I was never a patient of Dr. Bainsworth."

"You still could've hooked up," he said. "There are other places to meet than a dental office."

"Well, thank goodness for that," I said, "but I never even talked to Dr. Bainsworth before the night I called him on Myra's behalf."

"The night he was killed."

"Yes." I frowned. "I didn't kill him, Mr. Thompson. And neither did Myra. He was dead when we got there."

He was infuriatingly silent.

"Do you think I murdered Dr. Bainsworth?" I asked.

"Not that my opinion matters—especially to the police department—but no, I don't think you did. You have to admit, though, you look fairly good to the police for this crime."

"Killing someone makes you look *good* to the police?"

Mr. Thompson chuckled. "No. I meant you can see their reasons for thinking you might have motive. As I pointed out, you're a looker and a relative newcomer to Brea Ridge. You might've been having an affair with the dentist."

I started to protest, but Mr. Thompson held up his hand.

"You've also stumbled onto quite a bit of trouble since you've been in town," he said, continuing. "First Yodel Watson and then Fred Duncan. I know—and the police know—you had nothing to do with those deaths. But you have to admit, you keep turning up where there's smoke, and sooner or later, you have to be the one that started the fire."

"Please tell me what you found out about Angela Bainsworth," I said. "Did she have a motive for killing her husband?"

"Possibly. But it wouldn't be right for me to share that information with another suspect."

"Your client is dead! How could you be breaking his confidence?" I ran my hand through my hair. "I'm not saying you should share your information with me. I'm only asking that you turn it over to the police."

"I already have." He grinned. "The authorities know everything I know."

"Thank you," I said. "For some reason, I don't want to think Dr. Bainsworth was the scoundrel so many people are willing to make him out to be."

"Oh, you can be sure Jim was no saint," said Mr. Thompson. "But neither was his wife."

"The cleaning crew found photographs of some jewelry in Dr. Bainsworth's waiting room," I said. "Are those photographs something you might need for your records?"

"Nope," he said. "I believe I have everything I need. I wasn't hired on a jewelry case."

"Right. Well, again, thank you for seeing me and for providing your information to the police."

"You're quite welcome, young lady. And if you're ever in the market for a professional detective, please give me a call."

"I will, Mr. Thompson. Thank you."

Without actually coming out and saying so, Mr. Thompson had confirmed that Angela Bainsworth had been having an affair on her husband while—or possibly even before—he'd cheated on her. Bunni could be right. If both parties in the divorce had been at fault, there would have been a more equitable property resolution. I wondered if Dr. Bainsworth had confronted Angela with his knowledge of her affair, and if he had, how she'd reacted to the news.

AFTER TALKING WITH Mr. Thompson, I went by the dress shop owned by Maureen Fremont. It's a nice store, designed to look like an exclusive New York City boutique. All the clothes are on mannequins. You choose what you'd like to look at, and Maureen or a member of her sales staff goes to a back room to see if they have it in your size. I'd only been to the boutique once, and I really didn't care for it. I like to look for new clothes in peace without salespersons hovering the entire time.

When I walked through the door, a chime sounded. Maureen came from the back. She was dressed in a black pencil skirt, a white blouse, and a houndstooth jacket.

"Good morning," she said. "How may I help you?"

"Hi, Ms. Fremont," I said. "I'm not sure you'll remember me, but I'm Daphne Martin."

"Of course. You catered the party for my sister Belinda's guinea pigs, didn't you?"

I smiled. "That's right."

"What can I do for you, Daphne? Looking for a new dress?" She gestured toward a grouping of mannequins, all wearing combinations of black and white.

"Not exactly," I said. "I understand you were a patient of Dr. Bainsworth."

"Yes. Half the town patronized Dr. Bainsworth's practice."

"I wondered if you knew of anyone who might have it in for him," I said. "You see, Myra Jenkins and I found . . . the body."

"Lots of people might've had it in for him." She flipped her wrist. "A person who couldn't pay his dental bill, a person who felt wronged in some way, someone whose wife he was seeing, that nasty little man who was dating Angela—"

"Wait, you know who Angela was seeing?" I asked.

"I don't know his name, but I saw a photo of him that had been taken by the investigator. Not attractive in the least. I don't know why she'd cheat on Jim with *him*." She shrugged. "Perhaps he has money. Who knows?"

"Huh."

"Oh well, good luck with your search," she said. "I need to get back to work."

"Me too. By the way, did you ever lose an earring at Dr. Bainsworth's office?"

"Yes!" Her hand instinctively flew to her left ear. Today she was wearing jet button earrings. "It was a diamond stud. Did you find it?"

"I didn't," I said, "but the police did. You might give them a call about it."

"I'll do that, Daphne. Thanks for telling me."

Maureen certainly hadn't hidden the fact that she'd lost an earring in Dr. Bainsworth's office. If she'd lost it during a struggle on the night Dr. Bainsworth died, I don't think she'd have been so forthcoming.

WHEN I GOT home, I hung up my coat and went into the bathroom to wash my hands before resuming work on the *quinceañera* cakes. I examined my reflection in the mirror above the sink. Mr. Thompson had called me stunning. I wouldn't go that far, but I was able to see myself more objectively these days . . . I thought. My dark hair was layered, and I had just a bit of help from the hairdresser on keeping the gray at bay. My eyes were brown, and I had an olive complexion. My lips were full. My skin was smooth. I no longer saw myself as ugly, stupid, drab.

I'd gone through an abuse awareness and recovery program after Todd had been arrested. It was there that I'd regained a sense of self-worth. Images of verbal and physical altercations with Todd tried to invade my mind. I closed my eyes for a second and fought the urge to go lie on the bed. I knew that if I did that, I'd curl into a fetal position and stay that way for a long while . . . maybe even hours. I didn't have the time or the emotional energy to waste doing that.

My breathing became shallow, and I was suddenly cold. I sank to the floor, placed my head between my knees, and squeezed my eyes shut.

I will not faint. I will not be sick to my stomach. I will breathe normally. I will be fine.

Sparrow brushed against my ankles. I opened my eyes and

saw her beautiful little face looking up at me. I reached out and stroked her fur. She rubbed her head against my hand.

"You've been through a lot too, haven't you?" I asked her softly. "But we're strong, you and I. We're survivors."

I continued petting Sparrow until the sound of her purring filled the bathroom and made me relax. After a few minutes, I got up, washed my face and hands, and then went to the kitchen to resume work on the *quinceañera* cakes. And I made myself a mental note to give Sparrow tuna for dinner.

The bottom tiers of each cake were fairly simple to do—just white scrollwork on the rose-colored cakes—and the work went quickly. As I worked, I debated about calling Scottie. He could be a wonderful source of information about Dr. Bainsworth and his supposed mission trip to Nuevo Laredo. It was possible he could help me figure out if Dr. Bainsworth's visit to Mexico had anything to do with his death. Sure, the police had a flimsy case against Myra and me. But still. As more than one person had pointed out to me, this *was* the third suspicious death in Brea Ridge I'd been linked to, and I felt the need to prove my innocence once again.

I could just imagine the whispers at the Save-A-Buck. *Don't buy a cake from Daphne Martin. Everywhere she goes, death follows. And they never did find out for sure who killed that dentist. . . .*

I called Scottie. Naturally, the call went straight to voice mail.

"Hi," I said. "It's Daphne Martin. Please give me a call when you get this. Thanks."

*   *   *

I'D FINISHED ALL four of the bottom tiers of Isabel's *quincea-ñera* cake by the time I heard back from Scottie. But instead of calling, he came by.

"I brought the EIEIO information I promised you last night," he said as he strode into the kitchen. "Is everything okay? You sounded sort of upset over the phone."

"Everything is fine." I tossed the plastic gloves I'd been wearing into the garbage can. "I was just getting ready to make myself some lunch. Would you like a sandwich?"

He grinned. "Peanut butter and banana?"

"That'll work . . . only not fried. It might've been Elvis's favorite that way, but not mine."

"Suits me," he said. "So what's up?"

I took the bread and peanut butter from the cabinet, a banana from the stand on the counter, and a butter knife from the drawer. "I'm sure you've heard all the commotion about Dr. Bainsworth, the dentist who was murdered." I placed the sandwich fixings on the table and got out a couple plates and a bag of baked potato chips.

"Of course," Scottie said. "Not only has it been all over the newspaper, it's been the subject of gossip all over town."

"Did you know Myra and I found the body?" I asked, putting two slices of bread on each of the plates.

His brows shot up. "Um . . . no. No, I didn't."

"Really? I'd been at the jail since about ten thirty P.M. the night before the morning that I met you. I'd just got home when you drove up." I jerked my head toward the refrigerator. "Grab us a couple sodas, would you?"

Scottie opened the refrigerator, retrieved two diet sodas, and set them on the table. He then pulled out a chair and sat down. "That would explain your dazed and confused reaction to me when we met."

I laughed. "I think I'd have had a dazed and confused reaction to you no matter when I met you."

He lifted his soda can in salute. "Touché, madam."

I finished making our sandwiches, slid a plate over to Scottie, and sat down opposite him. "Had you ever met Dr. Bainsworth?"

He took a bite of his sandwich and shook his head.

I continued. "I thought you might've met him on a previous visit here or maybe on a mission. I heard he'd done some mission work himself. What do you know about Nuevo Laredo, Mexico?"

"It's a pretty tough place these days, now that the drug cartels are controlling the local government," he said, swallowing. "But it used to be a major tourist center and a market where the locals would sell their cattle, cotton, and sugarcane. You'd probably have loved Avenida Guerrero—it's their main street—where they sold handmade jewelry, blankets, and cheesy knickknacks."

"And you think I'd love cheesy knickknacks?" I looked around the kitchen to see how many cheesy knickknacks were in sight. A few . . . but not an abnormal amount.

He chuckled. "No. Actually, I believe you'd like the jewelry. But why the interest in Nuevo Laredo?"

"Are there a lot of religious or charitable missions there?" I asked.

"Quite a few," he said. "Why? Are you thinking of embarking upon a mission trip? If so, you don't want to go alone the first time. I can—"

"No, it's not about me," I said quickly. "Dr. Bainsworth went to visit Nuevo Laredo a few months ago. He was supposed to have been going on a medical mission trip, but one of his hygienists said he acted really weird after he got back."

Scottie inclined his head. "Something might have happened to him in Nuevo Laredo. In what way was he behaving strangely?" He helped himself to some chips.

"She didn't elaborate. She thinks the mission trip was just a ruse. She believes the real reason he went there was to visit the red-light district." I bit into my sandwich.

"It's odd he would go so far for that. From what I hear, the dentist didn't have any trouble getting girlfriends," he said.

"It doesn't make sense to me either," I said. "But there *are* missionaries there, right?"

"Yeah. The EIEIO has been there several times," said Scottie. "They set up Bible schools for children, build churches, provide medical care. . . ." He shrugged.

"That's why Dr. Bainsworth was supposed to have gone—to offer dental care." I sipped my soda. "So that's feasible, right?"

"Of course it is," he said. "But even if he went to Nuevo Laredo with honorable intentions, he might've stumbled across something that would make him come home and act weird."

I giggled.

"What?" Scottie asked.

"Myra was afraid that Dr. Bainsworth had gone down to Mexico and drank one of those drinks with the worms in it or got into drugs or something."

"Well, getting introduced to tequila could certainly affect a man." He stuffed a chip into his mouth. "Of course, getting introduced to a drug lord could too."

"A drug lord?" I asked. "That's a scary thought. What would a drug lord want with Dr. Bainsworth?"

"He'd want the dentist to transport drugs across the border," said Scottie.

"So do you think the drug lord would *hire* Dr. Bainsworth to do that?"

"I think that if Dr. Bainsworth was a willing mule, he and the drug lord would come to an agreement, sure." He took a drink of his soda.

"I'd heard the dentist was having a tough time financially," I said. "Maybe he'd decided to do this one bad thing for the money. . . . Maybe he acted strangely because his guilty conscience or the fear of getting caught was overwhelming him."

"Hard to say," Scottie said. "People do crazy things."

AFTER SCOTTIE LEFT, I drove to Bristol to get the rest of the supplies I needed for the *quinceañera* cake. I needed the staircases to join the two side cakes to the main cake and I needed a tiara topper.

As I drove, I thought about what Scottie had said. Could Dr. Bainsworth have become involved with a drug lord or some other unsavory character while he was in Mexico? Maybe the drug dealer forced Dr. Bainsworth to smuggle drugs into the United States. Being on a medical mission, the dentist would be expected to carry drugs along with other medical supplies. Would that make it easier for him to take the drugs back and forth across the border?

But how could the drug lord force Dr. Bainsworth to smuggle the drugs? Sure, he could threaten him and make him bring them across the border, but how could the drug dealer be certain the dentist would take them to their intended destination? What if he threatened Dr. Bainsworth's family? Could that be why Dr. Bainsworth had the rapid succession of affairs but still had the photo of Angela on his desk? Maybe he was trying to make the drug dealer believe he didn't care about his wife.

On the other hand, it was possible that Dr. Bainsworth needed money so badly that he made the fatal error of making what he believed would be a onetime deal with the drug lord. Or maybe the person who needed a smuggler wasn't a drug lord at all. Perhaps it was a jewel thief.

I pulled into the parking area of the strip mall where the small baking supply company was located. I got out of the Mini Cooper, beeped the door locked with my wireless remote, and nearly ran headlong into Belinda Fremont.

"Belinda, hi!" I said. "Please excuse my clumsiness."

"No problem," she said with a smile. "I heard about that dreadful business with the dentist. You have lousy luck when it comes to stumbling upon dead people, don't you?"

"I certainly do," I said, returning her smile. "Speaking of Dr. Bainsworth, is Maureen okay? I heard they'd been dating—"

"Oh, please." She waved away my concern with a flick of her wrist. "There must have been some gaps in that grapevine. Maureen and Jim went out a time or two, but she found out he was a gold digger and dumped him."

"Good for her. I spoke with her earlier today at the boutique, but I didn't ask about any romantic involvement she might've had with Dr. Bainsworth."

"He was a real piece of work. He came right out and asked Maureen for money on their very first date—which was dinner at a greasy pizza place." Belinda shook her head. "I called her when I heard about his death, but she appeared to be taking it just fine. She's dating Steve Franklin now."

"Great," I said. "Mr. Franklin strikes me as a nice man. I think they'll be good for each other."

"They're good *to* each other," Belinda said, "and that's a start. You wouldn't think of Steve as a suitable prospect for Maureen at first—at least, I didn't—but he's hardworking, he makes his own way, and he doesn't ask for handouts."

"And, as you said, they treat each other well. That's the main thing."

She smiled. "Isn't that the truth?"

"How are Guinevere and her companions?" I asked.

"They're doing well." She reached into her small shopping bag and took out some paper nut cups she'd bought at the bakery supply and party shop. "I bought them these for their snacks. Hilda usually puts their snacks in small glass bowls in their bedrooms, but I thought it would be nice to put some in their sitting room."

"How thoughtful!"

"Thank you. I thought it was a clever idea," she said. "You see, they can be in there playing and happen upon a cup of treats."

"And they'll be delighted." I beamed, wondering to myself if guinea pigs experience delight. Probably. Besides, if it pleases your best-paying customer, it's thoughtful, delightful, marvelous, and downright skippy.

Belinda dropped the nut cups back into her bag. "I'd better let you get your shopping done. Are you working on something fabulous?"

"I hope it's going to be," I said. "I'm making a *quinceañera* cake."

"A *quinceañera* cake. You will take pictures and post them on your site, won't you?" she asked.

"Of course." I could almost see the wheels in Belinda's head turning as she wondered what type of cake would be appropriate for Guinevere's *quinceañera*. I was almost positive guinea pigs didn't live to be fifteen, but I wouldn't have told Belinda that for half the gold in Fort Knox.

"By the way, who's having a *quinceañera*?" she asked.

"Juanita Ramirez's sister, Isabel," I said.

"Juanita from the Save-A-Buck?" Belinda asked.

I nodded.

"Oh, that's nice. For Isabel, I mean," said Belinda. "It must be rather hard on Juanita, though."

"It doesn't seem to be," I said. "She's the one planning the party."

Belinda looked confused for a moment and then said, "How . . . sweet."

"I think so too."

"She didn't get to have a *quinceañera*, you know," Belinda said. "She disgraced the family or something just before she was to have her party." She shook her head. "Pity, too. She appears to be a very nice girl."

"She is nice," I said. "What did she do that was so bad?"

"I'm not sure, but I believe it had something to do with a guy." Belinda laughed. "Doesn't it always?"

CHAPTER Fifteen

A s soon as I got home from the bakery supply shop, I called China and Myra using my phone's three-way conference feature. Myra and I needed to separate fact from fiction with regard to all the gossip we'd been hearing, and I figured China was the perfect candidate to help us do that. Both women agreed to come over to my house right away. Myra said we'd have to make it quick because she had plans with John later.

Before they arrived, I quickly dusted and vacuumed the living room. I put the teakettle on the stove and set some mixed nuts and some truffles on the coffee table. Being just next door, Myra arrived first. She deposited her loafers by the kitchen door and padded into the living room.

"What did you think of Jill?" she asked, curling up in the club chair.

"She wasn't anything like I thought she'd be," I said.

"She threw me for a loop too." Myra shook her head slowly. "I thought she'd be either young, cute, and giggly or else elegant, smart, and sensual. She was none of the above. In fact, it'd be safer to say she was as ugly as homemade soap and as dreary as old gym socks."

"I wouldn't go that far. But after meeting Jill, I started to wonder about all of those affairs." The teakettle whistled. "Be right back." I hurried to the kitchen, took the kettle off the stove, and poured the boiling water over white tea bags I'd placed into the teapot. I put the pot, matching teacups, napkins, spoons, and sweeteners on a serving tray and carried it back into the living room.

"What did you say you started wondering about?" Myra asked.

I sat the tray onto the table. "It made me wonder if Dr. Bainsworth was being threatened in some way, if maybe he was carrying on with these other women to downplay his love for his wife."

Before Myra could react to that, China arrived. She and I sat on the sofa, and while I poured the tea, Myra filled China in on our meeting Jill and my latest theory that Dr. Bainsworth had been "forced" into his numerous affairs.

China frowned at me. "How'd you come up with that one?"

I explained about the conversation about Nuevo Laredo I'd had with Scottie. "If Dr. Bainsworth did cross paths with a drug dealer, maybe Dr. Bainsworth double-crossed him or something and the drug dealer threatened his wife."

"So to counteract that, Dr. Bainsworth cheated on his wife in order to make it appear he didn't care what happened to her?" China asked.

"Precisely." I smiled triumphantly. "I mean, Angela's picture was still on his desk when we were there yesterday. He wouldn't keep out a photo of a wife he despised."

"Good try," China said, "but Dr. Bainsworth was cheating on his wife long before he went to Mexico. Remember? She found out. That's why she divorced him."

"But what if he'd had the run-in with the drug dealer *before* he went to Mexico?" I asked. "Isn't that possible? I mean, maybe that's why he went there."

Myra sighed. "After everything you've been through with your ex-husband, Daphne, you're still determined to find some good in Dr. Bainsworth?"

I shrugged. "I was surprised to see the picture still there, that's all. Todd didn't keep a photo of me on his desk when we were married. I thought Dr. Bainsworth had to have loved Angela to have her face sitting there on his desk where he'd see it every day." I shook my head. "It doesn't make one iota of sense to me. He was cheating on her. She was cheating on him. And yet, he had her picture on his desk. On top of that, he was using the photo to hide a hotel key card. I just don't get it."

"Nobody said he didn't love his wife," China said. "Some men think they can love their wives and everyone else's to boot."

"Wait a second," Myra said. "She was cheating on him? Did she tell you that?"

"No," I said, "Bunni did. And while Dr. Bainsworth's private investigator didn't confirm that fact, he didn't deny it. Bunni thinks Angela killed Dr. Bainsworth to keep him from exposing her affair in divorce court."

"I don't buy that," said China. "Angela was doing fine financially. I don't see her risking life in prison or the death penalty just to get a bigger slice of the pie."

"You're probably right." Myra plucked a truffle off the tray. "Even if Angela only wound up with half of Dr. Bainsworth's property and no alimony, she'd be fine. She has a good job. I think she's trying to move on with her life."

"That's what Violet seems to think too," I said. "And in my conversations with Angela, she doesn't seem terribly bitter or vindictive. I don't think she killed Dr. Bainsworth either. But what's up with that key card?"

"It's either his from an illicit affair *he* was having," China said, "or it could be proof of one of Angela's."

"How could a blank key card be proof of an affair?" Myra asked.

"It could prove she was at a particular hotel." China looked at me. "What hotel name was on the card?"

"There wasn't one. It just had a picture of a little redbird."

"It must be a logo," China said. "Did you run it through a search engine?"

"Not yet, but I will," I said.

"Don't forget, we still have our Elvis running into the Sunoco with his bloody sleeve," Myra said, popping the truffle into her mouth.

"And, as much as I hate the possibility, I think we need to consider Juanita a suspect," I said. "I ran into Belinda Fremont in Bristol earlier today. I told her about the *quinceañera* cake, and she mentioned that the reason Juanita didn't get to have a *quinceañera* was because she somehow disgraced her family over some guy. I know whatever happened was several years ago, but it could suggest a pattern of dating losers. Plus, her current boyfriend is an Elvis."

"Not too skinny, and not too fat," Myra said.

"I know what Belinda is talking about." China took a sip of her tea and then sat the cup and saucer on the coffee table. "Before she came to the United States, Juanita was courted by a man who promised her the moon and the stars. Even better, though, he promised to bring her family into the U.S., get them legalized, and marry Juanita."

"Did he renege on his promises?" I asked.

"No. He did everything he said he'd do," China said. "He and Juanita were to be married in a church in South Carolina, and the following weekend Juanita was to have her *quinceañera*."

My jaw dropped. "She was just fourteen when this marriage was to take place?"

"No, she'd turned fifteen already. But her groom was in a hurry to get married and told her he'd throw her the grandest *quinceañera* ever after their honeymoon." China picked up her teacup and took another sip.

"How could a fifteen-year-old get married?" Myra asked. "Ain't that illegal?"

"Not in the state of Mississippi if you have a notarized statement of parental consent," China said.

"So, basically, Juanita's parents were willing to sell her in order to have a better life," I said.

"Apparently, they thought they were doing what was best for all of them," China said.

"Did she love the man?" Myra asked.

"I couldn't say," China said. "But I do know Juanita stopped the wedding when the man's other girlfriends showed up."

"Girlfriends?" I asked. "Plural?"

"Yep," China said. "All three of them."

"Wasn't that convenient?" I mused.

I PUT THE finishing touches on the *quinceañera* cakes. All I had to do now was deliver them to the party on Saturday and set up the cakes. I gave Juanita a call and left a message asking her to come by when she could to see what she thought. I then boxed up the cakes and put them in the refrigerator.

I went into my office to check my e-mail and see how much traffic my website was getting. My home page loaded. Fifteen new e-mails. All junk. Site traffic was down.

I pulled up the photographs Myra had taken. The pictures of the jewelry photos were a little blurry, but I was able to crop and enlarge them and then print them out. Some of the pieces looked like heirlooms. Either that or they were really excellent fakes. But I didn't know why anyone would take pictures of fakes. Actually, other than for insurance purposes, I didn't know why anyone would take pictures of jewelry at all. Unless Dr. Bainsworth had been planning to sell it.

I took Ben's suggestion and checked the online classifieds of the *Brea Ridge Chronicle*. None of the jewelry listed matched any of the pieces in the photographs found in Dr. Bainsworth's office. I then looked through the classified jewelry ads in newspapers from the surrounding area, but those searches didn't produce any matches either. There was not even anything similar in the ads.

As I turned my attention fully back to the photos of Dr. Bainsworth's jewelry, the thought of insurance reoccurred to me, but this time with a different meaning. Maybe Dr. Bainsworth *had* taken pictures of the jewelry for insurance purposes. Maybe he had smuggled the jewelry out of Nuevo Laredo, and he'd taken the photographs for insurance against the thief.

I then did a search for redbird hotel key cards. The search turned up several Redbird Hotel locations, one of which was Nuevo Laredo.

The doorbell rang. I got up from my computer and went down the hall to the living room. I looked out the front window and saw that my visitor was Juanita.

"Hi," I said, opening the door.

"I hope you don't mind that I came on over," she said. "I got your message as I was getting off work and thought I'd see if this is a good time. If it isn't, I can come back later or tomorrow."

"No, this is a great time." I led her through the living room and into the kitchen. "I went and got the rest of the things I needed for the *quinceañera* cakes today. Let me set it up for you so you'll know how it's going to look on Saturday."

I cleared the place mats off the kitchen table and placed the fountain in the center. I got out the main cakes and constructed them over the top of the fountain. I then set up the side cakes with the staircases leading to the main cake.

"What do you think?" I asked. "Of course, I'll put the *damas* on the staircases on Saturday, and I'll put this tiara on the top tier."

Juanita didn't say anything, so I turned to look at her. Her eyes were glistening with tears.

"Is it all right?" I asked.

"It is magnificent." She blinked rapidly, causing the tears to spill down her face.

I grabbed a napkin off the island and handed it to her.

"I'm sorry," she said, wiping her eyes. "It's just even better than I had imagined it would be. It is perfect. Isabel will love it."

"Maybe—in a way—it can be your *quinceañera* cake too," I said quietly. "Since you didn't get to have one, I mean."

Juanita smiled sadly but didn't comment.

"While you're here, may I ask you a question?" I asked.

"I guess so." She looked hesitant.

"You don't have to answer me if you don't want to," I said, "but why did you leave Dr. Bainsworth and go to Dr. Farmer?"

She looked down at the floor.

"Was it because Dr. Bainsworth acted inappropriately toward you?" I asked. "I'm asking because it's my understanding he behaved badly toward several of his female patients and staff members."

Juanita raised her eyes. "He wouldn't leave me alone. Every time I had to go there, he pushed his luck a little further. When I protested, he acted like I was being childish. So I switched to the other dentist." She lowered her eyes again. "I know I probably deserved his treatment, but I did not appreciate it."

I pulled out a kitchen chair and invited Juanita to sit down. She did, and I sat in the chair to her right. "Why would you think you deserved to be treated disrespectfully?"

She didn't answer right away, so I tried to fill in the blank.

"Is it because you're so pretty?" I asked. "You expect men to give you a lot of attention?"

She shook her head. "It is because of how I came to be in this country. I was to be married to a rich American businessman. But then I found out he had other fiancées—or girlfriends—and I refused to marry him." Her lips turned down at the corners, and she had to take a steadying breath before she continued. "This man had already taken care of the paperwork for my family and me to come to America and not get in trouble, so he said my family owed him a lot of money. They paid this money—it took my *quinceañera* money and all the money they could borrow from relatives—but I disgraced the entire family."

"Juanita, you didn't disgrace your family! That horrible man did!"

She cocked her head. "I should have been more careful."

"But you were only fifteen years old," I said. "If anyone should have been more careful, it's your parents."

"So you had already heard the story?" she asked.

I bit my lip. "Just this afternoon. I'm sorry."

She nodded. "It's common knowledge to many of the people around here, especially those who frequent the Save-A-Buck. That is why I have a bad reputation."

"You don't have a bad reputation," I said. "The person who told me about the man who wronged you felt badly for you. You were put in a terrible situation. You didn't deserve that."

"Thank you, but I cost my family a lot of money," she said. "I am still paying them back."

Tears pricked the backs of my eyes. "Juanita, that's terrible. I'm so sorry."

Juanita placed her small hand over mine. "Now look. I have gone and made you sad. I never meant to do that. The reason I left your house so quickly yesterday is because I thought I saw him here."

"You thought you saw who here?" I asked.

"The man who caused me to disgrace my family."

My eyes widened. "He was here? He's one of the EIEIO members?"

She nodded. "I think so."

"Which one?"

"His name is George," she said. "But he sometimes goes by Jorge."

"I don't remember a George or a Jorge," I said, wracking my brain to try to remember the names of all the men who were there yesterday. "Tomorrow night at the party, will you come with me and identify the man?"

She shook her head. "No . . . I do not believe I could do that. It would be very difficult. I've already told Aaron, and we're not going." Her eyes filled with tears again. "That man caused such a rift between my parents and me."

"But, Juanita, that wasn't your fault. You were a child."

"I wasn't after that. I had to get a job and start paying my family back for the money I had cost them." She closed her eyes momentarily. "If you cannot find this man on your own, then I will help. Otherwise, I would prefer not to be involved. Besides, I'm not even sure it was him. It could have been someone who merely resembles him. People can change a great deal over the years."

"That's true." A thought occurred to me. "You said you had to get a job and pay your parents back. Are your parents paying for this cake, or are they making you pay for it?"

"I am paying for half, and they are paying the other half.

My half is going toward the amount I owe to them," Juanita said. "It is a generous thing they are doing for both me and Isabel. My mother and I did not have to try to make the cake ourselves, half the money for the cake will be credited to my debt, and Isabel will have a lovely cake. You see?"

"Then I'm giving half my fee back to you," I said. "Your parents will never know the difference."

"I cannot let you do that," she said.

"You can and you will. Besides, by allowing me to make this *quinceañera* cake, you've done me a huge favor. I can add this cake to the gallery on my website. It's the closest thing I have to a wedding cake so far, and people will be impressed with it."

"Are you sure?" she asked.

I smiled. "Positive."

"My parents," she said. "They are not bad people."

"Of course they're not," I said. I tried to sound convincing, but I was angry with Juanita's parents for treating her the way they had.

"They did the best they knew how to do," she said.

I nodded.

We both looked at the cake for a moment.

"It really is lovely," Juanita said.

"Thank you." I began dismantling it and boxing it back up. "I truly appreciate your business."

"And I appreciate your friendship, Daphne."

AFTER JUANITA LEFT, I sat down on the sofa in the living room and called Ben at the paper.

"Will you help me figure out if Dr. Bainsworth was dealing in something shady?" I asked.

"By the tone of your voice, I'd say you've already got a theory," he said. "Let's hear it."

"Remember the jewelry photos Myra found in Dr. Bainsworth's lobby? I think he smuggled the jewelry across the Mexican border." I pressed my lips together, waiting for Ben's reaction.

"How did you make that leap?" he asked. "I thought we'd deduced that the jewelry was his and that he was planning to sell it."

"Well, Scottie came by today with the brochure information, and I told him Myra's theory that Dr. Bainsworth had gone to Nuevo Laredo and become involved in smuggling drugs," I said. "Scottie agreed that the town has become rough these days and said that it was possible Dr. Bainsworth had encountered some members of a drug cartel while he was there."

"So what if he did, Daph? You're still not explaining how you got jewelry smuggling from photographs in the lobby combined with the suggestion that Dr. Bainsworth ran into some cartel in Nuevo Laredo."

"Have you heard rumors about Juanita and how she came to America?"

"Bits and pieces. I dismissed them, though, because they were either gossip or idle speculation—neither of which is reliable," he said.

I grinned. "Spoken like a true reporter. Still, when Juanita came by the house today to look at the *quinceañera* cake, she filled me in about the man who'd brought her from Mexico to America and agreed to marry her when she was fifteen. She said she couldn't be certain, but she thinks one of the EIEIO members is that man."

"And she didn't recognize him before now? I mean, her boyfriend is a member, isn't he?"

"Yes, but he's only been with the group for a month or two," I said. "But she thinks she saw the guy at the EIEIO meeting the other day whom she was supposed to marry and who scammed her parents. Doesn't it stand to reason that the same man who swindled a young girl's family—in Mexico—might be the same one who killed Dr. Bainsworth? What if the dentist also ran afoul of this guy in Mexico?"

"You don't think the guy wanted to marry Dr. Bainsworth, do you?" Ben asked with a chuckle.

"No," I said. "What I think is that if a man has been involved in one type of shady affair, he'd be a likely suspect to participate in another. Myra and I have suspected an EIEIO member ever since the Sunoco woman reported selling a Coke to an Elvis with blood on his sleeve minutes after the murder. You don't think those dots require connecting?"

"Possibly," he said. "But the fact remains that the EIEIO will be leaving town in a couple days. If we can't provide solid proof that this man—or any of the other EIEIO members—is guilty of Dr. Bainsworth's murder, then the police have to let him go. They have no reason to hold him. And you can be fairly certain that he'll never come back to Brea Ridge."

"I know. Still, I think I'm onto something. . . . Don't you?"

"I do, sweetheart," said Ben. "But it's a stretch to think that a man who conned a young girl's family has graduated to jewel smuggling within a few short years."

"I don't think so," I said. "A bad seed will either reform or become a worse seed. And I'm convinced Dr. Bainsworth was being manipulated. When Myra and I helped clean his office, I noticed there was a photograph of Angela on his desk. I think he still loved her. I mean, I met a married man once who asked me out but said he was devoted to his wife. His excuse was that he liked variety."

"If he'd loved her, he wouldn't have been cheating on her," Ben said. "Besides, you don't even know that this man set out to swindle Juanita and her family. After all, he *did* bring them to the United States as promised."

"But then his so-called girlfriends showed up just before the ceremony," I said. "Don't you think that was terribly convenient for the groom-to-be?"

"Maybe. I don't know."

"You think my theory is stupid," I said, letting my head drop against the back of the sofa.

"I think the part of it concerning Juanita is. She was a child who got manipulated into a situation by the adults in her life. But your idea about the smuggling might not be so far off base."

"Really?" I asked. "Do you really think so, or are you just patronizing me?"

"I don't think it's out of the question," he said carefully.

I sighed. "Maybe I am grasping at dandelion fluff here, but it makes sense to me. Dr. Bainsworth meets someone in Mexico who asks him to smuggle a few pieces of stolen jewelry into the country. Dr. Bainsworth either agrees or is forced to comply somehow, but then he double-crosses the thief."

"Why would he do that?" Ben asked.

"I don't know," I said. "Maybe he got a conscience, or maybe he decided to sell the jewelry and cut the smuggler out of the deal. But then the night Myra and I arranged to meet Dr. Bainsworth at his office, the smuggler got to the office ahead of Dr. Bainsworth with the intention of finding the jewelry. When Dr. Bainsworth came in and caught him, the thief killed him."

"If Bainsworth smuggled jewelry into the country two months ago, why hadn't he sold it before now? And why is the thief only coming after it now?"

"I'm thinking maybe Dr. Bainsworth didn't fence the jewelry right away because he knew the authorities would be looking for it," I said. "I mean, he knew it was stolen. And I believe he was too smart to behave rashly."

"Bainsworth? Too smart to behave rashly?" he asked. "Yeah. Run that one by his divorce lawyer."

"All right then, maybe he was trying to find someone who would melt it down or remove the diamonds and gemstones and sell the pieces that way. Finding someone to do that and keep quiet about it might take time."

"And the thief?" asked Ben.

"Maybe the thief came to Brea Ridge at a time when it was convenient for him or at a time when he was supposed to be here anyway. Maybe he came when he knew he'd have a pretty solid alibi."

"Like when the EIEIO was coming to town."

"It makes sense," I said. "The EIEIO does mission work all over—including Nuevo Laredo—and Dr. Bainsworth was killed the night the group came to town."

"I know I mentioned this the other night—mostly in jest—but do you think it could've been Scottie?"

"No. I don't think he's the type," I said. "Besides, Juanita said her guy's name was George or Jorge."

"That name could be one of many aliases he uses. Contrary to your belief, I think Scottie is perfectly the type. You were right in thinking that might've been why he hired you in the first place. He saw you and Myra arrive at the dental office. He knows you found Bainsworth's body, and he hired you to keep informed about the investigation."

"But Juanita has seen Scottie before, and she didn't freak then," I pointed out.

"Just because he isn't the villain in Juanita's story doesn't mean he isn't a villain in this one," Ben said. "Just be careful around him. That's all I'm asking. I need to get back to work. May I buy you dinner tomorrow night?"

"I'd like that. I have to go by and set up the EIEIO cake first. Would you like to pick me up here after I'm finished, or would you prefer to meet at the restaurant?"

"Why don't I pick you up at home? Just give me a call when you get back."

"Sounds good," I said.

After we hung up, I realized Ben had pointed out something I hadn't considered before. The killer probably had seen Myra and me going into the building. He had to have seen my car at the very least.

CHAPTER
Sixteen

THE NEXT morning, I got up, took a bath, and got ready to start my day. A cup of café au lait and a biscotti would help to clear my brain fog. I prepared my single-cup coffeemaker, poured a fourth of a cup of skim milk into my mug, and waited. Naturally, the phone rang.

"Daphne's Delectable—"

"Hi, it's me, Myra."

"Good morning," I said. "How are you?"

"I'm fine. Have you got a few minutes?" she asked. "I'd like to come over and talk with you."

"Come on over," I said. "I'll have a cup of hot coffee ready."

"Thanks," she said. "You're a doll."

When Myra got to my house, she was wearing her overcoat, boots, and pajamas. She deposited her coat on the hook by the back door and her boots on the rug.

"Are you all right?" I asked, aghast at her unkempt appearance. That was so unlike Myra.

"Yeah, I reckon. I've just got stuff on my mind." She slumped into a chair at the kitchen table.

I handed her a cup of black coffee along with some creamer and sweetener. I set the biscotti on the table, retrieved my café au lait, and sat in the chair across from Myra. "Spill."

"It's this Elvis thing," she said. She put creamer and sweetener into her coffee and stirred. "They'll be gone tomorrow."

"I thought you were prepared for that."

"I thought I was too," she said. "But I believe one of those Elvises killed Dr. Bainsworth, and we have to figure out which one it was before they leave here sticking you and me with the blame."

"I know." I sighed and took a drink of my café au lait. "Ben says there's not enough evidence to prosecute us for killing the dentist. And while I believe that, I don't want to take any chances."

"Neither do I," Myra said. "I figure we go to that banquet hall early and weed out the fat and skinny Elvises and see who we've got left."

"Ben thinks it's Scottie," I said.

Myra's jaw dropped. "He does?"

I shrugged. "I don't know if he really believes Scottie is guilty, but he made some pretty good arguments yesterday about Scottie being our guy. He believes Scottie saw us arriving at Dr. Bainsworth's office and that he invented the need for a cake in order to stay close to the investigation."

"He's not fat, and he's not too skinny," Myra said. "Wonder if he'd meet us out at the Sunoco."

I nearly choked on the drink I'd just taken. "What? You want me to call Scottie and ask him to take part in a lineup?"

"Hey, that's even better," she said, warming even more to her idea. "We'll go to the Sunoco and call Scottie after Hot Lips comes on duty. We'll tell Scottie that you've had a wreck and your car is on its side. We need him and some of the other Elvises—who are in good enough shape—to come and turn your car upright." She smiled smugly.

"Yeah, there are several problems with that plan," I said. "What if Hot Lips has the night off? And what will we do when the Elvises arrive and the car isn't on its side? And no, we are not somehow turning the car on its side. Furthermore, if the Elvises arrive and Hot Lips is on duty, then how would we get the Elvises to go inside and possibly be identified by her?" Before Myra could speak, I held up my hand. "And this last one's the kicker—I have to deliver the cake to the convention hall at five thirty."

"Well, there goes that perfect plan," she said glumly.

We sat in silence for about one entire minute.

"I've got it," Myra said, her face brightening. "I'll go with you to the convention hall to deliver the cake and to help set everything up. Then we'll mingle with all the Elvises—particularly the ones who fall within Hot Lips's description—and we'll talk about dentistry to see if any of them act like they're uncomfortable."

"If we talk about dentistry, everyone will be uncomfortable," I said. "I mean, how do you work that into a conversation?"

"I lost a filling, remember?" she asked. "I can talk about that."

"I guess it's worth a try," I said. I was thinking there had to be a better way. I just hadn't come up with one yet.

LONG AFTER MYRA had left, I was still trying to figure out how to draw out the guilty Elvis. I decided to talk with China. She'd helped me think things through before. Maybe she could again.

I phoned China, and she answered on the first ring.

"You sound worried," she said.

How I could sound worried saying only "Hi, China," I'll never know. But she was right. "You're right. I'm worried about who killed Dr. Bainsworth and the possibility that the killer will leave town without ever being caught." I explained to her about the jewelry photos Myra found in Dr. Bainsworth's office and how Angela said they weren't taken for insurance purposes because she wasn't into jewelry.

"And you think the killer went there to find the jewelry?" she asked.

"Yes." I laid out my theory about Dr. Bainsworth smuggling the jewelry across the border for thieves and then double-crossing them in some way. "What do you think?"

"I reckon anything is possible. And that makes a lot more sense than you and Myra clubbing the poor man with a giant toothbrush and a plastic molar." She snickered. "Any jury that knows Myra would realize she'd have never hurt Dr. Bainsworth—at least, not until *after* he'd fixed her tooth."

"Exactly," I said. "But I doubt that it would get that far."

"Oh, they just don't have any viable suspects to investigate right now. But if you're thinking the killer has an eye for antique jewelry, then come on over to my house. I might have just the thing that would draw him out."

WHEN I ARRIVED at China's modest gable-front house, I set off a cacophony of barking. At least five fairly large dogs jumped up on the back fence to "say hello," and I could hear the yaps of one or two smaller dogs as well.

China came to the door. "Don't mind them! They're loud but not vicious!"

I smiled and walked down the narrow sidewalk to her front porch. China's house was white, and she had navy blue metal furniture on the porch. There was a glider and two rockers, one on either side of the glider. The fact that it was sunny today—albeit cold—reminded me of how nice it must be to sit on this porch during the spring and summer evenings.

"Come on in," she said. "Can I get you anything?"

"No, thanks," I said. "I'm fine."

Though clean and smelling of lemon furniture polish, China's living room was cluttered with magazines. There were crime and detective magazines on the coffee table, cooking magazines overflowing from a basket beside a large burgundy recliner, and entertainment magazines stacked at one corner of the sofa. I sat on the uncluttered section of the sofa as a large orange tabby came into the room, gave me the once-over, and then hopped onto the basket beside the recliner and began licking its paws.

China retrieved a box from a tall table in the hallway and brought it to me. "Here. See if you think this might work to draw out your jewelry thief."

I opened the red velvet box and gasped. Inside was a large teardrop pendant. The outside of the pendant had a row of tiny diamonds followed by a row of blue sapphires. The next row was filigree leaves, and there was a large diamond dangling in the center of the row. It appeared the chain was platinum. The necklace looked very old and very delicate. I was afraid to touch it.

"Do you like it?" she asked.

"It's gorgeous," I said.

"Thanks. It was my mama's." She shrugged. "As you can tell, I'm a bit of a tomboy myself. I never went in for much fancy jewelry. But I figure I can live off this necklace for a few months if push ever comes to shove."

"For a few months?" I asked.

She nodded. "Yeah. The last time I had it appraised, it was going for fifteen thousand dollars." China reached over and gently tapped my chin. "Close your mouth, dear. You look like a fish. Do you have a low-cut blouse you can wear this with?"

"I can't wear this, China! What if something happens to it?"

"It's insured," she said, dismissing my concern with a wave of her hand. "And if you don't wear this necklace, how else are you gonna draw out the thief?"

"We don't even know there is a thief," I said. "I'm just jumping to conclusions."

"It seems like a fairly logical conclusion to me," said China. "Besides, if there's no thief, you can bring the necklace back to me tomorrow and we'll at least know we tried."

I looked at the necklace again. "But what if there *is* a thief? And he somehow manages to steal this necklace?"

"Then we'll catch him."

"How?" I sighed and glanced around the living room, once again zeroing in on the detective magazines. "Mark Thompson, Dr. B's private detective—"

"Mark? What about him?"

"You know Mark Thompson?" I asked.

"Sure."

"Call and see if you can get him to come over here. Tell him I'll pay whatever he charges." I hoped I could afford it.

China called Mark, and he came right over. By the time he got there, she and I were already putting together ideas.

"We need your help," I told Mark. "Or at least, I do."

"*We* do," China said. "You're my friend. Besides, our entire town needs to get a killer off the streets. It's your problem too, Mark."

He smiled. "Right you are. So, how can I help?"

"You tell us," I said. "We've got a pretty strong feeling that one of the Elvis impersonators in town murdered Dr. Bainsworth."

"And Daphne thinks it has to do with jewelry because of some photos she found in his office," China said. "Did Jim ever talk with you about any jewelry?"

Mark shook his head. "I was hired to investigate his wife, and that's what I did."

"His secretary believes you found evidence she'd been having an affair," I said.

The PI looked wary.

"Oh, come on, Mark," China said. "Jim's dead, and Daphne

needs your help. You won't be breaking confidentiality at this point."

"She was having a fling," Mark admitted. "Had been for quite some time."

"Maureen Fremont said you'd given Dr. Bainsworth a photograph of the man she was seeing," I said. "Do you have a copy of it?"

"Not with me," he said.

I told Mark about the Redbird Hotel key card I'd found. "Since Dr. Bainsworth had hidden the key card in the picture frame, I thought it might be a regular room he kept somewhere. But now I'm wondering if it was proof of somewhere Angela had stayed."

"Angela had been in Mexico. She and her . . . er, amigo would meet there on occasion." Mark inclined his head. "Her lover could have engaged Jim in some sort of theft or smuggling plot, I suppose . . . without realizing who he was dealing with, of course."

"Or maybe he knew exactly who he was dealing with," China said.

"Here's our plan," I said. "China has a really expensive necklace she wants me to wear to the convention hall this evening. We believe it'll draw out the smuggler, if there is one."

"It's dangerous for untrained people to try to perpetrate their own sting operations," Mark warned us.

"That's why we want you to help us," China said.

"And I'm willing to pay you whatever your rate is," I said. "What *is* your rate?"

"We'll get to that if and when I decide whether or not I'm willing to sign on for this harebrained scheme," Mark said. "What do you want me to do?"

"I thought if you could maybe wire me up somehow . . . you know, to a recording device . . . and you could be on the other end . . ." I trailed off. It did sound like a harebrained scheme when you said it out loud.

China picked up where I left off. "And you could have some law enforcement standing by."

"Actually, they've been following me and Myra anyway," I said. "It won't be hard to find them. I even got one of them to give me a ride home on Sunday night."

Mark closed his eyes and shook his head. "I might regret saying this until the day I die, but I'll help you."

"Great." I smiled. "I'll call Myra."

Mark opened his eyes. "No, you won't. The fewer people that know about this, the better. That way, her reactions are genuine."

"What about Ben?" I asked. "I have to let him know."

"Talk with him. If he wants in," Mark said, "he can be with me. What time do you need to be at the convention hall?"

"Five thirty."

Mark nodded. "Then I'll be at your house at four thirty."

CHAPTER
Seventeen

BY FOUR fifteen P.M. I was wearing a black dress with a deep V, black patent pumps, and China's $15,000 heirloom necklace while I paced the kitchen waiting for Ben and Mark. I'd even swept my hair up off my face to keep it from somehow obscuring the necklace.

After speaking with Ben, he and Mark had decided Ben would drive them to my house. Myra wouldn't be suspicious of Ben's vehicle in my driveway. Then before Myra and I left, Ben and Mark would leave. They'd switch to Mark's van, where they could remotely listen through the wire I'd be wearing.

Luckily for me, Ben and Mark arrived before my pacing ruined the floor.

"Wow," Ben said when he came inside. "Just . . . wow."

"Isn't this necklace incredible?" I asked.

"You're wearing a necklace?" Ben teased. "You look gorgeous."

"Yes, you do," Mark said.

"Thanks. Having this necklace on makes me so nervous." My hand went instinctively to the pendant. "Well . . . that and the fact that we're trying to catch a thief, smuggler, killer . . . whatever."

"Everything will be fine," Ben said. "Mark and I will be right outside in the van. The second we hear anything suspicious, we'll be in there."

I nodded. "I know. I just . . ."

"Let's get you wired up before your friend gets here," Mark said. He placed the wire around my neck. "Place this little transmitter there in your bra, and then we'll tape the wire to your body so it doesn't become visible."

I did as he instructed, turning my back to the men in order to tape the wire in place. "Are you sure this will work? Will I have to point my chest in the direction of whoever's talking?"

Mark chuckled. "No. By all means, don't do that. You'll give us away. Act naturally. We'll be able to hear everyone within twenty yards of you."

"All right." I took a deep breath.

"You're going to do great," Ben said. "And if nothing else, we'll get a funny story out of it."

"I don't want a funny story. I want to catch the bad guy and prove my innocence—again."

"You will." He kissed my cheek. "*We* will."

"When you get to the convention hall," Mark said, "don't

look around for the van. Just go about your business like we're not even there."

"Okay," I said.

The men left, and I put the cake in the car.

Within ten minutes of doing so, I heard Myra humming "Viva Las Vegas" as she traipsed up the walkway. I flung on an emerald wool cape, grabbed my car keys and purse, and hurried out the door.

"Hi," I said. "Are you ready to go?" When she didn't answer, I turned.

Myra was staring at me in slack-jawed confusion.

"What?" I asked. "What is it?" I was afraid the wire might be sticking out or something.

"You tell me."

"I'll tell you whatever you want to know once we're in the car," I said. "We really do need to go." I got into the car and strapped on my seat belt.

Myra followed suit. "I didn't know you planned to get so dressed up."

I glanced at her outfit—a beige suit with a dark brown sweater—before looking into the rearview and backing down the driveway. "You're dressed up," I pointed out. "And you look terrific, by the way."

"Maybe so, but you look like you could start a riot," she said. "Are you like Miss Scarlett going to the Wilkes' barbecue to woo every eligible man there?"

I merely smiled at the *Gone with the Wind* reference and restrained myself from calling Myra either Mammy or Aunt Pittypat.

"Nope," I said as I merged with the traffic. "Actually, Ben is picking me up from the convention hall, and we're going out to dinner tonight."

"In that case, the way you're dressed is kinda cruel, don't you think?" she asked. "Scottie might think you went to all this trouble for him."

"Myra, this getup is tame compared to your Ann-Margret costume."

"Yeah . . . but I was *trying* to attract attention," she said.

"I'm trying to attract attention too," I said. "Remember we're doing more than simply delivering a cake and setting up the display, you know." She didn't know just how *much* more we were doing, but I think Mark was right that it was best to keep her in the dark about the surveillance equipment. Myra had already proven her tendency to be a little over the top when it came to spying.

It wasn't until we arrived at the convention hall and got out of the car that Myra noticed the necklace. A shaft of light caught the large center diamond and nearly blinded her.

"Have you got on a new necklace?" she asked.

"Sort of. When we get inside and I set the cake down, I'll show it to you," I said, handing Myra a box containing the items I needed for the display. I carried the cake and resisted the impulse to glance around the parking lot. We walked into the convention hall and were immediately greeted by Scottie and John.

"Whoa," Scottie said. "If you were trying to take my breath away, you succeeded." He took the heavy cake from me and carried it to a nearby table. "You look incredible."

"So do you," John said to Myra. "My knees buckled the instant you walked through the door."

Myra laughed and playfully swatted his arm. "Oh, you silver-tongued devil."

John kissed her cheek.

Scottie stepped in closer to me. "I don't have a date for tonight."

I smiled. "I do."

Myra announced, "Daphne's got on a stunning new necklace. Let me see that up close." She all but elbowed Scottie out of the way as she zeroed in on my throat like a hungry vampire.

"That is stunning," Scottie said. "Was it a gift?"

"Actually, it's a loaner," I said. I looked at Myra. "Remember Pat, China's cousin who was hired to clean Dr. Bainsworth's office?"

"The hobbit?" She looked incredulous. "This necklace belongs to the freakin' hobbit?"

I laughed. "In a roundabout way, I guess. Or at least it did. She found it somewhere and gave it to China to thank her for helping her get the cleaning job."

"You say she *found* that necklace?" John asked.

"That's what she said, and—get this—she thought it was fake," I said. "But China had it appraised, and it's definitely not fake."

"Then how come she's letting you borrow it?" Myra asked.

"You know China," I said. "She's not really the type to wear such showy jewelry, and she's generous to a fault. When I admired it at her house earlier today, she insisted I wear it tonight."

Myra's brow furrowed. "Maybe she'd let me buy it from her. Did she say what it's worth?"

I lowered my voice. "Keep this under your hats because I

don't want to get mugged in the parking lot later, but this piece is worth fifteen thousand dollars."

Myra gaped, and John whistled.

"Where'd you say this chick was cleaning?" John asked. "The White House?"

I laughed. "Nope. It was a dentist's office. Can you imagine?"

"No, ma'am, I cannot," John said. "I believe I'm in the wrong profession."

"China didn't say exactly *where* Pat found the jewelry," I said. "I'm not accusing her of stealing anything from anyone."

"Of course not," John said.

"Well, did she find any more pieces?" Myra asked. "Maybe Pat would be willing to sell something else . . . something that hasn't been appraised yet."

"China didn't say," I said. "Call her tomorrow and ask her. But for now, I've got to get this cake set up." I looked at Scottie. "What're you guys doing here this early anyway?"

"I wanted to be here in case you needed me," he said.

That sentence was so loaded I didn't dare comment on it. Instead I just smiled and said, "Then let's get to work." I saw that the convention hall staff was starting to set up buffet warmers on long tables at the front of the room. "Will we be putting the cake on one of those buffet tables? If so, I need to try to get the convention staff to work with me to make enough room."

"It's okay," Scottie said, placing his hand at the small of my back and steering me toward the front of the room. "I instructed them to give you a separate table."

"Thank you."

He grinned. "I do what I can. See, it's the smaller table there to the right."

"That'll work great," I said.

"I'll grab the cake and—"

"No, wait," I said, interrupting him. "Get the box from Myra first, please. It has the tablecloth in it."

"Will do," he said.

I stepped over to the table Scottie had indicated and placed my wrap and purse on a chair. Scottie brought me the box, and I took the gold lamé fabric I was using as a tablecloth and arranged it—with some of the fabric to be pooled around the cake—on the table.

"I like it," Scottie said. "Elvis would have too."

"I know," I said with a smile. I started to go get the cake, but Scottie was way ahead of me. Literally. He sprinted in front of me so he could grab the cake. "Just don't run back with it. If you drop it, I'll kill you!"

"Gee whiz," he said as he returned with the cake. "You really are a femme fatale tonight, aren't you?"

"You know I wouldn't actually kill you," I said. "I'd cry and scream and stomp and pout. And I'd still charge you for the cake, but I wouldn't murder you." I thought I should make that clear not only to Scottie but to Mark and Ben as well.

He sat the box down, and I opened it.

When he saw the cake, Scottie laughed. "Man! That is amazing! John, get over here and look at this!"

I lifted the cake and placed it onto the gold lamé fabric.

Scottie laughed again. "Have you ever seen anything like it? Can you believe it's actually a cake?"

I turned and smiled at him. "I'm so glad you're happy with it."

He picked me up, took a big step backward, and then spun me around. "I love it. Thank you."

I laughed too, albeit nervously, and I desperately hoped I hadn't become unwired. "I'm not done, you know. Wait until you see the finishing touches."

"No," he said, sitting me down gingerly. "Don't do another thing to it. That Caddy is perfect exactly the way it is."

"I'm not doing anything else to the car," I said. "But the table isn't finished." I took out the little surprises I'd been working on to go with the cake. I unboxed a Hawaiian lei made of white and pink fondant plumerias and placed it on the table next to the cake. I also had some of the cake balls Ben, Leslie, Lucas, and I had made, and on these, I'd piped *E*s, *I*s, and *O*s. I put them on a light blue platter at the left side of the table so they would spell out rows of *EIEIO*. I had milk chocolate guitars, white chocolate guitar picks, and three-dimensional hound dogs molded out of modeling chocolate.

Scottie said, "All that's missing is—"

"The blue suede shoes?" I said, interrupting with a grin as I took out the last box. I opened the box to reveal a dozen cupcakes adorned with tiny blue suede loafers.

Scottie laughed and kissed my cheek. "Have I told you that you're amazing?"

"Just now," I said.

"Pretty cool," John said, nodding his head. "I'd kiss your cheek too, but my date might get jealous."

"Heck, I'd kiss her whole face myself if she'd let me wear that necklace," Myra said.

"I need to go get into costume," Scottie said. "Will you stay awhile? I want to make an announcement, introduce you to everybody—you know, for making the cake and all."

I nodded. "I'll be here."

He grinned. "Thanks."

"What about you?" Myra asked John. "Don't you need to get into costume too?"

"Yeah, but I'll wait until Scottie gets back," he said. "It'd be rude for both of us to leave you ladies unattended."

"I'll be back as quickly as I can," Scottie said. "I brought my costume over from the hotel, so all I have to do is go into the dressing area and change."

With a wink, Scottie jogged to the stage door.

I took my camera from my purse and took several photos of the cake and the other items I'd made for the display. They'd be a terrific addition to my website gallery.

John strode over to a table and pulled out two chairs. "Care to take a load off, ladies?"

"Sounds good to me," Myra said, sitting in one of the chairs John offered.

I still wasn't sure the table looked to suit me, and I went back over to fuss with it some more. John came over to get me.

"It looks wonderful," he said. "Come on over and chat with me and Myra for a few minutes."

"All right." I went over and sat at the table beside Myra, but I still kept stealing glances at the cake table. It was important to me that everything be just right.

John blew out a breath. "I'm telling you it's great. Ain't it great, Myra?"

"It's fantastic, Daphne," Myra said. "You've outdone yourself."

"What are you going to do when somebody cuts into that pink Cadillac?" John asked. "I hope Scottie is there to catch you if you faint."

"Oh, what's the fun of having a cake no one can eat?" I asked.

He looked thoughtful. "Could you ladies come with me a second?"

"Come with you where?" Myra asked. "What's wrong?"

"There's something out there in the parking lot I think you ought to see," he said.

I frowned. "It's awfully cold out there, John. What is it?"

"Come with me and see." His tone made me nervous.

"Just tell us what it is, and that way we'll know whether or not we want to see whatever it is," I said.

"Can't you go get it and bring it to us?" Myra asked.

"No." He looked around to make sure none of the convention hall employees were paying attention, and then he bent down and took a small pistol from an ankle holster concealed by his jeans. "Very calmly and very quietly get up and come with me outside, or I will shoot you. By the time anyone knows what's happened, I'll be gone."

Myra's jaw dropped. "Is this a joke?" she squeaked.

"No joke, sweetheart. Move."

A LOT OF crazy, jumbled-up thoughts tumbled through my mind while I was straddling the center console of a stolen rusty brown pickup truck and a madman poked a gun in my ribs. I wondered why Mark and Ben hadn't tackled John the minute we stepped out of the convention hall. After all, John had made it clear he'd shoot one of us and escape before anyone knew what was happening. Maybe they wanted us to get more solid evidence . . . but they weren't the ones being threatened right now. Where the heck were Halligan and Kendall? I thought about opening the passenger door and pushing John out into the road before he could get a shot off, but I quickly dismissed that as a bad idea.

I whipped my head around to look at John. "Just what do you want from us?"

"Don't make him mad, Daphne. Don't make him mad," Myra hissed. "He's already killed once. He'll do it again . . . and . . . again." She dissolved into another round of sobs.

"Is she right?" I asked John. "Did you kill Dr. Bainsworth?"

"Can't tell you," he said. "If I told you, I'd have to shoot you." He snickered.

"Is this about the jewelry?" I asked. "If this necklace is what you want, have Myra pull over and let us get out of this truck. I'll toss you the necklace, and we'll never say a word to anyone."

"You're cute," John said. "I don't just want that necklace. I want the whole stash."

"There isn't a stash!" I cried. "I lied! Pat didn't find the necklace at the dental office. It was China's all along. Her mother gave it to her. She let me wear it to draw out the killer."

"Sure, sweetness, and I just fell off a turnip truck yesterday afternoon." John nudged Myra with the gun. "Take the next right."

"But I'm telling you the truth," I said. "There is no stash of jewelry."

"Well, we're going to my hotel to talk all this over. I suggest you be thinking of a way for me to get my jewelry so you'll have a plan when we get there," he said.

"Had you ever seen this piece of jewelry before tonight?" I asked.

"Nope," he said, eying the necklace lasciviously. "It is a thing of beauty though."

"Okay," I said. "You hadn't seen this necklace before. That means it wasn't in whatever you gave the dentist, right?"

"I don't know what the dentist had," John said. "All I know is that he smuggled the jewelry out of Mexico for my cousin and was supposed to deliver it to me. He didn't. He decided to keep the money for doing the smuggling and keep the jewelry too. It don't work that way." He tugged at a tendril of my hair that had come loose from my updo.

I yanked my head away.

"You might as well play nice," John said, "because you *are* going to play."

Myra took the turn.

"Right up here," John instructed her. "Turn in at the hotel and go around to the back."

"Call your cousin," I said. "He'll tell you this necklace was not in the jewelry he stole."

"Just hold your horses, Daphne," he said. "We'll sort all this out once we get in the room."

"I wish I had a horse," I said. "A horse that would bite your hand off."

"Daphne!" Myra exclaimed. "Stop antagonizing the man!"

John merely laughed.

At John's instruction, Myra drove around to the back of the hotel.

"Room two thirty-three," John said.

"I see it," Myra said.

"Good. Pull up there to that empty space near the stairs."

Myra did as she was told, and John opened his door. "Don't either of you try anything or Daphne here will get a bullet in the ribs," he warned us. "Got it?"

Myra nodded.

"He's going to shoot me anyway," I said. "Try something, Myra. Try anything."

"You really do think you're cute, don't you?" John asked. "How's this? If either of you try anything, I'll shoot the old broad."

"The old broad?" Myra shrieked. "*The old broad?* You must not have thought I was too old last night when you were slobbering all over me at that dance club in Kingsport!"

"A man's gotta do what a man's gotta do." John shrugged. "Both of you get out of the truck and walk slowly up those steps. If you do anything—I mean anything—to draw attention to yourselves, I will shoot one or both of you." He jabbed me in the ribs with the barrel of the gun. "And you might act like you don't care what I do to you, but I know you don't want to be responsible for someone else's death. Do you?"

I shook my head.

"Good girl. Let's go." He made me go first with Myra in the middle so he could shoot Myra if need be. He felt I had all the valuable information about the jewelry, but I knew absolutely nothing. Still, maybe I could bluff and at least buy Myra and me enough time for Mark and Ben to come through.

I looked around and saw no one. You'd think at six thirty P.M. on a Friday night, there would be somebody hanging around a hotel parking lot—people going to their cars to leave for dinner . . . other Elvises en route to the convention . . . weary travelers checking in . . . Ben and Mark in the surveillance van. I did notice a silver BMW. It looked like the one Angela Bainsworth drove. If she—or anyone— was in the parking lot and would only look up here and see us . . .

When we got to the top of the stairs, John gave the metal door to his room two quick jabs with his foot. Again, I desperately scanned the parking lot.

Where are you, Ben?!

The door opened, and there stood Angela. John hustled us inside and shut the door. "Pull those two chairs away from the table."

Myra and I looked at each other as Angela complied with his order.

"Were you followed?" she asked.

He shook his head.

"Are you sure?" she said, pressing him.

"I know what I'm doing, all right?" He gave her a look that silenced her and then looked at Myra and me. "Both of you grab a chair and sit down."

We started for the same chair, and then I took the other one.

"Neither one of you is the brightest bulb in the light socket, are you?" John asked.

"Especially not me," Myra said. "I dated you."

He smirked at her. "That might've been the smartest thing you ever did. You know you like me. We don't have to let Daphne come between us."

"You called me an old broad and threatened to shoot me," Myra said.

"That was just to get her goat," John said.

"Well, it got mine too," she said.

"What about me?" Angela asked.

"Yeah, what about you?" I asked.

"Shut up," John said. "All of you. Now, let's get back to business." With his free hand, he took out the cell phone he'd removed from my purse and found China's number under *Contacts*. "I'm dialing China York's number, and I'm putting the phone on speaker so I can listen to every word you say."

"What do you want me to say?" I asked.

"I want you to find out where the rest of the jewelry is." He waved the gun toward Myra. "No tricks."

I was half afraid and half hopeful that China wouldn't answer her phone. If she didn't answer, it would give me more time to come up with a plan for escape. If she did answer, maybe I could clue her in to our situation.

She answered.

"Hi, China," I said. "I'm calling about the necklace."

"Did something happen?" she asked.

"No, no, no," I said. "Everything is fine. Myra is here . . . and—"

John slapped my arm and leveled the gun at my head.

"And lots of other people are here, too," I said, continuing.

"Really? Is that good?" China asked.

"Uh . . . yeah. In fact, I need to know where Pat got the necklace and where she might have stashed the rest of the jewelry." I silently prayed China wouldn't blow the Pat story.

"Oh. Well, I can't really say. I can call Pat, though, and ask her," she said. "You want me to do that and call you back?"

John was vigorously nodding his head.

"Please," I said. "Call me back on my cell phone as soon as you can find out something, okay?"

"All right." She paused. "This won't get Pat in any trouble, will it?"

John shook his head.

"Oh, no," I said. "I wouldn't let that happen. In fact, nobody would even guess she took that jewelry from Dr. Bainsworth's office."

John made a slashing motion across his throat.

"I have to go now," I said.

"Well, I'll call Pat and call you right back."

John nodded.

"Thanks, China."

John ended the call. "Now we wait."

I looked over at Myra. She looked weary, worried, and tired. I imagined I did too. John, on the other hand, looked more animated and alive than I'd ever thought he could be. Angela looked annoyed.

"Angela, how did you get involved with this?" I asked. "I thought you weren't into jewelry."

"I'm not into jewelry," she said. "I'm into investments that ultimately pay off."

I shook my head. "And you truly feel that this investment will pay off?"

"Shut up," John demanded. "Leave her alone."

"Are you just stringing her along like you did Juanita?" I asked John.

His eyes narrowed. "Don't make me hurt you."

For the next few minutes, the only sound in the room was our breathing and the sound of the digital clock flipping over.

John broke the silence by asking Angela to see if he had a beer in the fridge.

She got up and looked into the room's mini-fridge. "No. It's empty."

He shrugged. "I guess I'll have to do something else to keep my mind occupied then. Let's play strip poker without the cards." He looked at an imaginary hand. "What do you know? I win." He waved the pistol in my direction. "Daphne, I'll have that necklace now."

When I hesitated, he said, "You can do it, or I can have Angela hold the gun while I take it off you. Your choice." He gave me a leering grin. "Let's see how badly you want my hands on you."

I quickly unfastened the necklace and handed it to him.

He laughed. "She doesn't like me as much as you two do." He rubbed the barrel of the gun against his chin. "While it's always good to start with the crown jewel, I have to wonder if you're hiding anything else, Daphne."

"No. That's the only thing China had," I said. "She should've called back by now, don't you think? Maybe we should call her again."

John shook his head. "Be patient."

Fortunately, I didn't have to be. There was a sudden crash against the door. The police had used a battering ram to get inside the room. With about half a dozen guns all pointed at his head, John dropped his own weapon and meekly allowed the officers to handcuff him. At first, they didn't know what to do about Angela.

"Is she with the two of you?" one officer asked me.

"Definitely not!" Myra shouted. "She's with him! Bunni was right about her all along!" Her tirade ended in heaving sobs.

I started to hug Myra but Ben, Mark, Officer Kendall, and Officer Halligan rushed into the room. Ben swept me out of the chair and into his strong arms.

"Thank God," he said. "Thank God. I don't know what I'd do if anything happened to you."

I clung to him, releasing my pent-up anxiety in a flood of tears. "What took you so long?"

"Your microphone cut out. But it's all right," he told me. "It's over. I'm here now."

"Take us home," Myra said. "Just please take us home."

I glanced over to see that she was speaking to Mark, who was holding her hands and talking to her softly.

"Myra's right," I said. "We need to go home."

Ben nodded. "I'll see if the police officers will agree to talk with the two of you tomorrow morning rather than tonight." He stepped over to the officer in charge.

China stepped into the motel room and grinned at me. "Didn't I tell you I'd make a good detective? I called the police and had them trace your call to this hotel."

"You're the best detective I've ever seen," I said.

Epilogue

As it turns out, Juanita was right. John was her George/Jorge and whoever else he claimed to be. He and his cousin ran all sorts of small-time criminal operations between Mexico and the United States. One of those operations was bringing the families of Mexican girls into the United States with the promise of marriage for the girl and a better life for her family. The groom would then do something—like have other girlfriends show up—to make the girl call off the wedding, and they'd stick her parents with a huge, bogus bill.

John's cousin also knew some prostitutes who would steal hotel room keys from men visiting the Nuevo Laredo red-light district and sell the keys to him. The cousin would then use the keys to get into the men's rooms and steal their valuables. Their favorite? The Redbird Hotel, of course.

The cousin had an accomplice who lived in Laredo, Texas. This man would get the valuables to John for him to fence at various locations during his travels with the EIEIO. When the cousin's accomplice was arrested and jailed on an unrelated theft charge, John's cousin needed another mule. Dr. Bainsworth was willing to do the job for the money offered him.

The police had found jewelry appraisals at Dr. Bainsworth's home that indicated he'd had a couple pieces of the jewelry appraised when he crossed the border back into the United States. Bainsworth realized the thief didn't know what valuable pieces he had. He decided to hang on to the jewelry rather than meet John as he'd promised.

When John learned the EIEIO was coming to Brea Ridge for a benefit concert and to enjoy some downtime, he did his own reconnaissance. He learned Dr. Bainsworth was separated from his wife, and he started seeing Angela. Angela was more bitter than she'd let on about the divorce. Like Myra and me, she couldn't figure out why her husband would cheat on her with the ugly duckling Jill. Her vulnerability had left the door wide open for John to step through.

When he was comfortable enough in their affair, John told her about Dr. Bainsworth's transaction with his cousin in Mexico. Angela was only too willing to give John a key to the office in order to recover the stolen jewelry. She stood to gain a small finder's fee and the satisfaction of thwarting her estranged husband.

That Friday night after the EIEIO got into town, Angela drove John to the dental office. She dropped him off and drove to the back of the Sunoco to wait. Neither of them could have anticipated Myra would lose a filling that night and require Dr. Bainsworth to come into his office. When Angela saw her husband's SUV pull into his office, she panicked and left. Her conscience got the best of her, though, and she returned to the Sunoco to pick up John, whose thick winter coat hid his bony frame.

John had already looked through the office and was in the exam room when Dr. Bainsworth came in. He hid behind the door and smashed Dr. Bainsworth over the head with an iron doorstop. The police had already found the doorstop and tagged it as evidence, but there had been no fingerprints on it since John had wiped it clean. He claimed to Officers Halligan and Kendall that he never meant to hit the dentist so hard.

After Scottie picked me up and swung me around at the convention hall, the microphone had started going in and out. That's why Ben and Mark weren't sure what was going on when John first threatened Myra and me. Prior to setting up outside the convention hall, Mark had brought Officers Halligan and Kendall up to speed. Upon seeing the two of us come out with John, they decided it would be best to hang back and secure further evidence against him. Mark recognized John as Angela's lover, but they had no idea the man had a gun.

Scottie and the rest of the Elvises have left town. Scottie told me he "sure hated" that John turned out to be such a worm and gave me a bonus, what he called hazardous duty pay. Who knew you could earn hazardous duty pay for feeding a bunch of Elvis impersonators?

So, for the time being, things are back to normal . . . whatever *that* is. Myra is dating Mark now. She's hoping to put her trench coat, sunglasses, and fedora to good use again soon.

If you'll excuse me, I need to check on my cake. I'm making a coconut cake for Ben. It's his favorite. He's bringing pizza and a movie, and we're celebrating his decision to let his assistant editor take over some of the responsibilities of the paper so he can spend more time with me.

ACKNOWLEDGMENTS

FIRST OF all, I'm thankful to God as always for the many blessings he's given me and my family. I'd also like to thank my agent, Robert Gottlieb, for his encouragement and belief in me and this series; editors Danielle Poiesz and Kathy Sagan; publicist Ayelet Gruenspecht; DeeDee, Lora, and Regina for contributing recipes; and, as always, Tim, Lianna, and Nicholas for their love and support.

Daphne's Kitchen Recipes

Pat Tolbert's Banana Pudding

(Submitted by her daughter DeeDee Kitts)

3½ tablespoons all-purpose flour

1¾ cups plus 2 tablespoons sugar

dash of salt

3 eggs, separated

3 cups milk (can use evaporated milk)

2 teaspoons vanilla extract

1 12-ounce package vanilla wafers

6 medium bananas

Combine flour, 1½ cups sugar, and salt in heavy saucepan. Beat egg yolks and milk, mixing well. Stir in dry ingredients. Cook over medium heat, stirring constantly until smooth and thickened. Remove from heat and add 1 teaspoon vanilla. Let pudding cool some before putting together. Layer about ⅓ of vanilla wafers in the bottom of a 13 x 9–inch (3-quart) baking dish. Slice 2 bananas over them and pour ⅓ of custard over; continue to layer, repeating twice. Beat egg whites until foamy (should be at room temperature). Gradually add remaining sugar and beat to stiff peaks. Add 1 teaspoon vanilla. Spread meringue over custard, sealing to edge of dish. Bake at 425 for 10–12 minutes. Yields 8–10 servings.

If you're counting calories, you might want to try this lower-cal version:

Lora's Good-for-You Banana Pudding

(Submitted by Lora Rasnake)

3 cups fat-free (skim) milk

2 boxes (4-serving size each) Jell-O French Vanilla Instant Pudding and Pie Filling mix

4 containers (6 ounces each) Yoplait 99% Fat-Free Banana Crème or French Vanilla yogurt

8 ounces frozen fat-free whipped topping, thawed

48 reduced-fat vanilla wafer cookies

6 small bananas, sliced

Additional banana slices for garnish, if desired

In large bowl, beat milk and pudding mix with electric mixer on low speed until well mixed, then beat in yogurt. Fold in whipped topping. Place 24 vanilla wafers in a single layer in ungreased 13 x 9–inch (3-quart) glass baking dish. Spoon half of the pudding mixture over wafers. Place 6 sliced bananas over pudding mixture. Spoon remaining pudding mixture over bananas. Arrange remaining 24 vanilla wafers over top of pudding. Cover; refrigerate at least 3 hours but no longer than 8 hours. Just before serving, garnish with additional banana slices.

Regina's Peanut Butter and Banana Cake

(Submitted by Regina Shinall)

CAKE INGREDIENTS

½ cup butter, softened

1½ cups sugar

2 eggs

1 cup mashed ripe bananas (2 to 3 medium)

1 teaspoon vanilla extract

2 cups all-purpose flour

2 teaspoons baking powder

1 teaspoon baking soda

½ cup 2% milk

FROSTING INGREDIENTS

⅓ cup creamy peanut butter

⅓ cup 2% milk

1½ teaspoons vanilla extract

3 cups confectioners' sugar

To prepare the cake, in a large bowl, cream the butter and sugar until light and fluffy. Add eggs, one at a time, beating well after each addition. Beat in bananas and vanilla. Combine the flour, baking powder, and baking soda; add to creamed mixture alternately with milk, beating well after each addition.

Transfer to a greased 13 x 9 (3 quart) baking pan. Bake at 350 for 30–35 minutes or until a toothpick inserted near the center comes out clean. Cool on a wire rack.

For frosting, in a small bowl, beat peanut butter, milk, and vanilla until blended; gradually beat in confectioners' sugar until smooth. Spread over cake.

How to Make a 3D Cake Template

Print out a photo of the item you'd like to make. Enlarge the photo to the desired size. Use onionskin paper to trace the photo; more than one sheet might be necessary depending on the size of the cake you're making. Tape the onionskin or tracing paper onto a piece of thin cardboard or poster board. Carefully cut around the design.

With Daphne's car cake, she used templates to do each side. A separate template would have to be done for the front and back of the car. Of course, some bakers are able to carve the design freestyle!

Read on for an excerpt from the first
Daphne Martin mystery,

Murder Takes the Cake

Available now from Gallery Books!

CHAPTER
one

M RS. WATSON?" I called, banging on the door. I glanced
up at the ever-blackening clouds. Although I had Mrs. Watson's cake in a box, it would be just my luck to get caught in a
downpour with it. This was my third attempt to please her, and I
couldn't afford another mistake with the amount she was paying
me. Whoever said "the customer is always right" had obviously
never dealt with Yodel Watson. I should've listened to all those
people who'd told me Yodel was the meanest old lady in town. But
she was my first customer. How could I turn away her business?

I heard something inside the house and pressed my ear
against the door. A vision of me falling and dropping the cake
when Mrs. Watson flung the door open made me rethink it,
though, and I pulled my head away from the door.

"Mrs. Watson?" I called again.

"Come in! It's open! Come in!"

I tried the knob and the door was indeed unlocked. I stepped inside but didn't see Mrs. Watson. "It's me—Daphne Martin. I'm here with your cake."

"Come in! It's open!"

"I am in, Mrs. Watson. Where are you?"

"It's open!"

"I know! I—" Gritting my teeth, I walked through the foyer to the kitchen and placed the cake on the table. A quick glance around the room told me Mrs. Watson wasn't in there, either.

"It's open!"

Man, could this lady get on your nerves. The voice sounded like it came from the left, so I moved slowly down the hallway.

"Mrs. Watson?" I poked my head inside a den on the right.

"Come in!"

I turned toward the voice. A gray parrot was sitting on a perch inside its cage.

"It's open!" the bird squawked.

"I noticed." I'd heard about parrots that could mimic their owners' voices to perfection, but this was the first time I'd experienced it. Great. She's probably not home, and I'll get arrested for breaking and entering . . . though, technically, I didn't break.

It was then that I saw Mrs. Watson lying on the sofa in a faded, navy blue robe. A plaid blanket covered her legs. She appeared to be sleeping, but I'd heard the parrot calling when I was outside. There's no way Mrs. Watson could have been in the same room and slept through that racket.

I stepped closer. "Are you okay?" Her pallor already answered my question. Then the foul odor hit me.

I backed away and took my cell phone out of my purse. "I'm calling 9-1-1, Mrs. Watson. Everything's gonna be all right." I don't know if I was trying to reassure her or myself.

Everything's gonna be all right. I'd been telling myself that for the past month.

AFTER CALLING 9-1-1, I lingered in the doorway in case Mrs. Watson woke up and needed something before the EMTs arrived. Mrs. Watson was old enough that she could be my mother lying there.

I turned forty this year. Forty seems to be a sobering age for every woman, but it hit me especially hard. When most women get to be my age, they at least have some bragging rights: successful career, happy marriage, beautiful children, nice home. I had none of the above. My so-called accomplishments included a failed marriage, a dingy apartment, and twenty years' service in a dead-end job. Cue the violins.

So when my sister Violet called and told me about a "charming little house" for sale near her neighborhood, I jumped at the chance to leave all the dead ends of central Tennessee and come home to southwest Virginia. Surely something better awaited me here.

I'd already moved into my house—which seems to have come with a one-eyed stray cat—and started my own cake decorating business. It took a while to come up with a name and a logo, have business cards made, set up a website, and do other "fun" administrative duties, but now I was settled. The cake and cupcakes I'd made for my niece and nephew to take to school on Halloween had been a hit, leading to some nice word-of-mouth advertising and a couple orders. Leslie's puppy dog cake and Lucas's black cat cupcakes were the first additions to my website's gallery.

But my first real customer was Yodel Watson. She'd considered herself a world-class baker in her heyday but no longer had the time or desire to engage in "such foolishness."

"I want you to make me a cake for my Thanksgiving dinner," she'd said. "Nothing too gaudy. I want my family to think I made it myself."

My first two attempts had been refused: the first cake was too fancy, and the second was too plain. I'd been hoping—*praying*—the third time would be the charm. I laboriously prepared a spice cake with cream cheese frosting and decorated it with orange and red satin ribbons for a bottom border and a red apple, arranged in a flower petal pattern, on top. And now it was on Mrs. Watson's kitchen table while Mrs. Watson herself was slumped on her sofa as deflated as a December jack-o'-lantern. Oh, yeah, things were looking up.

I was startled out of my reverie by a sharp rap.

"EMT!"

"Come in! It's open!" the bird called.

I hurried to the living room to open the door, and two men with a stretcher brushed past me.

"Where's the patient?" one asked.

"Back here." I showed them the way to the den, and then got out of the way.

"Come in!"

I moved next to the birdcage. "Don't you ever shut up? This is serious."

"I'll say," agreed one of the EMTs. "Are you the next of kin?"

"Excuse me?" My hand flew to my heart. "She's dead?"

"Yes, ma'am. Are you related to her?"

While one EMT questioned me, the other was on his radio asking dispatch to send the police and the coroner.

"I barely know her," I told the man. "I just brought the cake."

AFTER CALLING IN the reinforcements, the EMTs sent me to the formal living room. They didn't get any argument from me. I sat down on the edge of a burgundy wingback chair and studied the room.

There was an elaborate Oriental rug over beige carpet, a pale blue sofa, and a curio cabinet with all sorts of expensive-looking knickknacks. Unlike the messier den, this room was spotless. Except for a small yellow stain I noticed near my right foot. Parrot pee, I supposed.

"Ms. Martin?"

I looked up at one of the deputies. "Yes?"

"I'm Officer Hayden. I need to ask you some questions."

"Um . . . sure." This guy looked young enough to be my son—scratch that, *nephew*—but he still made me nervous.

"Tell me about your arrival, ma'am."

Ma'am. Like I was seventy. Of course, when you're twelve, everybody looks old.

I cleared my throat. "I, uh, knocked on the door, and some-one told me to come in. I thought it was Mrs. Watson, so I opened the door and came inside." I pointed toward the kitchen table. "I'm Daphne of Daphne's Delectable Cakes." I patted my pockets for my business card holder but realized I must have left it in the car. "I brought the cake."

Officer Hayden took out a notepad. "Let me get this straight. Someone else was here when you arrived?"

"No . . . no, it was the bird. The bird hollered and told me to come in."

He closed his eyes and pinched the bridge of his nose.

"I thought it was her, though," I added quickly. *Please, God, don't let me get arrested.* "It told me the door was open, and it *was.*"

Officer Hayden opened his eyes.

Never being one to know when to shut up, I reiterated, "I just brought the cake."

ABOUT AN HOUR later, I pulled into my own driveway. I didn't make it to the front door before I heard my next-door neighbor calling to me.

"Hello, Daphne! I see you're bringing home another cake."

"Afraid so."

She beat me to the porch. For a woman in her sixties, Myra Jenkins was pretty quick. "What was wrong with this one?"

I handed Myra the cake and unlocked the door. "Um . . . she didn't say."

"She didn't say?" Myra wiped her feet on the mat and followed me inside.

I dropped my purse onto the table by the door. I'd let Myra hang on to the cake. She'd kept the other two rejects; I figured she'd want this one, too.

I went into the kitchen and took two diet sodas from the fridge. I handed Myra one can, popped the top on the other, and took a long drink before dropping into a chair.

"This is beautiful," Myra said, after opening the cake box and peering inside. "What kind of cake is it?"

"Spice. With a cream cheese icing."

Myra ran her finger through the frosting on the side of the cake and licked her finger. "Mmm, this is out of this world. You know the Save-A-Buck sometimes takes baked goods on commission, don't you?"

"No, I didn't know that."

She nodded. "They don't keep a bakery staff, so they sometimes buy cakes, cookies, doughnuts—stuff like that—from the locals and sell them in their store."

"I'll definitely look into that. Thanks."

"You should." She put the lid down on the box. "Are you going to take in this one?"

"No," I said. Her poking the side had already nullified that possibility. "Why don't you take it home?"

"Thank you. I believe I'll serve this and the white one with the raspberry filling for Thanksgiving and save the chocolate cake for Christmas." She smiled. "Do I owe you anything?"

"Yes. Good publicity. Sing my praises to the church group, the quilting circle, the library group, and anyone else you can."

"Will do, honey. Will do."

"Um . . . how well do you know Yodel Watson?" I asked cautiously, unsure of how much information I should spill.

Myra pulled out a chair and sat down. "About as well as anybody in this town, I reckon. Why?"

"She—" I said quietly. "She's dead."

She gasped. "What happened? Car wreck? You know, she drives the most awful car I've ever seen. All the tires are bald, the—"

"It wasn't a car wreck," I interrupted. "When I went to her house, I thought she told me to come in, so—"

"Banjo."

"I beg your pardon?"

"It was probably Yodel's bird Banjo tellin' you to come in."

"Right. It was. So, uh, I went in and . . . and found Mrs. Watson in the den."

"And she was dead?"

I nodded.

"Was she naked?"

"No! She had on a robe and was covered with a blanket. Why would you think she was naked?"

Myra shrugged. "When people find dead bodies in the movies, the bodies are usually naked." She opened her soda. "So what happened?"

"I don't know. Since there was no obvious cause of death, she's being sent for an autopsy."

"Were there any opened envelopes lying around? Maybe somebody sent Yodel some of that amtrax stuff."

"I don't think it was *anthrax*," I said. "I figure she had a heart attack or an aneurysm or something."

"Don't be too sure."

"Why do you say that?"

"Because Yodel was *mean*." Myra took a drink of her soda. "Heck, you know that."

I shook my head and tried to steer the conversation away from murder. "Who'd name their daughter Yodel?"

"Oh, honey."

In the short time I've lived here, I've already learned that when Myra Jenkins says *Oh, honey,* you're in for a story.

"The Watsons yearned to follow in the Carter family's footsteps," she said. "Yodel's sisters were Melody and Harmony, and her brother was Guitar. Guitar Refrain Watson—Tar, for short."

I nearly spit diet soda across the table. "You're kidding."

"No, honey, I'm not. Trouble was, nary a one of the Watsons had any talent. When my daughter was little, she'd clap her hands over her ears and make the most terrible faces if we sat behind them in church. Just about anybody can sing that 'praise God from Whom all blessings flow' song they sing while takin' the offering plates back up to the alter, but the Watsons couldn't. And the worst part was that every one of them sang loud and proud. Loud, proud, *and* off-key." She smiled. "I have to admit, though, the congregation as a whole said a lot more silent prayers in church before Mr. and Mrs. Watson died and before their young-uns—all but Yodel—scattered here and there. 'Lord, please don't let the Watsons sit near us.' 'Lord, please stop up my ears just long enough to deliver me from sufferin' through another hymn.' 'Lord, please give Tar laryngitis for forty-five minutes.'"

We both laughed.

"That was ugly of me to tell," Myra said. "But it's true! Still, I'll have to ask forgiveness for that. I always did wonder if God hadn't blessed any of them Watsons with musical ability because they'd tried to write their own ticket with those musical names. You know what I mean?"

"I guess so."

"Now, back to Yodel. Yodel was always jealous of China York because China could sing. The choir director was always getting China to sing solos. China didn't care for Yodel because Yodel was spiteful and mean to her most of the time. It seemed Yodel couldn't feel good about herself unless she was puttin' somebody else down."

"She must've felt great about herself every time I brought a cake over," I muttered.

Myra frowned. "I don't know why she would. Those cakes were beautiful, and I know they'll be delicious."

"Thanks, Myra. I didn't mean to interrupt your story. Please, go on."

"Well, a few years ago, our old preacher retired and we got a new one. Of course, we threw him a potluck howdy-get-to-know-you party at the church. It was summer, and I took a strawberry pie. I make the best strawberry pies. I'd thought about making one for Thanksgiving, but I don't have to now that you've given me all these cakes. I do appreciate it."

I waved away her gratitude. "Don't mention it."

"Anyhow, China brought a chocolate and coconut cake. She'd got the recipe out of *McCall's* magazine and was just bustin' to have us all try it out. Then wouldn't you know it? In waltzed Yodel with the very same cake."

"If she loved to bake so much, I wonder why she gave it up. She told me she didn't have time to bake these days. Was she active in a lot of groups? I mean, what took up so much of her time?"

"Keeping tabs on the rest of the town took up her time. When Arlo was alive—he was a Watson, too, of course, though no relation . . . except maybe really distant cousins once or twice removed or something. . . . There's more Watsons in these parts than there are chins at a fat farm. Is that how that saying goes?"

"I think it's more Chins than a Chinese phone book."

"Huh. I don't get it. Anyhow, Arlo expected his wife to be more than the town gossip. That's when Yodel prided herself on her cooking, her volunteer work, and all the rest. When he died—oh, I guess it was ten years ago—she gave it all up." Myra shook her head. "Shame, too. But back to the story. Yodel told the new preacher, 'Wait until you try this cake. It's my very own recipe.'

"'It is not,' China said. 'You saw me copy that recipe out of

McCall's when we were both at the beauty shop waitin' to get our hair done!'

"'So what if I did?' Yodel asked. 'I subscribe to *McCall's*. How was I supposed to know you'd be making a similar cake?'

"China got right up in Yodel's face and hollered, 'It's the same cake!'

"Yodel said it wasn't. She said, 'I put almonds and a splash of vanilla in mine. Otherwise that cake would be boring and bland.'

"At this point, the preacher tried to intervene. 'They both look delicious,' he told them, 'and I'm sure there are enough of us here to eat them both.'

"Yodel and China were like two snarling dogs, and I don't believe either of them heard a word he said. China had already set her cake on the table, but Yodel was still holding hers. China calmly placed her hand on the bottom of Yodel's cake plate and upended that cake right on Yodel's chest."

I giggled. "Really?"

"Really. And then China walked to the door and said, 'I've had it with her. I won't be back here until one of us is dead.' And she ain't been back to church since."

"Wow," I said. "That's some story."

"Makes you wonder if China finally got tired of sitting home by herself on Sunday mornings."

Seeing how serious Myra looked, I stifled my laughter. "Do you honestly think this woman has been nursing a grudge all these years and killed Mrs. Watson rather than simply finding herself another church?"

"There's not another Baptist church within ten miles of here." She finished off her soda. "People have killed for crazier reasons than that, haven't they?"

"I suppose, but—"

"And if it wasn't China York, I can think of a few other folks who had it in for Yodel."

"Come on. I'll admit she's been a pain to work with on these cakes, but I have a hard time casting Mrs. Watson in the role of Cruella de Vil."

Myra got up and put her empty soda can in the garbage. "I didn't say she made puppy coats. I said there were a lot of people who'd just as soon not have Yodel Watson around."

I WAS RELIEVED when Myra left. She seemed to be a good person, and I liked her, but she could be a bit much. Everything was so dramatic with her. She even had me wondering whether or not poor Mrs. Watson died of natural causes.

I got up and walked down the hall to my office. It had a sofa bed so it could double as a guest room if need be. It also held a desk, a file cabinet, and a bookcase full of cookbooks, cake decorating books, small-business books, marketing books, and one photograph of me with Lucas and Leslie. The photo had been taken last year when I was at Violet's house for Christmas.

I booted up my computer. As always, I checked my e-mail first. E-mail is a procrastinator's dream come true. There was a message from my friend Bonnie, still holding down the fort at the company I'd worked for in Tennessee:

> Hey, girl! Are you up to your eyebrows in cake batter? I can think of worse predicaments. We get off half a day Wednesday. I can hardly wait. Do you have tons of orders to fill before Thursday? I hope so. I mean, I

hope business is off to a good start but that
you have time to enjoy the holiday, too. I really miss you, Daph. Write when you can and
fill me in on everything, especially whether or
not any of your neighbors are HAGs!

I smiled. HAG was our acronym for Hot Available Guy. It
wasn't a flattering acronym, but it worked.

I marked the e-mail as unread and decided to reply when I
had better news to report. As I deleted my junk messages, I
thought about Bonnie. We had met while I was taking culinary
classes at a local college. She was taking business courses and
was desperate to get into the field I wanted out of so badly. One
evening, we were two of the oldest people in the student
lounge. That night even the faculty members present were in
their twenties! Bonnie and I were both in our early thirties, and
after that initial meeting we had fun people-watching over coffee before all our evening classes.

When a job opened up at the company I worked for, Bonnie applied and got the job. It wasn't long after that my college days came to an abrupt end. Not believing that I could
actually be good—make that, great—at something, dear
hubby Todd came by the school one evening and saw Chef
Pierre. Admittedly, Chef Pierre was impressive in every way,
but Bonnie and I had already dubbed him a HUG—Hot Un-
available Guy. Chef Pierre was married, had three young children, and was devoted to his lovely wife. Todd couldn't get
past the chef's stellar looks, though. I was the chef's star student, so Todd thought I *had* to be sleeping with the man and
made me drop out.

But I'd already been bitten by the baking bug. I watched

TV chefs, bought cake decorating books, rented how-to videos, and practiced decorating every chance I got. I'd practice on vinyl place mats. And I'd tell myself "Someday."

Now it seemed my "someday" had come. I was an excellent cake decorator, I'd finally taken a chance, and I was finally tuning out Todd's taunting voice in my head. I was believing in myself for the first time in years. I knew I could make this business work.

I started when the phone rang.

"Hey, I heard about Mrs. Watson. You must've freaked out when you found her," my sister said as soon as I picked up.

"How'd you know?"

"I saw Bill Hayden's wife at the school when I picked up Leslie and Lucas this afternoon."

Bill Hayden. *Officer* Bill Hayden. Married . . . and with children. He must be older than he looked.

"Why didn't you call me?" Violet asked.

"I don't know." Because you're perfect, and in three years when you turn forty, all you'll have to be concerned about is laugh lines? Because I didn't come back home to have a babysitter? Because I promised myself I wouldn't be the one thorn in your bouquet of roses? "Myra came over as soon as I got home, so I really didn't have a chance to call."

"No, I don't suppose you did. Did you tell her about Yodel?"

"Yeah. Should I not have?"

"Eh. I guess it'll be in the paper tomorrow anyway."

"Plus, it's a really small town, Vi. There were probably a dozen messages on Myra's answering machine when she got back home. I mean, you heard it at the school, right?"

"I didn't mean anything by it," Violet said. "I'm merely cautioning you to be careful of what you say to Myra."

"With Myra I find myself mostly listening."

"I know that's true." Violet laughed. "Just be careful. As a witness in a homicide investigation, you have to watch what you say to the general public."

"A homicide investigation? The coroner didn't send the woman's body to Roanoke for autopsy until this afternoon. The results couldn't possibly be in."

"No, of course not, but Joanne told me Bill said there were indications of foul play. They believe Yodel was poisoned."

"Is that ethical?"

"He only told his wife, Daphne."

"And she told you and who knows who else. What is it with small-town drama?"

"Excuse me, Ms. Big City. I forgot how boring we must be to you now."

"Sarcasm doesn't suit you, Vi. I just think Officer Hayden should learn a bit about confidentiality, that's all."

"Please don't get him in trouble."

"I won't. I—"

"Let's just talk about Thursday. What time will you be here?" Violet asked.

"I was thinking eleven, but I can come earlier if you'd like."

"No. Eleven's good. Mom's spending the night, so I'll have plenty of help in the kitchen."

"Then eleven it is."

After hanging up with Violet, I went out the kitchen door to sit on the side porch. It was cool outside, but I was feeling a little sorry for myself and I always felt better in the big wide open than I did in an empty house.

Violet had a lot to be proud of. She'd been married for the past fifteen years to a dreamboat of a guy. She had gorgeous eleven-year-old twins. She was a successful Realtor. She had a lovely home. She had curly, blond hair, blue eyes, and a bubbly personality—as opposed to my straight, dark brown hair, brown eyes, and more serious demeanor. *And* she had a great relationship with our mom.

I, however, had been married for ten years to an abusive manipulator who is currently serving a seven-year prison term for assault with a deadly weapon after trying to shoot me. Fortunately, he'd missed, and, in my opinion, he was sentenced to far too little time simply because his aim was off. He'd called it a "mistake." Whether he meant shooting at me or missing, I have no idea. Mom called the whole ordeal a mistake, too. Neither of them could understand why I filed for divorce.

"He said he was sorry," Mom had scolded me over the phone. "You made the man angry, Daphne. You know how you can be. A person can only take so much."

I'd hung up on her. A person *could* only take so much. That was nearly five years ago. Of course, Mom and I had talked since then, but our conversations were more strained than baby food.

I heard a plaintive meow and looked up to see the fluffy gray and white, one-eyed stray sitting a short distance away.

"Me too, baby," I told the cat softly. "Me too."